Dedicated to Caterina. Federico. Augusto.
Margherita and my father Duilio, who has
always been my inspiration.

Printed by Amazon
Copyright © 2021 Enrico Coletti
All rights reserved.
ISBN-9798714755446

THE DAY OF ALL DAYS

TUTANKHAMUN The Story Never Told

Enrico Coletti

translated by:

Bill Lee

"Get ready for an amazing journey back in time, in search of a secret kept for 3300 years".

CHAPTER I
The Attack

The youthful fans of the pop star Ariana Grande were ecstatic. But at 22:31 pm, the joyful mood at the Manchester Arena was transformed into an unimaginable darkness. Just a few minutes following the end of the show, as the youthful concertgoers were leaving, still aglow with the thrill of the event, two tremendous blasts in the foyer of the arena, not far from where they had been sitting, sent metal bolts and nails ripping into their dreams, killing twenty-two of them and wounding another one hundred and twenty-two, including a number of very young children. A pungent odour of TATP, or triacetone triperoxide, a substance already used in other savage attacks in Europe, hung in the air. In the midst of the mayhem, the dust, the blood, the cries of the wounded, there was no mistaking the deep holes gouged out of the walls by the flying bolts. One wounded young girl, deafened by the explosion, was unable to find her mother in that tragic silence. Salman Ramadan Abedi, a 22 year-old of Libyan descent who had converted to the most radical form of Islam, that founded on blind obedience of Sharia law, had blown himself up to become a martyr, having fallen under the crazed spell of a terrorism so pitiless it was happy to end the lives and dreams of so many young, innocent victims, one of them a girl of no more than eight.

"Broken. From the bottom of my heart, I am so so sorry. I don't have words", wrote Ariana Grande on her official Twitter account after suspending her tour.

A distraught Queen Elizabeth appeared on television to offer comfort to the families struck by the tragedy:

"The whole nation has been shocked by the death and injury in Manchester last night of so many people, adults and children, who had just been enjoying a concert".

"...I know I speak for everyone in expressing my deepest sympathy to all who have been affected by this dreadful event and especially to the families and friends of those who have died or were injured.

"I want to thank all the members of the emergency services, who have responded with such professionalism and care.

"And I would like to express my admiration for the way the people of Manchester have responded, with humanity and compassion, to this act of barbarity".

The next day, the British Prime Minister, Theresa May, stated outside 10 Downing Street: "All acts of terrorism are cowardly attacks on innocent people, but this attack stands out for its appalling, sickening cowardice – deliberately targeting innocent, defenceless children and young people who should have been enjoying one of the most memorable nights of their lives".

Giorgia Newman, an elegant lady even at the venerable age of ninety, makes her way into the Royal Manchester Children's Hospital with the aid of her inseparable walking stick. People rush in and out of the building in continuation, its entrance is guarded by police officers, while agents of the Special Protection Service wait outside, standing alongside a line of limousines that have brought high-ranking officials to the scene. Inside the hospital, Mrs. Newman walks up to the reception desk and asks where she can find her granddaughter, Elsa Newman. The nurse consults a register and points Giorgia down a hallway along which she encounters, at a certain point, a group of plainclothes officers who are escorting Queen Elizabeth to the hospital exit. Having come to visit and comfort the victims of the attack and their families, the Queen's gaze is saddened but, as always, firm and resolute. Giorgia Newman reaches room #123, where she finds her son David, a man in his fifties. His hair flecked with grey, his face unshaven, David has an exhausted, anguished look. "Thank you for coming, Mother". Giorgia's worried gaze looks past her son, seeking out her thirteen year-old granddaughter Elsa, a lovely girl, blond, slim and rather tall for her age. But she looks so fragile in the hospital bed, her face covered with cuts and scratches, two massive, blood-stained bandages on her head, an arm wrapped in dressings and a bulging eye that is nothing but an ugly bruise. There are wires attached to her chest, to control her heartbeat, and an IV drip sends antibiotics into her arm through a needle. Not having slept all night, David is drained, but he still appears to be in a hurry. "I have to go, Mother. Please stay with her as long you can. I'm not sure when I'll be back". Worried, Giorgia asks: "How is your wife?". Fighting back the tears, David answers in a whisper, to keep his daughter from hearing: "They have her in an artificial coma. Her heart is still beating, but they've got to wait before they try to bring her around... they took twelve nails and bolts out of her body... Good lord, if only there was something I could do..." Giorgia reassures him: "Your wife is strong. I'll stay here with Elsa. You go ahead". As David leaves, she adds: "Be sure to talk to her, even if you don't think she can hear you. Tell her that Elsa is fine and that the two of you need her... don't give up on her". David gathers his mother in a close embrace. Drying his eyes on the back of his hand, he leaves the room. Giorgia moves closer to her granddaughter's bed. "Hello darling, it's me, grandma... can you see me?". Elsa struggles to open her good eye, managing a faint smile as her grandmother takes her hand. "Your mother is doing well. Now we have to concentrate on you". Elsa squeezes her grandmother's hand as a tear slides down the girl's cheek. Her grandmother dries it with a piece of gauze before saying: "... You'll be fine... I have something for you". She pulls a chair up to the bed: "I'll stay here with you, don't worry. I've always wanted to tell you about this ... it's a story, actually. You know, it's very important that memories get handed down". Giorgia takes an old binder from her purse. The dark, worn leather is closed with a cloth ribbon. "These are notes that my mother, your great grandmother, kept. A sort of diary". She holds it up to her nose. "I can almost smell her scent, though that's probably my subconscious playing tricks on me. Your great grandmother was a brilliant lady, way ahead of her time. She studied mankind from a social and cultural perspective as an anthropologist, a field she developed a passion for after reading Kant's "Anthropology from a Pragmatic Point of View", a work that emphasises the difference between the pragmatic and the practical. As a rule, anything having to do with human activities, no matter what end is being pursued, is pragmatic, whereas the practical sphere focusses on moral action, making it synonymous with ethics. The acts of man can be divided into those meant to achieve the various empirical objectives of life, all of which can be traced back to a search for the greatest possible pleasure, and those geared towards establishing a categorical imperative, meaning a law that governs nothing less than morality itself. In one of his reflections, Kant stated that knowing the world involves knowing man in an unequivocal, categorical manner. Your great grandmother was especially enthusiastic about the second half of the text, in which Kant makes the distinction between "natural character", meaning what nature makes of man, and "moral character", or what man makes of himself: in other words his ethics, his morality. She firmly believed that human events repeat themselves in cycles which are gradually forgotten, only to play themselves out at a later date, sometimes many years later. She had lived in England, and she knew the language, which led to her being offered the opportunity to travel with her family from Italy to the Sudan, so that she could study and analyse in greater depth the historical and cultural realities which gave rise, between 1884 and 1898, to the harsh, unforgiving Shari'a law, also known as Sharia. This body of law was first established by Muhammad Ahmad bin Abd Allah, a Sudanese Arab from Dongola, a city on the banks of the northern portion of the Nile. It was in Dongola, the capital of north Sudan, that Muhammad Ahmad proclaimed himself the Mahdi, or spiritual guide of the people. With his proclamation of Sharia law, he was declaring war against "evil" while leading a popular revolt against Egyptian domination, with the ultimate goal of creating a fundamentalist theocracy. He wanted to enact a form of government under which everything that the people did, and all government procedures, were in accordance with the divine will. In other words "Islamic fundamentalism", a concept that originated with the Shi'a sect in Iran, under a conservative political-theoretical current of thought that preached, based on certain interpretations of the Koran, a return to the "fundamentals", to the "origins" of Islam, all of which Muhammad Ahmad held to be infallible, flawless and authentic. The thing is, Arabs see the world in black or white. They are absolutists who ignore the different shades of grey that we take into consideration. Having wiped out anybody who failed to embrace his orthodox regime, and after reconquering much of the Sudan, Muhammad Ahmad died of typhus. A few months later,

Abdallahi ibn Muhammad, another Sudanese Arab and a native of Dafur, an area in the Sahara Desert that was one of the nine historic provinces of the Sudan, took command, proclaiming himself the "Khalifa" or successor. Abdallahi also laid claim to the title of Mahdi, or spiritual guide, as a proponent of orthodox Islamic fundamentalism. He declared war on Ethiopia and Egypt, and on Equatoria, which included southern Sudan and northern Uganda. Later, he went to war with Eritrea, which was an Italian colonial domain at the time. Italian troops moved into the Sudan and occupied the city of Kassala, the capital of the Sudanese region of the same name, from 1894 to 1897. After fighting off a number of counterattacks, but ultimately suffering a crippling defeat at Adua, the Italians, their forces badly depleted, asked the English for help. Anglo-Egyptian troops launched their own counterattack against the Mahdi Islamic State, driving it back into the southern portion of the Sudan, where it still controlled the region of Dafur. In 1898, near the village of Umm Diwaykarat, Abdallahi ibn Muhammad, the successor or "Khalifa", was killed, leading to the final defeat and disappearance of the army of the Islamic State. My mother always held that events were cyclical. She was convinced that one day, unfortunately, perhaps many years in the future, the fundamentalist Islamic State would come back to life, though it was impossible to say where, with what amount of violence, or for how long.

"Are you awake?". Elsa nods yes.   Her grandmother opens the diary: " ... Let me tell you why your name is Elsa...or maybe you're not interested?". The girl gives a faint smile. "Your name, Elsa, holds a special place in my heart. It was my sister's name, so it is very important to me. But there is so much more to the story...I'll read you what my mother wrote in her diary". From her bed, young Elsa asks: "...But great grandmother, your mother, was named Olga, wasn't she?". "Yes, Olga Mittieri...and here is what she wrote". The grandmother puts on her glasses and begins reading:

"The desert has always held an irresistible attraction for me. It has an otherworldly, indescribable scent. When the wind, stirred by the sudden changes in temperature, plays amidst the sand, it can startle you with the unpredictable, almost infernal sounds it makes. The desert's colours never fade, while its nights, which wrap you in a blanket of stars, seem to last forever. But how could I ever imagine that such beauty would cause me so much pain, turn my life completely inside out... and with a violence I never would have thought possible."

"After completing my ethno-anthropological analysis of the underlying motives of Sharia law, I decided to take up residence in the Sudan, in the city of Kassala, which sits between the Nile and the Sahara Desert, with the Taka Mountains towering majestically off in the distance, their peculiar shapes making them seem like so many giant holiday cakes. Inside this dusty city, the open-air stores were filled with an unexpected bounty of vegetables and other produce, the fruit was rich and colourful, thanks to the fertile land along the banks of the Nile. Carts pulled by donkeys were used to haul abundant supplies, including heavy sacks of rice and an endless stock of red onions. If one of the carts tipped over, littering the street with bananas, that two boys in charge of the load would hurriedly gather up again. On account of the heat, practically all the men wore long, white flowing robes and headpieces in the form of turbans. The women dressed in the traditional Chador, a garment that came in a variety of vivid colours: orange, yellow, turquoise, red and purple. It left their faces uncovered, as only a few, the most devotedly orthodox, wore the niqab, behind which only their dark, piercing, beautiful eyes can be seen. The women of this region had the good fortune of not being forced to wear the burqa, a garment that closed them off in absolute darkness. The streets were always abuzz with lively chatter. I loved these warm, friendly people with their ready smiles. Once I spotted a thin, toothless fellow stationed under a portico, trying to sell an assortment of sabres, knives and daggers that he had laid out on the ground, atop a white cloth, though his items were not meant to do harm, but rather to adorn belts or be used to cut the canes from which fences were made. A small herd of oxen might move lazily by, led by two boys driving the animals forward with branches that they used as switches. Placed on a wall by the entrance to a government building was a brass plaque that stated: "Muhammad Ali Pasha 1840". Ali Pasha was the Ottoman commander who founded the city of Kassala, at first nothing more than an outpost, the site of a large military camp from which the Ottoman troops set out to conquer eastern Sudan. Muhammad Ali Pasha is considered the founding father of modern Egypt, a fascinating historical event that I am now studying in the context of an analysis of human behaviour as it manifests itself in various social groups. This is why, in 1910, I settled in Kassala, by then a city governed by the English. I have now lived there for almost four years with my family, whose roots are in Italy. My husband Giorgio Mittieri, a descendent of an Italian noble family, has not met with good fortune in his business ventures, eventually losing all of our assets. At present, we get by thanks to my clearheaded practicality. Those who know me say that I am a good-looking woman of thirty, though I am well aware that I have my defects: I am quite tall and a bit too thin, though I do seem to have the right curves in the right places. After earning my degree in anthropology, I had a chance to move to this region in order to further my studies of the social origins of this famed figure, the father of modern Egypt.

They say that I am a brave, emancipated woman, and the truth is that, for the female sex, finding a place in the professional world is no easy task. Through perseverance, and thanks to my knowledge of foreign languages, I was able to write, as mentioned, a number of texts on emerging figures and the underlying cultural forces that motivated them, all viewed from the perspective of various social contexts. A number of my writings have been included in the curricula of prestigious universities, where I have also been invited to speak on occasion. They send me the funds needed for the trip and they reimburse me for what I spend on lodgings. I certainly have no reason to complain, seeing that relations with my publisher have also grown more positive, thanks to the enthusiast reception of my books in the West. I love my family, always travelling together with my husband and with Elsa, my thirteen year-old daughter, a lively, fun-loving, inquisitive girl whose features are so fine that, when she smiles, she gives off an enchanting, irresistible glow".

Elsa interrupts her grandmother: "Elsa was thirteen, Grandma, just like me?". Her grandmother smiles: "That's right. She was pretty and full of energy, just like you. I still hadn't been born at the time, so I didn't even exist". The girl turns to face her grandmother more directly, to follow the story better: "... Please read to me, Grandma". The Grandmother begins reading again...

"The preparations for our upcoming departure were in full swing inside the house. We were moving. In the large drawing room, I was packing everything up with care, helped by Muna, our beloved governess, and two other women hired especially for the occasion".

In the next room, a number of books have been stacked on a crate. All of them are written by Olga Mittieri. Another book is in the hands of a black man who, strangely enough, is also portrayed on the cover. With his typically Sudanese face, he was selected by Olga to be the model for the cover illustration, but he is also the family's loyal domestic helper, Ackur, a man well along in years, with exceptionally dark skin and a strong, kind, dignified bearing. Next to him sits Elsa, who is listening to Ackur do his best to learn how to read: "...its way of life.. and its.. its very.. evolution are directly tied to the culture of the polly ..." Elsa laughs in fun: "... Polly?!..." She laughs again ... Ackur lowers his eyes, embarrassed. Realising that she may have gone too far: "...I'm sorry Ackur, I shouldn't have. But Polly! It's "polity", not "Polly": po.. li.. ty. You see? "Polly" is this..." She gets up, imitating the pecking motions of a parakeet, "Polly want a cracker!". Ackur smiles too, enjoying the joke. But when Elsa's mother enters the room, he hides the book. Having noticed his sudden movement, she asks: "What are you hiding?". Ackur sheepishly shows her the book, and she realises that it is the one with his portrait on the cover. "... I didn't know you were learning to read". "Yes, Miss Elsa is helping me, but it is so hard". "Reading is very important, Ackur. Just think: you can travel to faraway places without leaving this room. It's miraculous". "...That would be so far to go, Ma'am". "Ackur, if you learn to read, then those faraway worlds will become yours. Start with this book, you can have it as a gift from me". An overjoyed Ackur shows his dazzling teeth in a broad smile: "...It will be my pleasure to travel while staying in my room...". Olga changes the subject, saying in a teasing tone: "Well for now, please put away that smile. We can't afford to get to the Taka Mountains too late. Would you please go find my husband? He's bound to be at the usual tavern."

Ackur arrives at the tavern, but he does not see Giprgio Mittieri. Asking the man behind the counter, he gets a knowing smile as the man indicates a table in the back where someone seems to be sleeping with his head propped on his folded arms. "Raja, Raja, my Lady says to come back, she wants to leave. Raja?". A drunken Mittieri accidentally knocks his glass to the floor. Ackur picks it up and helps him get to his feet. "Raja, my Lady will not be happy. Come, I will help". The two of them struggle as they make their way out of the tavern.

A strong wind is kicking up dust and sand in an arid, rocky zone. The Sahara is a desert of breath-taking allure, but it can also be unpredictable, dangerous. The camels advance in one long, straight line, the Bedouins forced to shield their faces with the cloth of their turbans as they push forward. Ackur leads the caravan from atop his camel. He rides up to Giorgio Mittieri, who is having a hard time staying in the saddle. "Raja, we need to reach the foothills of the Taka Mountains as soon as possible. There we will find shelter in the caves. The wind will be getting stronger. The storm will last all night". Giorgio nods in agreement. He turns in the direction of his wife, who is as elegant as ever, even in Bedouin garb. Olga signals to him that everything is fine, then she turns to look at their daughter Elsa, who unlike the others, seems to be totally unconcerned with the tempestuous wind. She laughingly teases Muna, the Sudanese governess, who clings to her saddle, poor thing, barely able to keep from falling off her camel. In high spirits, Elsa remarks: "Muna! You look like one of those monkeys in the marketplace!". Muna gives her a grimace that makes Elsa laugh all the harder. The caravan moves on, quickening its pace.

It is almost nightfall. The wind, more violent than ever, practically stops the camels in their tracks. Olga rides up to her husband and yells, to make herself heard over the howling wind: "We'll take shelter in those hills! Can you make it?!...Her husband signals yes with a glance and then shouts to her: "Where is Elsa?" Olga: "Back with Muna!" "I'll check on her", says the husband in a reassuring before heading off in Elsa's direction.

A Bedouin has taken the reins of Muna's camel in order to try and pull the animal forward. Giorgio Mittieri reaches Elsa in the middle of the caravan. Having gotten off her own camel, the girl refuses to get on another one being ridden by a Bedouin. "No! Can't you see? I want to stay with my camel!", she insists, protecting her eyes from the flying sand. The Bedouin is just as insistent: "... this camel is too nervous. You can't ride him any more!" Pointing to the sloping sand: "... It is too dangerous!". Ackur rides up, and her father joins the discussion too: "Come along Elsa, ride with me!" says Mittieri, before telling Ackur: "You take her camel and go on up ahead to Mrs. Olga!" Ackur seems uneasy about the idea, but he obeys, leading the camel off. Elsa tries to mount her father's camel as the caravan continues moving towards the hills. Olga turns around: in the midst of the swirling wind and sand she can barely make out her husband and her daughter, who have fallen behind and are slowly disappearing in the storm. Alarmed, she wants to stop, but the Bedouin leading her camel has hold of the reins. She shouts, hoping to make herself heard, but her voice is lost in the storm. Desperately trying to grab the reins back, she spooks the camel, who sends her tumbling down the side of a sand dune. The Bedouin who was walking in front of her yells in Sudanese to Ackur, who jumps down from his own camel to run to her aid, until he too is swallowed up by the storm.

CHAPTER II
The Funeral

An overcast sky foretells rain on the way. A light breeze sets the leaves of the palm trees astir. In the military cemetery of Khartoum, my husband Giorgio's has come to a close. I feel an incredible sadness, an enormous emptiness inside. Of late, his business affairs offered him little in the way of happiness, but I know he was proud of me, I was convinced that everything would soon fall into place, because the bond between us was strong, we were happy. We laughed and had fun together, and there was still so much we had to do. But now all that is over. I am left with nothing but darkness, mourning, my tears, a deep, enduring pain. The desert I so cherished has taken away my beloved companion of the last sixteen years. We found him the day after the storm, lifeless, his body curled up to protect Elsa, who lived, thanks to his sacrifice. This is why I loved him. He was far from perfect, but his love for us was always generous, it was what he lived for and, all too tragically, what he died for. I had lost him, and it seemed as if my torment could cause me no greater suffering. Little did I know what fate had in store for me just a short time later.

A stately home in Khartoum, the capital of Anglo-Egyptian Sudan, which had become a British protectorate in 1914, as had Egypt itself. Found in the residential quarter that houses the majority of the Western diplomats live, the villa is sun-drenched, filled with colour. Its window and spacious doors open onto gardens arranged in the traditional Sudanese style. A portico of elegant, white arches wraps much of the home in its embrace. From off in the distance comes the sound of a local woman, possibly a domestic, singing a song of the past. Elsa lies on a bed in one of the rooms of the villa, her face still bearing the harsh burn marks left by the sandstorm. A Sudanese physician has finished examining the girl. Olga, dressed in mourning, looking distressed, waits to hear what he has to say. Muna the governess stands next to her, looking equally anguished.

The doctor returns his instruments to his bag. "Continue applying the compresses. And do your best to get her to eat. She needs to regain her strength. You must be patient Ma'am ... Stay by her side, talk to her frequently. I'm sure she can hear you".

His words do little to sooth Olga, while a tear slides down Muna's cheek, only, to be humbly brushed away by the governess. The doctor takes his leave in as reassuring tone: "I'll be back tomorrow".

Moving closer to her daughter, Olga softly caresses the girl. "Darling, can you hear me? If so, please blink. Let me know you're there", but Elsa remains motionless, her eyes staring straight up at the ceiling, as if no sound could reach her. "I'm here with you. Mama will never leave you, sweetheart".

A shaken Olga kisses her daughter on the forehead and leaves the room. Muna, equally unsettled, takes a seat to stay and keep the girl company, though Elsa does nothing but stare into space. Muna can hardly bear to see this girl, whose teasing and tricks she misses more than she would ever have imagined, lie there so lifelessly. Hoping to distract herself, Muna picks up a book as a slow, drowsy breeze sets the curtains to rustling.

Outside the house, beyond the portico, the doctor is being led out of the villa by Ackur. He waves one last time to Olga, before the gate closes behind him. Walking back through the large entryway, Olga enters the partially open drawing room found along one side of the portico and sits down next to her friend Maggie Wilson, an Englishwoman who is being served a cool drink by one of the servants.

"He's an excellent doctor," Maggie offers, "trained according the English school of medicine".

"Thank you, Maggie," answers Olga.

Maggie, doing her best to cheer her friend up, "As soon as Elsa is better, the two of you simply must come see me in Sussex. You have no idea how beautiful that countryside can be". With a forced smile, Olga observes: "That would be nice. Just as soon as Elsa is feeling like herself again. We'll see".

The sun filters through the open end of the drawing room, from where a wisteria plant climbs in the direction of the roof. The lush vegetation is in full bloom. The birds in an aviary put their vast array of brightly coloured feathers on display as they hop from branch to branch. The morning breeze sets the branches and leaves astir, causing the grass to lean gently over to one side. From one corner of the room, the tick-tock of a grandfather clock can clearly be heard. Suddenly a gust of air shakes the windows, as if a storm had arrived. But then the curtains stop fluttering. Everything goes still. The leaves are motionless. Even the grass seems frozen in place. The breeze has simply disappeared, as has the bittersweet, distant sound of the woman's song. The birds no longer chirp. Everything has gone still. There is not a single sound to be heard, not even the tireless ticking of the grandfather clock over in the corner. Olga looks towards it in surprise, only to see the pendulum hanging there motionless. Something in the air leaves the two women both puzzled and shaken. The silence is complete.

Muna interrupts her reading in Elsa's room, having sensed that something is amiss. The girl has shut her eyes, and her hand has slid down her side, until it hangs over the edge of the bed. Back in the drawing room, Maggie also looks startled, while Olga has the terrible feeling that all is not right. Her hands begin to shake, her heart pounds, her throat tightens up. In the other room, Elsa takes a deep breath, as if she were winded, and then opens her eyes again, looking about her in bewilderment. The curtains go back to swaying gently up and down, the leaves once again rustle in the breeze. The sound of a woman singing of a distant past returns. Olga's incredulous eyes seek out those of her frightened friend, hoping to find some hint of an explanation. Muna lets her book slip from her hands as she breathlessly takes in scene. Elsa looks around, her eyes locked in a startled stare, only to pronounce a short phrase in a strange, unknown language.

Muna runs frantically into the drawing room. "Ma'am! Come quickly! I've no idea what has happened, but please come now!" Olga runs to Elsa's room, followed by Muna and Olga's friend Maggie. They find the girl gazing around the room, her eyes locked in a bewildered stare, as if she had no idea where she was or who these women who have come rushing in might be.

Olga walks up to her. "Elsa, what is it? Please tell me!"

But the girl bolts away, running towards the door while pronouncing words which appear to have no sense. Her mother runs after her in astonishment, while the governess tries to block her path. Ackur comes rushing in too, together with a number of the servants. Maggie, Olga's English friend, watches the scene in stunned silence. The girl reaches the door and pushes at it, presses up against it, as if she had no idea how to use a door handle. She breaks away from Muna, still speaking words that seem incomprehensible, and runs straight towards the glass door that leads out to the garden, cutting her arms and her face as she crashes into it. Her mother, in a state of sheer panic: "Muna, help me!" Elsa, looking dazed and astonished to have been stopped by that transparent wall, gazes at the glass as if it were something she has never seen before. Her hands and face are covered with blood, but she keeps struggling as her mother pins her arms, trying to help her: "Darling, what is it!...Calm down, be still! ...Will someone do something please!!!" Maggie turns to Ackur: "Run and get the doctor from the garrison".

In trying to keep Elsa calm, Olga's own clothes have been soaked in blood. "Darling, you're losing blood!... Please stop, no one wants to hurt you!"... "Enough, my child!" she cries out.

A few hours later, a medical officer in a colonial uniform finishes bandaging Elsa, who once again lies in her bed. She looks calm, almost distant, though her eyes are very much alert, filling at times with a look of terror. Her face and arms have been bandaged, while her wrists and ankles have been tied to the bedframe using strips of gauze.

"Mrs. Mittieri, there is nothing wrong with your daughter physically. She is in perfect health, though what happened is quite strange. I am a military doctor, and your daughter exhibits a condition which is completely unknown to me".

Olga, at her wits' end, is still wearing the clothes stained with her daughter's blood. "What can we do?"

"A psychiatrist," says the doctor. "I suggest moving in two directions at once, though always being very careful not to upset the child's nervous system, because, let me repeat, there is nothing wrong with her physically. I also think it would be a good idea to see a specialist in glottology, simply to get an idea of what language your daughter might be speaking, or to see whether she is making it all up on her own".

The mother, in a troubled tone, "Can we free her hands? I can't stand to see her like this".

"I understand how you feel, but it's for her own good, to keep her from hurting herself again". But then he realises how much pain the mother is in.

"All right, but it would be better if you did it".

Olga, hesitates, trying to give her daughter a caress first, but Elsa, as alert as ever, pulls away from her again. Though sick at heart, the mother refuses to give up. Softly stroking her daughter, she overcomes an initial moment of resistance, until Elsa seems to relax a bit, finally letting her mother untie first one hand and then the other, only to dart away again, fleeing from her mother's caresses to a darkened corner of the room.

Olga instinctively starts to go after her, but the doctor cautions, "You should wait... give her time. Let's all leave, so that she can calm down".

Elsa watches them closely, with a frightened look, as they all leave for the drawing room.

"Ma'am, it would appear that your daughter no longer recognises you. I don't think she even knows where she is. It's as if she had lost all contact with reality. Most likely the trauma of losing her father that way, the violence of the sandstorm... Let's not pressure her, but give her a chance to get her bearings once again. I'm certain we'll soon see some improvement. Draw closer to her, but gradually. After then I recommend that you take her to Cairo, where you'll find physicians much far more qualified to examine her than I am".

Olga, worried sick but still sure of herself, says, "Yes, of course. We will take her to Cairo".

CHAPTER III
The Fate

In springtime, in the month of May, the German countryside is especially charming and richly scented with the smells of nature. The fields are starting to bloom, and the towering forests have shed their snowy winter coats. An automobile is travelling at a brisk pace along a straight road, with no other vehicle in sight, leaving cloud of dust behind it as it makes its way through the vast woodlands. A road sign announcing "TAUNUS Bad Langenschwalbach" passes by in the bat of an eye. On this gorgeous morning, fate is plotting to bring together two exceptional men whom are destined, in the not too distant future, to join each other in a marvellous but terrifying adventure. The chauffeur at the wheel of the automobile is Edward Trotman, while behind him sits a man dressed in the unerring elegance of an Englishman, complete with a red carnation adorning the buttonhole of his jacket. This is someone who could only be a native of the British Isles: Sir George Edward Stanhope

Molyneux Herbert, Earl of Carnarvon. A collector, a gentleman, a global traveller, he has a passion for both finely crafted automobiles and speed. A realist when he acts, he is a romantic when it comes to his sentiments. The car moves down the road at no small speed, slicing between two flowered hedgerows, when suddenly, from out of a narrow side-road just a short distance away, a pair of oxcarts appears, partially blocking the way. In an attempt to manoeuvre around them, the driver veers towards the edge of the roadway, but a tyre clips a pile of stones and bursts, causing the vehicle to flip over and end up in a ditch. Trotman is able to free himself from the wreck, but Carnarvon, knocked unconscious, remains trapped inside. Two farmers come running, carrying a bowl of water for the driver. He takes it from them, hurriedly soaking a handkerchief that he places on Lord Carnarvon's forehead. The injured man opens his eyes and, through the pain, observes: "I assume we rolled over?"

"Sir, I never saw them coming". The driver shakes his head apologetically, reserving an icy glare for the farmers. "In 23 of service to Your Lordship, no incident of this type has ever befallen me. I am truly sorry, Sir".

"And so am I, Edward. This experience was quite unnecessary".

"Yes Sir, most unnecessary indeed".

Lord Carnarvon grimaces in pain as he tries but fails to get back on his feet. "Would there happen to be anything stronger than water?"

Trotman retrieves a steel flask from the wrecked automobile and fills the cap of the flask, which also serves as a cup, before handing it to his employer, who drinks the contents straight down.

In a wild and barren area between the Tigris and Euphrates rivers, in Iraqi territory, the legendary land of Abraham, a group of men are hard at work, digging down to a depth of roughly twelve metres below the ground level. Supervising their efforts, three archaeologists sit beneath a makeshift tent. One is Professor Howard Carter. Next to him, busy drying the sweat from his brow, is Sir Leonard Wooley, an archaeologist much esteemed in his field. The third overseer is destined to become world famous, though not for his accomplishments as an archaeologist, but rather for his role, as T.E. Lawrence, or Lawrence of Arabia, in leading the Arab insurrection during the First World War.

The workmen break through a sheet of clay, revealing the opening of a vast, unlit cave.

Drawn by their excited chatter, the three archaeologists come running. This may be what they have been hoping for! One by one, they lower themselves into the cave. The workers hand them lamps that are already lit, so they can disappear into the darkness. The lights held by the three men illuminate the inside of the cave, revealing a discovery that leaves Carter, Woolley and Lawrence staring in shocked silence: there, in the middle of the large cave, is a burial room which holds the tombs and bodies of a KING and a QUEEN, plus other bodies found all around them. Four millennia before Christ, this must have been the site of a massacre: the ladies of court, arrayed in two lines, still display the splendid manner in which their hair was styled for the funeral celebration; the soldiers of the royal guard still wear their copper helmets, and their lances are still at the ready, by their hands. Even servants were sacrificed, with the skeletons of two drivers sitting upright on the seats of their heavy wagons, thanks to the cartilage that still connects their bones. In one corner of the room, a man who must have been a musician is poised by his harp, looking like the bones of his arms are ready to play the magnificent instrument, though they too are held in place by nothing but cartilage. Kneeling next to the coffin of the Queen, the most richly adorned, are the skeletons of two men who appear to have been killed at the very moment in which they were demonstrating their respect and reverence. Precious draperies, shawls and ornaments are on hand in large supply. The three archaeologists receive another shock when the oxygen-rich air entering the cave causes the harpist's hand to fall off his wrist and slide down the chords of the instrument, producing a bizarre sound that seems to cue the disintegration of the rest of the frightening scene. The wreaths of flowers crumble into so much dust, while the bones of the skeletons, no longer held together by their cartilage, clatter to the floor. The trio of archaeologists, their eyes heavy with dread and astonishment, can only stand there, powerless to keep the chilling treasure of their discovery from falling apart.

England's Cambridge University offers a wealth of colours in the spring, when a flowery scent can be noted even in the large lecture hall on the ground floor of a building of Trinity College where archaeologist Howard Carter is giving a talk to a mixed audience of students and other ladies and gentleman. Sitting among the students, one young woman in particular, Lady Evelyn Carnarvon, follows Carter's presentation of a number of photographs taken at the tomb in Mesopotamia with rapt attention.

"What is the meaning of this massacre? The only possible explanation is that, to honour man, what he holds most precious was offered up as a sacrifice: human life. Perhaps the goal was to establish a divine reign? For even if these massacres, so to speak, can be seen as attempts to deify the first kings, not even the most important gods of the distant past ever demanded a similar rite, showing just how far back in ancient times the tombs at Ur can be dated, though I should add that, at present, our knowledge of this era still rests on little more than legend and mystery".

The students and guests applaud enthusiastically, including a smiling Lady Evelyn. One of the students asks, "Professor Carter, I've read in the Times that you think a sovereign who lived many thousands of years before Christ may be waiting to be discovered in Egypt's Valley of the Kings. Can you tell us anything more?"

Carter answers as he puts his photographs back in a leather briefcase. "Journalists always write too much, while there is actually very little to say. Still, I have good reason to believe that somewhere in the Valley of the Kings there lies the tomb of a sovereign of whom, to date, we know very little. And what information we do have is often contradictory".

Taking a piece of chalk, Carter goes to the blackboard and sketches the outline of a valley, writing in the centre: VALLEY OF THE KINGS.

"Here," he says while drawing a triangle inside the Valley of the Kings, "the sovereign we are searching for has been found somewhere in this general area since roughly 3,300 years BC".

The students follow him attentively, as does Lady Evelyn, who asks: "Is there much of a chance that the tomb will still be intact?"

Carter dusts the chalk off his hands. "Unfortunately, not much at all. But even if the tomb allows us to add just ten more lines to the history of that period, I say it is well worth the effort to search for it".

Another admiring student: "When will you begin to look for it again?"

"If we obtain the necessary funding, we could start very soon. After all, our work as archaeologists is to discover how things once were, based on what has survived to the present. We have the privilege of living an adventure like no other. And at the end, we shall owe you an account of what we find".

The students and the many other enthusiastic listeners give Carter a standing ovation. Some even leave their seats to congratulate him in person. Moving nimbly, Lady Evelyn makes her way to the end of her row, in order to catch the professor's attention as he passes by.

"Professor Carter, Howard!"

Carter stops, turning to look at the young woman, who continues with a smile: "Perhaps you don't remember me. Of course I was a lot younger, just a girl, back when you worked together with my father".

Carter responds in a gallant tone: "I'm afraid I'm terrible with names, but I never forget a strikingly pretty face. If I'm not mistaken, you must be the daughter of Lord Carnarvon?"

"Evelyn", says the delighted young woman as she holds out her hand.

Carter bows to kiss it, though he only brushes the hand with his lips, as is the custom.

"How is your father? I hope he has finally recovered from that unfortunate accident".

The two of them leave the lecture hall and begin walking down the hallway together, as Evelyn observes: "A man as energetic and active as my father, suddenly forced to spend all his time in a wheelchair, you can imagine how he is! He'll have to pass the winter months in Egypt for a number of years, doing nothing but resting, or so the doctors say. But you know full well how he is".

Carter smiles. "Egypt is delightful this time of year. He won't regret the trip".

As they continue down the hallway, side by side, Evelyn asks in a sly but light-hearted tone: "Howard, forgive my unseemly curiosity, but the newspapers say that you have tired of your solitary existence, and so you've returned to find somebody to be by your side when you go back to Egypt. Is this true?".

Carter smiles, "For once, the newspapers have written the truth".

Evelyn seemed to have hoped for rather a different answer. Momentarily at a loss for words, she finally manages to get out: "Well can I ask... do you in fact intend ... to marry? Is it someone who is well known? Who exactly is "she"? Or must it remain a secret?"

Carter smiles, murmuring in a tone of mystery: "A secret yes, but one that I can reveal, assuming you have the time and the patience to come into town with me".

Inside a store filled with birds and their cages, the countless varieties of chirping make for a raucous din. Evelyn asks in a discrete whisper: "Is this her store? I mean, does "she" work here?"

In an equally hushed tone, Carter answers: "This where I shall find the companion I need to relieve my solitude".

Evelyn looks in surprise at the premises: "And here I thought...." She laughs in relief. "But don't they have pet birds in Egypt?"

Carter, in a playful tone: "Few of the birds in Egypt sing, and those that do, sing in Arabic".

As Evelyn's gaze takes in the store, the site of Carter carefully examines the occupants of the different cages sets her to laughing. When a dark-grey bird with white breast feathers catches her eye, the sales attendant steps forward.

"Mimus Polyglottus, Ma'am. Much valued for the beauty and virtuosity of its singing. Originally from the woods of South Carolina, in the United States, with the ability to imitate every imaginable species of bird, plus a full range of other animals".

Carter does not appear convinced: "It's not quite what I had in mind…"

But the salesman insists: "Its tones range from the crystalline song of the songbird of the forest to…"

This time it is Carter who cuts him off: "I've no doubt that's the case".

The salesman refuses to give up: "Trust me Sir, it is capable of every possible inflection, even the shrill cry of the vulture. In all of nature, I doubt there is another bird that can match its mastery of song, a skill acquired directly from Mother Nature".

Evelyn moves closer, until she's practically face to face with the bird, at which point she makes the sound of three notes. The bird repeats all three flawlessly. Carter glances at Evelyn, who smiles back at him.

The two of them leave the store. Evelyn is carrying the birdcage. "Howard, why don't you come pay us a visit at Highclere?" she says, immediately adding, so that he cannot raise any objections: "I am certain that my father would be delighted to see you before he leaves. He is still passionately interested in archaeology, and I know he would appreciate the company of another man".

Carter smiles obligingly: "Highclere must be beautiful this time of year".

Evelyn, intent on pressing her point: "Howard, where will find the funds for your next expedition?"

The topic seems to intrigue Carter, though good manners keep him from showing just how much.

"There are some potential sources of funding, but nothing definite yet. I'm negotiating with the Egyptian government. An excavation concession was given to Theodore Davis, a New York businessman, for twelve years, only he passed away a few months ago".

Evelyn's enthusiasm gets the best of her: "But if you found someone who's not only a financer, but a patron as well? You and my father made such a good team!"

Carter smiles at the compliment.

Scattered around the vast, magnificent grounds of Highclere are cedars of Lebanon. Approaching the castle along a road which skirts a lake, Lady Evelyn arrives at the entryway, which sits at the foot of a large tower. Atop the tower flies the flag of the Earl of Carnarvon.

After entering through the massive front door, Evelyn finds Lord Carnarvon, her father, sitting in a rocking chair, absorbed in a classic of ancient Greek literature. His Lordship's favourite dog, lying by his feet, acknowledges Evelyn's arrival with a twitch of its brow and its tail. The young woman goes to her father, who kisses her on the forehead. Turning to her mother, Lady Almina, Evelyn recounts: "Oh Mother, I went to the most stimulating lecture. Professor Carter provided a fascinating account of an archaeological discovery! It was marvellous".

Her mother sits by the fireplace in a comfortable velvet armchair.

"That's wonderful, my dear. Would you like some tea?"

Lord Carnarvon puts down his book. "A new archaeological discovery, you say?"

Drawing closer to her father, Evelyn sits on the armrest of his chair.

"Yes Father. Carter is convinced that he can find the tomb of a pharaoh of the 18th Egyptian dynasty. If I'm not mistaken, that would be four thousand years before Christ".

"If we're talking about the 18th dynasty, then I would say roughly three thousand and three hundred years ago, based on Georg Steindorff's division of the different reigns. In any event, a period in which the arts and literature of Egypt flourished".

A butler arrives to serve tea, accompanied by two footmen.

Evelyn continues, her enthusiasm undiminished: "The thing is Father, he is certain that he will discover the tomb ..."

"... Who is?" asks her father, now quite curious.

"Why Professor Carter," explains Evelyn. "He believes that the sovereign he is looking for must be buried somewhere in the Valley of Kings. He is convinced of it! But I fear he still needs to find the funding for the dig".

Her father smiles, "Short on funds, is he?"

Evelyn continues, undaunted: "He says that he has some potential sources of financing, but nothing definite".

Lady Almina, between sips of her tea, "Exactly what they all say".

Lord Carnarvon ponders the matter: "The concessions to dig in the Valley of the Kings were held by Theodore Davis. It was he, together with Carter, who discovered the tomb of Yuya and Tjuyu, the parents of Tiye, the Great Royal Wife of Amenhotep III, and that tomb was intact. But Davis is an avid hoarder of fame and success. He'll never loosen his grip on those concessions".

Lady Almina interjects: "Unless I'm mistaken, Theodore Davis has died in Florida".

Lord Carnarvon lifts his eyebrows, a sign of interest that does not escape his daughter Evelyn's notice. She adds: "Yes, he is dead. Carter told me so. Father, you know Howard from before the war. A new archaeological exploration for the two of you two, it would be like old times! And the adventure would make your convalescence in Egypt fly by, don't you think?"

Lord Carnarvon clears his throat rather loudly before he too starts to sip his tea, but his daughter will not let the matter rest: "All those glorious days in Egypt, and you having to sit stock-still in a wheelchair".

Carnarvon practically chokes on his tea as his wife declares: "Evelyn, your father will never be stock-still, certainly not mentally, much less physically or spiritually. He adores Egypt".

The look on Carnarvon's face confirms the wisdom of his wife's diagnosis.

But Evelyn will not be denied: "What if those days were filled with activity, and with archaeological activity at that? You've always had a passion for such projects, and the heat would do wonders for your bones!"

Lord Carnarvon considers the idea. "You're right, but I still have my doubts ...."

Refusing to give up, showing the same persistence as the salesman in the Cambridge bird shop: "You've always said that you wanted to invest in archaeology again. Here's your chance! Become Professor Carter's patron!"

Her father looks at her wordlessly before turning to his wife: "There's something extraordinary about this girl. I've always said she resembles me".

Evelyn smiles, as Carnarvon observes: "Patron, you say? It sounds like something that could cost a pretty penny. Howard is definitely a man of considerable talent, and I would be most happy to be involved once again... to play a part in the history of archaeology".

But then he catches his wife's disapproving glance. "It would certainly brighten up the prospects of the time I have to spend in Egypt, a trip that we have already planned. I'll speak with Professor Maspero as soon as I arrive in Cairo. He has the last word on the concessions".

A visibly contented Evelyn hugs her father. "Of course, Father. And I'll go with you to Egypt!"

In a wry tone, her mother observes: "Evelyn dear, unless memory fails me, Professor Carter is a rather handsome man, isn't he?

Letting go of her father, Evelyn says to her mother, her eyes the picture of innocence: "I wouldn't have any idea, Mother. What can I say? It's not his appearance that interests me, but rather what he speaks of and how he says it".

"Yes my dear, of course".

CHAPTER IV
The Nile

Cairo is a hot, noisy, vibrant city found on the right bank of the Nile, just south of the point where the river splits into the pulsating flows that make up its delta. Off in the distance, beyond the far bank of the river, the Mokattam Hills can be seen, along with the desert, keeper of glorious reminders of the past, such as the massive Sphinx, a sitting lion with the head of a man, all carved from the limestone of the Giza plateau. A short distance away is the Pyramid of Cheops, the oldest and the largest of the three pyramids of the Giza necropolis. Thirty kilometres further south is the Saqqara necropolis, site of the Step Pyramid of Djoser, a monument dating from the 3rd dynasty and considered to be the oldest of the pyramids that inspired the "perfect" pyramids, or the ones which we picture in our mind's eye.

The sprawling old portion of Cairo barely seems to fit inside the city's eight monumental gateways. Magnificent buildings tell of a flourishing wealth tied to trade. Just a short walk away is the famous Khan el-Khalili, an enormous market souk. The setting sun lights up a golden dust, giving the enchanting city a magical glow. Further south from Cairo, moving downstream along the Nile, is Luxor, once known as Thebes, where the winters are mild and the summers are hot and dry, with temperatures that can reach 40°/45° centigrade. Continuing southward, between the second and third cataracts of the river, is a region known as Nubia, which means "gold" in ancient Egyptian. Here the climate is a challenge for even the hardiest adventurers, with peak temperatures that can reach 50° C in July and August, though the nights are surprisingly cold.

The Greek historian Herodotus was of the opinion that: "The people of Egypt are a gift of the Nile", a river that comes to life 6,400 kilometres south of its delta, where two tributaries give birth to its vigorous, flowing waters: the Blue Nile, whose origins lie in the mountains of Nubia, today's Ethiopia, thanks to the ample monsoon rains that saturate those lands, and the White Nile, whose headwaters form in the Rwenzori mountain range, known in ancient times as the "Mountains of the Moon", thanks to glaciers and snow-topped peaks that can reach more than 5,000 metres above sea level, such as Mount Stanley, whose highest point, the Margherita Peak, touches the sky at no less than 5,109 metres.

At similar altitudes, the mountains trap the humid air arriving from the Congo basin, turning it into clouds, and then rain or snow. It is no accident that "Rwenzori", in the language of the local Batoro people, means "Rainmaker". It is here, along the border between Uganda and the People's Republic of the Congo, where the rivers earliest waters plunge into Lake Victoria, that the young, impetuous White Nile is born, destined to keep growing as it travels towards the site of its marriage with the Blue Nile, in the lowlands of Sudan, from where the wealth of minerals born of the embrace of the two rivers' will continue along its way.

In the summer months, when the waters flood their banks, they deposit their rich, fertile silt, the eroded sediment that was the lifeblood of the magnificent civilisation of Egypt.

In Cairo, a carriage pulled by two horses moves through the joyfully frenetic babel of the city's day-to-day activities. Sitting inside are Lord Carnarvon and Lady Evelyn. The young noblewoman gazes out the window, watching in rapt fascination as worshippers remove their shoes before entering the Great Mosque to answer the Muezzin's call to prayer.

The carriage stops in front of the building that houses the Bureau of Museums, site of the Office of the Superintendent of Antiquities. Lord Carnarvon and his daughter get out and enter the building through its massive, wide-open entryway. Inside, two manual labourers are working hard to carry a sarcophagus down a hallway under the supervision of an orderly. Lord Carnarvon and his daughter step aside to let them pass, before arriving at a door with a name plate announcing: 'Professor Gaston Maspero'.

When they knock, the door is quickly opened by an orderly. Once inside the office, they receive a warm welcome from Dr. Maspero. A servant wearing white gloves, with a red fez on his head, offers glasses of ice tea to the guests, who include, in addition to Lady Evelyn and Lord Carnarvon, her father, the archaeologist Howard Carter, plus a pair of "experts on antiquities".

One of these two experts, speaking with a German accent, observes to Lord Carnarvon, "My Lord, I share Professor Maspero's opinion, and namely that the valley offers no further possibility for new discoveries. And I say so with the utmost respect for Professor Carter, who was the first to discover the tomb of Amenhotep I, together with that built for Princess Hatschepsut. Both of which, sadly enough, had already been violated and plundered".

Carnarvon turns to Carter. "Howard, on what do you base your hopes of finding a tomb, and the resting place of a specific sovereign at that?"

As Evelyn listens to the various participants in the discussion, she is secretly hoping that Howard will have the last word. Removing them from a case he has brought with him, the archaeologist lays out four gold leaves, a piece of pottery shaped like a cup, a pair of clay vases and some seals.

"On these objects, Gentlemen. The cup bears the name of Tut-ankh-amun, as do the golden leaves".

Gaston Maspero looks the objects over quickly, while the two "experts" go on sipping their tea, highly sceptical expressions on their faces.

As for Lord Carnarvon, he is giving Howard his utmost attention as the archaeologist adds, "Plus the fact that we discovered, in a crack between the rocks, fragments of pottery and linen bandages that first seemed to be of little importance. But then, once Winlock of the Metropolitan Museum had examined them, they were identified as the remains of materials used in a funeral ceremony, presumably that of the sovereign whom we are looking for.

"Theodore Davis himself, when he discovered the last refuge of the heretic Akhenaton, also came across a quite a few clay seals that bore the name of Tut-ankh-amun.

"All of which leads me to conclude, Gentlemen, that the tomb of this this particular sovereign is almost certainly found, despite all the failed attempts to uncover it to date, in the vicinity of where these objects were discovered, meaning somewhere in the Valley of Kings".

"But these things, my dear fellow," interjects Maspero, "were among the artefacts discovered by Professor Davis".

While paying close attention to the discussion, also does her best to decipher the almost imperceptible changes of expression on her father's face.

Maspero adds, "And when he finished his explorations, one thing seemed certain: that the Valley of Kings, in that specific location, had been used as a "hiding place" for the remains of burial sites dating to the end of the 18th dynasty and tied to leading figures of the Amarna religious revolution.

The second expert, who has been silent until now, finally says, "Everything that was used in a funeral banquet, whether made from fabric or pottery, was jealously hidden by worshippers of the new faith and buried at the site where Mr.

Davis and you yourself, Professor Carter, found the objects. But the tomb would have been sacked in ancient times, either by grave robbers or by the general who eventually became pharaoh, Horemheb, when he set out to persecute the 'memory' of his blasphemous predecessors".

Visibly annoyed, Carter replies, "Suppositions. Nothing but suppositions, my dear Sir!"

A shroud of silence falls over the encounter. Evelyn would like to say a word or two of her own, but she holds her tongue while Maspero, pouring himself another glass of tea, wonders out loud, "Couldn't it be, my dear friend, that all you actually found were the very last remains of the tomb you are looking for?"

The German expert also speaks up, "My opinion exactly, Professor Maspero. These are simply the final remains".

Professor Maspero goes on, as if the expert had not even spoken.

"My dear Howard, Professor Theodor Davis, may he rest in peace, was probably not especially well liked by any of us, but he was still an archaeologist of enormous stature, and five years ago he said: 'The Valley of Kings has no more secrets to divulge.'

"And yet you, who worked alongside him," continues Maspero, "do not share that opinion? Is that what we are to understand?"

Carter, after a brief moment of silence, "Yes sir. As I see it, Davis was wrong".

Evelyn brushes her father's knee with her own, nodding her approval while keeping her lips tightly closed.

Professor Maspero falls silent, turning instead to Lord Carnarvon, who points to the gold leaves, the cup and the two clay bowls laid out with the seals before softly exclaiming to Carter, "I see!"

"So your hope," continues Lord Carnarvon, "or better yet your unshakeable conviction that you can discover the tomb of this sovereign is based on nothing more than this handful of objects?"

Carter, undaunted, "Exactly!"

There is no question how fervently Evelyn supports Carter. Lord Carnarvon rises and, aided by his daughter, uses his cane to take a step or two, absentmindedly rubbing his ear along the way.

Ending the anguished wait of his daughter, he turns and declares, "Howard, it's good to see that you have the utmost confidence in your good luck. I offer you my heartfelt congratulations!"

To Professor Maspero, "Professor, will you please issue a permit for the dig, the responsibility for which shall rest with this man, the most stubborn archaeologist I have ever met!"

Unable to hide her enthusiastic approval, Evelyn gives her father a kiss that, at first, leaves Lord Carnarvon disoriented, but ultimately puts a smile on his face.

In the very same city of Cairo, just a few blocks away, in the al-Abbasiya quarter, at the edge of the desert, is a recently built hospital named after Umberto I, the King of Savoy and Italy. The project was undertaken by Cairo's growing Italian community, and specifically the Italian Beneficent Society of Cairo, which collected funding, contributions and generous legacies, such as that provided by donor Giacomo Rizzo, all of which allowed it to engage the services of architect Luigi Tosi, as well as those of the Sarozzo construction firm.

Though a small institution, the finished hospital has proven to be quite effective, thanks to the efforts of the nuns of the Verona chapter of the order of the "Devout Mothers of Africa", as well as the excellent medical service provided by the School of Medicine and Surgery of the University of Rome. In one of the hospital hallways, Olga Mittieri listens to a psychiatrist as he gives his opinion to three fellow physicians who have called him in to consult on a case.

In the background, on the other side of a window, Elsa sits in silence in one of the rooms, wearing a long, flowing garment typical of the Sudan. By her side is the faithful governess Muna.

"The girl has been kept under observation for quite some time now. These attacks of anxiety that she suffers at night are undoubtedly a subconscious reacting to the loss of her father, to the traumatic experience of his death.

"In certain cases, Ma'am, the violent death of a father, especially in a girl in puberty, can become deeply entangled in the subconscious, revealing itself only when she lets down her defences and relaxes. In other words, when she sleeps.

"At the same time, though for reasons we have yet to identify, she finds it impossible to communicate. She makes these strange sounds, speaking a language which she is probably making up by herself, and which we certainly don't understand. Just as she, and for quite some time now, appears unable to understand us".

Each time she meets with the doctors, Olga comes away more discouraged than before.

"Doctor, Elsa used to speak not only Italian, but English as well. And she also knew some Sudanese. Then she stopped talking altogether, apart from these bizarre sounds that, after listening to them at length, and while paying close attention, I must say that they strike me as belonging to some strange language all its own".

The physicians exchange glances of helpless frustration as a pained Olga continues, "It may be as you say, that she's completely closed herself off to the outside world, but if there is any chance of understanding, of making her better, please don't hesitate to do whatever is needed".

The psychiatrist tries to offer some small comfort.

"There might be something, in order see if we can pull her out of this totally unresponsive state. I would try language lessons, given that she appears to have forgotten even Italian, her mother tongue.

"And I would also include lessons in English, the other language she was familiar with. It might all bring back memories which she could then use to communicate, helping her to finally return from the limbo in which she seems to be trapped.

"And remember, it would be best if you brought her back to us from time to time".

Taking an anguished look at her daughter on the other side of the window, Olga reassures the doctors, "We shall stay in Cairo. I have lost my husband, and I have no intention of losing my daughter too".

Olga had already arranged for any number of doctors to examine Elsa. Perhaps, as some were recommending, the only thing left to try was to communicate with the girl. She contacted some language teachers, and the lessons began.

CHAPTER V
The Prince's Palace

The sounds of picks and chisels reverberate in the Valley of Kings. Hundreds of men of varying degrees of youthfulness dig amidst clouds of dust, while a long line of other workers removes the earth produced by the digging, all to the accompaniment of an ancient, forlorn chant

The journey from Cairo to Wadi Biban al-Moluk, the Arab name for the Valley of Kings, covers more than six hundred kilometres of dusty, daunting roads. Or the Valley can be reached by travelling the mere five kilometres that separate it from the banks of the Nile, near the city of Luxor, known as Thebes in ancient times, when the city was the sacred site of the royal residences. With the Valley being so close to the river, the dust of the difficult roads can be avoided by taking a luxurious riverboat along the Nile. Though of all the ways to get to the valley from Cairo, the train remains the safest and the most rapid.

On the terrace of Luxor's exquisitely elegant Winter Palace Hotel, Carter speaks with Lord Carnarvon while pointing to different areas on a map.

"We have removed almost the entire upper layer within this triangle. Right now we are working here, between the tomb of Ramses IX and that of Ramses VI".

Lord Carnarvon pours himself a glass of scotch.

"In the same spot where you found the gold leaves and the bowls?"

"Yes, my Lord".

They are joined by Callender, Carter's assistant.

"Excuse me, but we have found something".

Carter, Carnarvon, Callender and Lady Evelyn reach the Valley of Kings, where they examine what appear to be only insignificant pieces of cloth. Carter's two illustrators have already sketched the pieces found.

Out of curiosity, Lord Carnarvon observes, "These would seem to be remnants of a hut, possibly from the 20th dynasty, at least based on what we can still see of their features".

Carter, with a satisfied expression, "Exactly my Lord! From the same type of workers huts discovered by Davis. Most likely we will also find flint deposits, which in the 'Valley' almost always means that a tomb is nearby".

A contented Evelyn, "Congratulations, Howard! Congratulations to everybody!"

The sun sets on the Nile as a barge moves across the broad river, ferrying back to Luxor those returning from the Valley of Kings. Carter gets on a horse, having helped Lady Evelyn lift herself onto the saddle of her mount. A servant gives Lord Carnarvon a hand as he gets into a car.

Evelyn is clearly enjoying herself. Carter, in taking his leave of Lord Carnarvon, says, "We'll be back soon!"

And with that, he and Evelyn ride off into the desert.

The immense, eternal desert pulsates with heat. Pointing to an ancient ruin from the Roman period, Carter tells Eveyln, "The Bedouins say that it was part of the palace of an illustrious prince".

Evelyn, her face red from the sun taken earlier in the day, "But why build a palace in the desert?"

Carter gazes at the ruins.

"They say he built it for his beloved. And to make the construction all the more precious, rare and valuable flowers were used to scent the water that was mixed with the clay.

"Legend has it that, if you scratch the walls, you can still smell the jasmine, the violets and the roses. Or so I was told by my dear friend and former colleague, T. E. Lawrence".

Evelyn, impressed to hear as much, "The man known as Lawrence of Arabia? The 'White Devil'? The hero who fought alongside the Arabs?"

"Yes, he was once an archaeologist who toiled in the dust of Syria, as an assistant to the esteemed Leonard Woolley".

Carter adds in a pensive tone, almost to himself, "I wonder what's became of Lawrence? I haven't heard from him in a while".

Evelyn breathes in the wind from the east. "The air has a scent that I can't quite put my finger on!"

Carter smiles.

"That's the aroma of the desert. It has no scent, but it's my favourite smell. The most delicate perfume of them all".

Evelyn takes another deep breath. The desert, spread out in front of her, is aflame with the colours of the evening sky. The sun has just set, giving way to a breeze heated by the sun-baked rock formations standing off in the distance, on the promontory. The breeze blows on their face and in their hair, having travelled a considerable distance, amidst the dunes and the oases, to do so.

Seeing the rapt expression on the young woman's face, Carter smiles.

"Be careful! The desert bewitches those who live in the city. A good many have come away burned".

Staring out at the sand, Evelyn notes, "There is no fertility".

Carter, in a tone of bemused admiration, "No human effort to be witnessed".

Evelyn, "Simply eternal".

After a moment of silent, grateful contemplation, Carter adds, "That's precisely why it's the only place in which you can find God".

Then, in a lighter, less pensive tone, "We should start heading back. It's getting later, and out here in the desert, there's no evening to warn you that night is coming".

Carter lives in a two-storey house with a handsome terrace that looks out on the river. He avoids staying in hotels, even luxury ones, preferring to be in the company of his own things, in a setting that he manages to render intimately personal, which also allows him to feel close to the country where he is staying, and which he loves.

Dinner is almost over. Seated at the table are Carnarvon, Carter, Evelyn, Callender and Professor Maspero. The Mimus Polyglottus performs its perfect imitations of the ibis and the owls that sing off in the distance. Ali, the trusted servant, carries out his duties with the utmost care and attention to detail, pouring wine for the guests while making sure that everything proceeds as it should.

The delicate linen curtains covering the windows lift with every breath of air, showing glimpses of the desert by the light of the moon.

Maspero, sipping at his glass of red wine, "A superb dinner. Well done, Ali! I truly hate to have to go and spoil it all".

Maspero takes three random objects from the table and arranges them as the points of a triangle.

"You're digging inside this triangle, where the tomb of Ramses VI was discovered. In other words, the same exact spot where Belzoni and Davis dug for years, with no further results".

Carter gets to his feet, taking his glass of cognac with him. Glancing out at the flashes of moonlight that dance on the surface of the river, "My sixth sense tells me that we are precisely the right place."

Maspero shakes his head.

"That may be, but in the past, we had nowhere near the same number of tourists in the Valley. You see, my friends, the Bureau of Antiquities has received any number of complaints from foreign visitors who are unable to visit the three tombs.

"And so I must ask you to work only during the summer months, when there are considerably fewer tourists".

Evelyn, hoping to arrive at an accommodation, "But the flow of tourists could be shifted elsewhere. And if Howard meets with success, that would be far more important ..."

Maspero interrupts. "I'm sorry, Lady Evelyn, but it simply cannot be done".

Carter and Carnarvon are ready to argue with Maspero as well, but he holds up a hand to head them off.

"Please understand, I in no way approve of the situation. I fought on your behalf, but there was no changing their minds.

"In the winter months you must explore elsewhere. In summer, you can once again dig where you are now. Perhaps this misfortune will ultimately bring you luck".

Carter is irate.

"In the summer!? When the temperature in the valley can reach 50-60 degrees centigrade!"

Lord Carnarvon states in no uncertain terms, "I shall speak with Lord Allenby. As Field Marshall and High Commissioner for Egypt, he has the last word on everything!"

Maspero, sounding apologetic, "There's no point in that, Lord Carnarvon, and you've no idea how sorry that makes me".

Turning to Carter, Maspero adds, "I'm convinced that the change will make you lose time, and the State will lose additional revenue as well, but as I've already said, even though I firmly opposed the decision, there is nothing more I can do".

Lord Carnarvon glances at Carter.

"If there's absolutely no way to change the minds of these melon heads...."

Carter, trying to calm things down, "We'll have to move further north, and hope that we aren't making a fatal mistake. Then, come summer, we can return to where we are now".

Callender, who has been closely involved in the dig from the start, "It will be no picnic working in that heat. But if there's nothing else we can do ...".

Evelyn puts a record on the turntable of the gramophone, an early model with a speaker horn, and rapidly cranks the handle, priming the machine to play an English song from years gone by.

"This reminds me of when I was a girl. Those September evenings when the temperature was just right, we would be out in the country, heather plants all around us. There was music and singing. You and I danced together, Father. Do you remember?"

Lord Carnarvon smiles at the memory. Evelyn does a dance step or two, inviting Howard to come join her. He works up his courage, goes to her side and does his best to join the dance. Finding the rhythm contagious, Lord Carnarvon also gets to his feet, and though his leg is not yet fully healed, he uses his cane to do some dancing of his own, as Maspero and Callender clap along.

CHAPTER VI
Elsa's Studies

The summer heat is excruciating. The bearers and the diggers toil in the stifling air, with the further torment of the sand whipped up by the constant gusts of wind. Some of the labourers, pushed beyond endurance by the heat, lie down to try and escape the wind, but the always vigilant overseers get them right back up again.

Wearing nothing but an undershirt that hangs loosely outside his trousers, Carter pours water over his own head. Meanwhile Callender is taking the dirt from the dig and sifting it through his hands, while Carter also picks up a hoe and starts toiling away. The wind starts blowing even stronger.

In Cairo, at her home, Olga Mittieri is sitting by a window, working on notes for her writings. A blackboard has been set up by the couch, where Elsa is seated between an English teacher and an Italian teacher.

The Italian teacher asks her, "Elsa, please write the word 'madre'".

The girl gets to her feet and writes 'madre' on the blackboard.

The English teacher asks her, "And how do we say that in English?"

Elsa looks at the teacher and says, "Mother," before writing the word on the blackboard.

Pointing towards Olga, the English teacher says, "Now write, 'This is my mother'!"

Elsa starts to write 'my mother', but then she stops, looks towards her mother and says in a perfectly innocent, guileless tone, "No, that is not my mother."

Olga's hands freeze. She looks stricken. Hanging her head, she sinks into a lengthy silence. The two teachers exchange puzzled glances. The distraught mother goes to her daughter and hugs her.

"Oh my darling!"

The railway station in Luxor is abuzz with tourists coming and going, plus affluent Egyptians who dress in Western garb, trying to look like Europeans. A train is getting ready to depart, as its locomotive makes the slow, rhythmic, muffled sound of steam boilers being stoked for the journey.

The day is windy, meaning that the desert air carries no small amount of sand. Lord Carnarvon and his daughter are heading back to England. The servants have finished loading their luggage onto the train.

The stationmaster walks up to Lord Carnarvon and asks, "Is everything to your satisfaction, my Lord? May we leave?"

Lord Carnarvon smiles in replay. The stationmaster readies his horn to signal the departure and waits. Carnarvon shakes hands with Carter and Callender.

"The best of luck, my friends!"

In saying goodbye to Evelyn, Carter hands her a lotus flower. Lord Carnarvon boards the train and, as a final parting gesture, turns to waive his hat. The stationmaster sounds his horn, sending the train on its way amidst clouds of steam and smoke from the locomotive.

The sun is setting in Cairo. At the home of Olga Mittieri, the governess Muna is serving tea to Olga, as well as to an Italian psychiatrist by the name of Gianfranco Dettori and to an Englishman who has arrived in town only a few days before, Professor Carl Newman. A scholar of sensorial phenomena and an expert Egyptologist, Dr. Newman is a well-built, handsome man of roughly fifty, with salt and pepper hair and a reassuring gaze.

Wiping at his lips with his napkin, the psychiatrist asks Olga, "Mrs. Mittieri, would you be so kind as to repeat to Professor Newman what happened last Sunday?"

Olga replies, "I had taken Elsa to visit the Bulaq Museum here in Cairo, when, at a certain point, she drew my attention to an inscription on a statue and told me: 'That means ....'

"I can't remember exactly what she said, but the episode reminded me of how, a year earlier, while we were travelling along the Nile to Cairo, I happened to be holding Elsa's hand while she stood on the boat, looking out at some grey slate stone covered with ancient hieroglyphics along the riverbank. All of a sudden, an ecstatic look came onto her face and she began pulling at my sleeve while pointing at the stone and pronouncing words in that strange language of hers.

"I simply smiled, thinking that she was trying to say something about the stone, and didn't pay any more attention to the episode. But the other day at the Bulaq Museum here in Cairo, when she read the inscription, using the strange sounds of that language of hers, I thought back to what had happened on the boat and realised that Elsa can read and speak the language of ancient Egypt".

Professor Newman seems sceptical, but he also looks like his curiosity is about to get the best of him, having finally run into an intriguing case.

He gets up from his seat, walks a few paces in one direction and then turns back towards Olga.

"I am an Egyptologist, Ma'am. In our field, we can translate, or rather decipher, a text written in hieroglyphics, but we have no way of knowing how those words were pronounced.

"I happen to have an Egyptian text with me right now, one that a great many specialists are already familiar with. If you have no objections, I would like to show it to your daughter".

The mother glances over at the psychiatrist before answering, "Of course ..."

Then she asks Muna, "Please bring Elsa in".

Newman is searching for something in his briefcase when Elsa, two years older than before, enters the room. The professor is clearly taken aback by her beauty.

Olga says to her daughter, "Elsa, this is Dr. Carl Newman, a specialist in Egyptology. He would like to get to know you better and have you take a look at a document".

The girl smiles. Newman takes the document from his briefcase and hands it to her. On the sheet of paper is a lengthy ancient inscription. Elsa looks at it and starts pronouncing the language's unknown sounds, her face the picture of contentment.

A pleasantly surprised Newman interrupts her.

"Excuse me Elsa, but you are reading in a language whose pronunciation is totally unknown to us. Could you translate what it says?"

The girl starts over:

"The pomegranate in the orchard speaks:
My fruit is like your mouth,
It is as sweet as your breath.
My seeds are like your teeth.
My form is like your breast".

Having reached the end of the first verse, Elsa puts down the sheet of paper and starts reciting from memory:

"I am the most beautiful tree in the orchard.
My flowers bloom all year long.
What the beloved does with her lover,
I do in the shelter of my leaves".

Along with everyone else, Newman is both thrilled and astounded.

Elsa's mother murmurs, "Good Lord...."

A smiling Elsa says to Professor Newman, "I've known it for a long time," and she goes back to reciting the poem, murmuring the words of the ancient Egyptian language to herself.

Overcome with emotion, Muna watches with her mouth agape, her eyes filled with tears.

Elsa's mother lets herself collapse onto the couch.

"That day, sadly enough, I realised that a part of my daughter was lost to me forever. Her ability to speak that language was not something I could possibly have passed on to her in the womb. Elsa had been set apart by a magnificent but terrifying gift that dramatically came between us..."

The pyramids of Cheops and Chephren stand out against the horizon, lit by the rising moon. Off in the distance, where the desert begins, the sphinx sits partially covered by sand, while the Nile reflects glimmering flashes of the evening sky. The Muezzin's call to prayer arrives from afar. In the meantime, the river leads to Luxor. The linen curtains of Carter's home are set aflutter as the warm night wind, arriving from the desert, blows onto his terrace.

The next morning, the sun lights up Carter's bedroom-study, where the singing and chirping of the Mimus Polyglottus make it seem as if the day has dawned in the middle of a forest. Ali is making breakfast for Cater, who walks out on the terrace in his robe, carrying the cage of his faithful feathered companion with him.

The bird continues making his joyful noises. The rider of a passing camel briefly stops in front of the terrace, astonished by the sounds, but then hurries away in fright. Ali's dog, curled up on his sleeping mat, dreams on, undisturbed by the bird's joyful celebration of morning.

Carter gets up from the table, takes a bowl and pours part of the contents into a food holder that he places inside the birdcage, while the bird tones down his singing until, perfectly still, he is ready to enjoy his own breakfast. Ali comes back out on the terrace with a bowl of water and whistles for the dog, who leaves the sleeping mat, tail wagging, eager for a drink. The curtains puff up in the breeze.

"The wind's blowing stronger, Ali. It won't be an easy day out there in the valley".

At the dig site, the wind gusts headlong through the excavation areas, raising furious whirlwinds of dust. The bearers and the diggers, their heads wrapped in large white shawls, try to protect their faces by ducking into the crevices and holes where they are working. Beneath a tent with no walls, Carter and Callender are doing their best to protect their maps and notes from the angry wind. Suddenly, the heavy matted roof of the tent flies away. The two set off in pursuit, but the wind, not letting up in the least, slams the woven roof against a rock formation. Then an especially violent gust sends it crashing into the sided of a cliff, causing a number of large boulders to fall from above.

The rocks hit an outcropping halfway up the cliff, shattering its face, behind which a tall, narrow stele, or commemorative stone, appears. Inscribed on the stone are six columns of ancient characters, together with a pair of images of infernal divinities: a lion's head with two cobras depicted on the forehead and a ram's head with horns that run horizontally.

The stunned diggers whisper to each other in alarm, while Carter and Callender look on in shocked astonishment as the slab slowly breaks away from the rock wall and falls to the ground, shattering into countless pieces.

Callender, shouting to make himself heard above the wind, "Damnation! We could try and put it back together again".

Carter, also doing his best to shout over the wind, "Not possible, Alan. That slab was made of sand. It was already very fragile".

Callender, trying to protect his eyes from the swirling sand, "What do you think the writing said? ..."

A group of cobra snakes comes pouring out of the large hole left by the fallen slab. Callender runs for a tent, using a stick to fight off the snakes. Carter wards the off by throwing with both hands. The cobras scatter in the wind-whipped sand. Every man defends himself as best he can. Some of the workers start screaming, others try to run to safety, their terrified faces appearing and disappearing amidst the sand raised by the gusts of wind. A cobra strikes one of the porters, who cries out in terror.

More than four years have passed since the dig began, but the few artefacts retrieved have failed to lead to any major discoveries. Carter is at home, finishing dinner with Callender. Ali is tidying up in the kitchen. The hot, muggy evening is perfectly windless. The bird sits silently in its cage. Ali's dog is snoring away on its sleeping mat, at peace with the world.

Callender lights his pipe and stretches his legs to relax. Carter pours himself a cognac, saviours the aroma and starts sipping away contentedly, when suddenly a photograph in the newspaper catches his eye.

"Alan, listen to this headline: 'The Uncrowned King of Arabia!' Why if it isn't my old friend Thomas Lawrence, dressed all in white, with a turban and a gold dagger at his waist. He's become a genuine hero of the Arab world!"

Callender, coming closer, takes a look at the photo.

"Can you imagine, Alan? Just a few years ago he was an archaeologist digging in the dust, the same as us, and now he's a beloved hero, admired by no less a figure than Winston Churchill.

"Apparently there will be a major conference in Cairo in a few weeks, to decide what to do with the territories conquered from the Turks during the World War. It says here that the participants will include Gertrude Bell. Finally, a woman with a role of real importance in the British government. They describe her as the person responsible for Mesopotamia".

Carter goes on reading the article, while Callender returns to his seat and his pipe. The silence is broken by the intermittent snoring of the dog, who draws a glance from Callender. A desk clock makes its tick-tock sound.

The dog moans in a peculiar way, as if it were dreaming. The noise appears to bother the bird, which shakes its head, rubs its wings together and lets out a whistle identical to the one that Ali uses to call the dog.

The sound causes the dog to wake up, jump from its sleeping mat and run off into the kitchen to its master, an astonished Ali, who had also heard the whistle. Ali signals to the dog to go back to sleep, and it obeys, once again makes itself comfortable on the mat, while the bird, which appears to be resting, is perfectly still.

Carter sees what is going on and smiles, wondering what the bird will come up with next. Callender is also follows the scene, while Ali, anxious over what the bird might be plotting, peeks out from the kitchen.

The dog's snoring starts up again. The bird does another faultless imitation of Ali's whistle, causing the dog to jump back onto its feet and run off to the kitchen, where a bewildered Ali is standing in the doorway. Thoroughly amused by the scene, Carter and Callender have a good laugh.

As always, Cairo is filled with both people and the constant din of their voices. Tourists and locals curious to inspect the goods flock to the Grand Bazaar. Business is thriving, as shown by the fact that more and more cars travel the streets, along with the traditional buggies and local carts. The Egyptians wear their traditional multi-coloured garb, some of them with white turbans on their heads, while small donkeys are used by their riders to carry bundles of sticks.

A group of English soldiers snaps to attention as an automobile with diminutive British flags flying on its fenders passes by, only to be slowed down further up the street by a herd of goats. Sitting in the car, visible from the outside, are two high-ranking officers, together with no less a personage than Winston Churchill, whose wife Clementine is also by his side, dressed in white and wearing a large, wide-brimmed red hat. Both Carter and Callender get to their feet, out of respect, and then take in the surrounding mayhem as they return to their seats at a café located on an open veranda.

Carter observes, "With all the fuss they're making, this conference must definitely be of critical importance to the political future of the Middle East".

"Here it says," he reads from the newspaper, "that the goal is to approve a plan which will place the two large areas that the English, with the help of the Arabs, took from the Turks under the control of the Hashemite princes. Prince Faisal, Lawrence's friend, is to be crowned the king of a new country that will be called Iraq, while his brother, Prince Abdullah, will govern a country formed from half the territory of Palestine, together with the region to the east of the River Jordan. The name still has to be chosen, but apparently it will be either Transjordan or Jordan.

"Of course it won't be easy getting the Shias and the Sunnis, as well as the Kurds, to live together in this large, new country of 'Iraq', seeing that they've never gotten along with each other".

Callender, taking a look at the newspaper, "But if Lawrence fought together with the Arabs to make this happen, and even managed to win Churchill's support, then the possibility of future conflicts can hardly be that much of a worry".

Turning to another page of the newspaper, Carter reads, "'Disaster at the Centocelle Airfield in Rome, Italy! A massive Handley Plage bomber of the Royal Air Force's 58th squadron crashes upon landing. The two pilots, twenty-seven year-old Frederick Prince and nineteen year-old Sydney Spratt, both perish. The heavy biplane, arriving at night, seems to have crashed into a row of trees at the end of the runway, having tried, to no avail, to regain altitude. Also on-board was a Welsh officer who, trapped amidst the wreckage with a broken collarbone, had to be pulled to safety by one of the two surviving mechanics. The officer is the same Lieutenant Colonel Thomas Edward Lawrence who led seventy-thousand Arabs in their victorious rebellion against the Turks in the Middle East'.

"Imagine that! We were just talking about him".

Carter continues reading.

"'King Victor Emanuel III of Italy went to the Addolorata Hospital in person to visit Sir Thomas.'"

Callender interjects, "But what was Lawrence doing in Rome?"

Carter notes, "The plane took off from Paris, and the plan was for that beast of a machine to stop for fuel in Marseille, Pisa and Rome, before continuing on to Greece, Crete and, finally, Egypt".

"'But the 'Devil', a nickname given to Sir Thomas, insisted on resuming the trip to Cairo immediately, even with his arm in a sling, being concerned that England and France may have reached a secret agreement which allows them to disregard their promise to unite the Middle East'".

"Poor Lawrence, politics appears to have done him a bad turn," comments Carter as he gets up from the café table.

"Well, I'm off to fight my own battle! Wish me luck. I'll fill you in later".

Carter, who has gone to the Office of the Superintendent of Antiquities for an important meeting with Professor Maspero, is making his case.

"I realise that the results of the dig, to date, are not what we had hoped for, but all too often you have made us stop and move to accommodate the tourists, and now I must ask you once again to renew the permit for at least another year. Just one more year!"

But Professor Maspero seems to have his doubts.

"I need to talk with Lord Carnarvon. He is the one providing the funding. The permit expires in a month, and he does not seem willing to renew it. As he sees it, he has already spent too much!"

A disappointed Carter observes, "We can't just throw away five years of work!"

Maspero tries to reason with Carter, "But with all that your sponsor has spent, and still no return in sight?"

Carter insists, "I know, I know. But just one more season of digging. I assure you it will be the last".

Faced with so much stubborn determination, Maspero can only shake his head, but Carter will not give up.

"If Lord Carnarvon wishes to withdraw, then you can issue the permit to me. I'll pay out of my own pocket!"

Most mornings Highclere Castle is cloaked in a light fog that gives everything a somewhat hazy look, but this morning a warm, glorious sun has cleared away the humidity. In one of the castle's many rooms, Lord Carnarvon is sitting atop a special wooden horse used to measure new clothes for the fox-hunting season. Two tailors busy themselves around him. The more senior of the two, standing on a stepladder, takes notes while noting the alterations to be made in a lowered voice.

There is also a boot-maker on hand, ready to have his Lordship try on the upper portions of some boots, together with a shirt-maker and a hat-maker. Lord Carnarvon, sitting atop the wooden horse, holds a telegram from Carter in his hand.

The tailor murmurs to his assistant, "Shoulders, half an inch on the right. The left is fine. The waste measures 33 1\2, the shirt, 2 inches, I believe…"

Carnarvon stops reading the telegram.

"Five years of failure, five years of exploration that have led to nothing. That's a decidedly negative result".

Lady Evelyn, ready, as always, to come to Carter's defence, "Just one more year, Father. All he asks is another year! He's bound to succeed".

Carnarvon, sounding tired of the whole question, "Just as he was five years ago. Only an idealist totally wrapped up in his own work would ever ask for so much! Perhaps Davis was right to think that the Valley had nothing left to offer".

But Evelyn will not let the mater rest, "You're always saying that archaeologists have to be patient, that they must wait for fortune to lend them a hand".

Being so fond of her, Evelyn's father finds it hard not to give his daughter what she wants.

"But my dear, why must my patience be tested a full five years? Who's to say we aren't simply chasing a fantasy?"

But Evelyn is highly skilled at "getting to" her father.

"Actually," she discloses, "Carter said to Professor Maspero that, if you give up, he'll be willing to provide the funding himself".

Carnarvon, in annoyance, "And where will he find the money? He'll wind up drowning in debt.

Evelyn, slyly leading her father on, "But if he finds what he's looking for?"

Carnarvon falls silent for a moment.

"All right, damnation! One more year! Just one! Which will be the sixth and last!"

In Egypt, at the Office of the Superintendent of Antiquities in Cairo, Professor Maspero is meeting with his pair of trusted experts.

The older of the two declares, "To just throw away so much time and money, all of which could have been put to much better uses. My colleague and I have a project that we wish to propose to Lord Carnarvon. It includes restoration efforts, the opening of new museum and exhibition facilities, in short, initiatives with tangible results".

The younger expert chimes in, "Carter is leading him down the garden path, encouraging him to keep spending money for no good reason".

Maspero, who has known Carter for quite some time, defends him, "No, Carter is acting on good faith!"

The more senior expert retorts, "You say good faith, Professor? But who can say to what extent? All we want is to be able to speak with Lord Carnarvon before you renew his permit?"

Maspero, who has always admired Carter as both an archaeologist and a man, "I have no idea when and if Lord Carnarvon will be coming back to Egypt. But, in any event, his permit has already been renewed for one more year".

CHAPTER VII
The Nightmare

In the villa of the Mittieri family, Elsa's room is lit only dimly. The girl is sleeping, but the anguished expression on her face shows that she is in the middle of a dream.

From off in the distance comes the steady beating of drums. In a marshy area, the sound of the drums draws ever closer. A young man appears from out of the undergrowth, propelling his small boat with a pole. Judging from his richly appointed garments and the heavy make-up on his eyes, he is probably a pharaoh.

From amidst the rushes, someone is spying on him. The young pharaoh searches the sky. Then the person spying on him becomes aware that someone else, a man with an "unsettling, unreliable" face, is not only following the Pharaoh but also carrying a pair of spears.

The white garment worn by the person spying on the other two, who happens to be a young girl, snags on a branch of thorns. Her hands try to free the cloth from the thorns, but she cuts herself. Unable to follow the pharaoh, she loses sight of him.

A sweat-soaked Elsa tosses and turns in her bed. The drums go on beating. Elsa, her face filled with fright and pain, is still dreaming. Meanwhile her hands frantically try to free the sheet from the springs of the old-fashioned bedframe, but in doing so, she cuts herself.

Now she is back in the marshlands, where the girl in white finally manages to pull herself free of the thorns. She runs into the underbrush, desperately searching for the pharaoh, when suddenly she hears the honking of wild ducks. The drums stop as a flock of ducks takes to the sky, but a boomerang hits one of them, sending it crashing to its death in the rushes.

The door to Elsa's room flies open and Olga enters. Finding the girl covered in splotches of blood, she screams in fright. Elsa, startled awake, takes deep, troubled breathes as she looks at her bloodied bedclothes, stares into her mother's eyes and bursts into tears.

The frantic mother wraps the girl in her arms, calling to Muna for help.

In Luxor, the dawn light of a splendid morning seeps its way into Carter's bedroom. On the bedside table, as Carter continues sleeping, sit the remains of what appears to have been a mighty bout of whisky drinking. The curtains sway gently in the morning breeze. The bird also seems to be resting in its cage.

Suddenly, the glass door to the terrace opens with a sinister creaking noise, letting in a sliver of light from the outside. The bird stirs in its cage. Carter goes on sleeping. Another soft, creaking sound come from the glass door as a cobra pokes its head through the opening and enters the room in menacing fashion, lifting itself to the full height of its majestic pose.

The bird, sensing the danger, starts to flutter about in its cage.

The cobra reaches Carter's bed and slithers between the sheets, reappearing right along the archaeologist's face. The bird gives a whistle, drawing the attention of the snake, which immediately lifts itself into the fully erect attack position, puffing up in a display of all its terrifying might.

The bird, aware that it has been spotted, flaps its wings inside the cage, as if to draw the cobra away from its master. Carter is still deep asleep, blissfully unaware of what is happening, most likely due to the whiskey.

The cobra slithers off in the direction of its prey. The bird hops from one side of the cage to the other, until finally the noise of the cage falling to the ground pulls Carter out of his sleep.

He looks around, sees the fallen cage and hears the noises coming from the floor. He spots the cobra, which immediately resumes its attack position.

Moving slowly, Carter opens the drawer of the bedside table, pulls out a revolver and takes a number of shots at the snake, not hitting it even once. The cobra quickly slithers out the glass door.

Carter tries to reload the revolver, but he spills the box of bullets into the floor, and when he finally makes his way out onto the terrace, the cobra is nowhere to be seen.

On coming back inside the room, he is heartbroken to see the feathers of the companion who shared his solitude scattered all over the floor, and little does he know that the bird gave up its life to save his.

A few hours later, Carter is riding on horseback through a canyon in the vicinity of the Valley of Kings, on his way to the dig site. The sound of men wielding picks can be heard off in the distance. A dreamy Arab litany echoes in the air. A small group of Bedouins are sitting off by themselves, chatting with one another, as roughly a dozen camels are left free to graze.

The routine proceeds in the same way that it has every other day, until all at once a shrill, terrifying scream breaks the sleepy morning lull. An astonished Carter slows his horse. Hearing more shouts and excitement, he rushes forward at a gallop.

When he reaches the Valley, he sees that all the workers have stopped digging and moved off to one side. Some have even fled, hiding themselves on higher grounds, where they are waiting.

Carter gets off his horse and approaches the men. No one makes a sound. A boy moves out of the way, causing a jar to fall to the ground.

The atmosphere is different than on other days, as the workers wait for him, their voices stilled. He sees that something exceptional must have taken place.

Callender, kneeling next the fallen jar, turns towards Carter, his eyes glistening with the thrill of the moment.

"What day is today?" he asks.

Carter, not quite following him, "The fourth of November..."

Callender completes his sentence, "Of the year 1922! A date that will go down in history. Congratulations, my friend!"

Callender's gaze draws Carter's attention to a step carved out of the rock. Partially covered with sand and debris, it sits at a level three metres and eighty centimetres lower that of the tomb of Ramses VI.

Superstition has Ali, along with the other workers, frightened.

Callender, who has never doubted Carter, declares, "Howard, back when we started, five years ago, this is exactly where we were digging. You were right, and if Maspero and the others from the Office of Antiquities hadn't made us move elsewhere, due to the tourists, we would have found this step way back at the start".

Carter is too happy to add anything but a measured, "Finally! Congratulations, Alan. Thank you everybody!"

He grabs a pickaxe and begins loosening the ground below the step. Callender helps, but the workers stay off at a distance on account of their superstitious fear.

Ali finally works up the courage to draw closer and begin working. He gestures to the workers, who are still torn, but cautiously return to the dig all the same. The area uncovered by Carter and Callender brings to light another step, until finally, after almost three hours of painstaking work, there are fifteen more steps, making for a stairway 4 metres in length and 1 metre and sixty centimetres in width.

The stairs lead to a door, a rectangular opening atop of which sits a heavy wood lintel that is completely blocked by stone, with traces of a number of seals visible on its surface.

Evening is approaching, and Carter says in a low voice to Callender, Ali and a small group of the diggers, "This is the first time a door with its seals still intact has been discovered in the Valley of Kings".

Callender, enthusiastically, "Howard, do you think this is what we are looking for?"

Carter, patting the door contently, "I'm still not sure. We need to..."

He wants to say, 'break it down', but he is unable to get the words out.

He stands there perfectly still, the evening wind playing in his hair, before adding, "We may find everything behind this wall. Or perhaps nothing at all!"

The burnished red sunset of Egypt is on display in the sky.

Carter turns to the workers and says, "You three go get the rifles. Everybody is to stay here all night long," he instructs the group of roughly ten. "Not a single stone is to be touched. Use the guns if you have to".

Carter hands his pistol to Callender. "You stay here and watch over them. They'll guard the door and you guard them. I'll be back in just a few hours".

He rushes over to his horse, jumps in the saddle and gallops off, riding straight through the valley, all the way to the ferry that will take him back across the river to Luxor. All around him are the mute remains of ancient times, vaguely threatening in their majestic solemnity as they gradually shed the sombre red light of sunset for the pale-hued veil of the moonlight. The sacred falcon stands guard at the Temple of Horus. The immense unfinished statue of Osiris, the master of eternity, lies partially submerged in the sand. Reflected in the proud face of Pharaoh Chephren is all the glory of ancient Egypt. The mysterious symbols of death appear brooding and dramatic, as the tomb of Ramses II shares the landscape with colossal statues and the temple of Hatshepsut sits cloaked in the shrill cries of owls.

In Cairo, inside Elsa's bedroom, the owl's piercing cry is transformed into Elsa's shriek as she suddenly awakens, terrified and drenched in sweat. Two more years have gone by, and she is now a beautiful eighteen year-old girl.

She gasps for breath, in the throes of a panic attack, and looks around fearfully, as if there were thousands of dead souls coming towards her. She draws back in horror, like someone trying to avoid a hand that is reaching out to grab her.

The door bursts open and in comes her mother, who draws her in close, trying to comfort her. But Elsa breaks down in tears, shouting in her incomprehensible language, "No! ... leave him alone! I beg you... let him be!"

The mother wraps the daughter in her arms, "Elsa, calm down. It was just a bad dream. Nothing more, my darling."

As Elsa's calm returns, he says to her mother, "They must let him rest in peace".

Olga does not understand. "Who darling? Who has to be allowed to rest in peace?"

In the early hours of the morning, as a brisk wind blows from the north, a delicate cloak of snow covers the Castle of Highclere, together with its leaves, its meadows and the oaks that surround the grounds. The silence is broken by the frantic, agitated yelping of dogs off in the distance. A fox hunt is in full swing, with horns blaring and horses galloping furiously over the large, snowy expanses of the great estate.

Lady Evelyn comes running out of the great house. She slips, risks falling, but finally manages to grab a heavy brass handle and enter the stable. A few seconds later she gallops out, having saddled her splendid thoroughbred.

She rides at a fast clip, the horse kicking up great clouds of snow, and then directs him into the forest, where he flies like the wind amidst the thick hedgerows and trees branches that come perilously close to hitting her face.

She gallops toward the sounds of the mounted hunters, catching up with them and then leaving behind a number of riders who are shocked at her breakneck pace.

Finally, she reaches her father, rides up to him and, without hiding any of her tremendous happiness yells out, "Father, a telegram has come from Howard! Stop!"

Lord Carnarvon pulls at the reins of his horse, bringing it to a halt. Evelyn hands him the telegram, which her father reads out loud.

"Have finally made extraordinary discovery in the valley. Magnificent tomb with the seals apparently still intact. Have covered everything back up until you arrive. Congratulations".

Evelyn is beside herself with satisfaction.

"I knew it, Father! We have to leave now. We must get out of these hunting clothes".

But despite his daughter's enthusiasm, Lord Carnarvon, who never forgets the obligations of his rank, manages to stifle his own burning desire to ride away from the hunt.

"Have a telegram sent saying, 'Believe I will arrive in Alexandria on the twentieth. Congratulations!"

Evelyn cannot believe what she is hearing.

"But father, that's seventeen whole days from now!"

The sound of the horns and the yelping of the dogs can still be heard off in the distance. Carnarvon folds the telegram away in a pocket.

"This is a great day, Evelyn. But first I must conclude a number of important negotiations. Please trust your father!" he says to her as he gallops off.

In Cairo, in Professor Maspero's office, Carter is visibly upset as he holds the telegram for Maspero to see while exclaiming, "Seventeen days! That means he won't get here until the 23rd! We have to wait all that time?!".

Professor Maspero also seems puzzled.

"But there is nothing we can do. He is the one paying for everything. The permit is his. Now, would you please go speak to the press. They've been waiting all morning".

"No, I'm sorry," Carter informs him, "but I have no intention..."

But Maspero, not even giving him the chance to finish his sentence, opens the office door, letting in a small crowd of journalists who surround Carter and begin besieging him with questions.

"Did you find any evidence that the tomb belonged to royalty?"

"Your first impressions, Professor Carter!"

"Congratulations! Well done!"

Carter, trying to restore some calm, "Gentlemen! Gentlemen!"

He gestures for silence before adding, "Congratulations for what? Of what discovery do you speak? We still know nothing for certain.

"It could turn out to be an unfinished tomb, or one that was never used. Maybe a tomb that was profaned or sacked, like so many others. Over the centuries, a total of 62 tombs have been discovered, all of which had been sacked, while none of them were the tombs of kings.

"I can't even rule out the distressing possibility that the mummy, assuming we find one, might turn out to be only that of an official, or perhaps of an important priest!"

The reports murmur to each other.

"Gentlemen!" insists Carter, "So far all we have are sixteen steps and a sealed door, nothing more! Please be patient!"

Carter tries to leave, but the reporters flock around him, asking question after question.

The next day, once again in Cairo, only a few blocks away from the Office of Antiquities, in the home of Olga Mittieri, Muna is finishing setting the table for lunch.

Olga and Professor Newman, who has won the trust of the family and become an invaluable friend, are seated on the couch.

Olga shows him something in the newspaper, saying, "Elsa finally seemed to be finding some peace. Then last night she had another one of her attacks, and today... have you seen what's in the papers?"

Newman looks at the newspaper, "It's all anyone is talking about. Definitely a major achievement".

Elsa comes into the room, looking strangely content.

Newman gives an astonished smile. "Elsa, you look marvellous. I find you in excellent form."

Elsa smiles before replying in a surprisingly playful tone, "You're not looking bad yourself, Professor."

Elsa kisses the professor on the forehead. Surprised to find her in such a good mood, Newman smiles contentedly as Elsa asks, "Has my mother already asked you for a progress report? Aren't you tired of hearing about my bizarre dreams?"

Newman, light-heartedly, "Actually, I come for the delightful lunches that Muna prepares."

Elsa, in a mischievous tone, "And for Mother, I presume...."

Newman exchanges a furtive glace with Olga, who seems slightly embarrassed, indeed, somewhat taken aback by her daughter's lack of discretion.

"Elsa," she scolds the girl, "what on earth are you talking about?"

Then to the professor, "I beg your pardon, Professor Newman".

Newman, not wanting to miss his chance to make such a remark, adds in a semi-serious tone, "I am obviously attracted by your mother's enchanting beauty, and along with the opportunity to admire it, I naturally appreciate Muna's delicious meals meaning that two of my senses are overjoyed whenever I have the good fortune to be invited to this home.

"And then there is you, Elsa, a rare and delightful creature who gives a sense to my days".

Elsa smiles, enjoying the playful exchange. Even Olga, though Newman's words have made her blush, smiles with pleasure while getting a distinct feeling of butterflies in her stomach.

Newman, sensing that he is onto something, and happy about the fact, asks the girl, "Have you seen the news?" while showing her the paper.

Elsa neither answers nor looks at the newspaper, but simply goes to the table and pours herself a glass of water from a crystal pitcher.

Newman exchanges an understanding glance with Olga before adding, "Your mother told me that yesterday, when you woke up, you said, 'They must let him rest in peace!' Who were you talking about?"

Elsa drinks some water before saying, "About the one who is buried in front of the tomb of Ramses VI.

"At times I see things," she continues, "but they are only bits and pieces, recollections which come out all mixed up and confused. And then they get swallowed up again by memory.

"None of it is clear in my head. I need to understand, to remember better. And now that they have discovered a stairway down in the valley, it too has entered my head, joining my other recollections."

Elsa looks straight into her mother's eyes with an expression of absolute determination, "I must go to him, in the valley".

Muna comes into the room, smiling with pride over the lunch she has just finished preparing. In her hands she carries, as if it were a precious relic, a succulent stuffed turkey.

Elsa, shifting her attention to Muna, exclaims, "How delightful!", before adding in a playful tone, "Muna, my dearest Muna, I'm dying of hunger! And did you know that you've won the Professor's heart with your cooking?!"

Muna smiles with satisfaction, while Olga and Newman are clearly enjoying the moment as well. Finally the family can enjoy some much needed peace and harmony. Olga reaches for the knife and fork to serve the turkey, just while Newman is making the exact same gesture. Their hands touch each other softly as the two of them smile to one another, with Newman ultimately pulling his hand back, so that Olga can go ahead and serve the turkey.

In the Valley of Kings, the workers, under Callender's supervision, have cleared all the dirt from the stairs that end at the walled-off entrance to the tomb. Visible in the lower portion is a seal in the form of a beetle, together with some writing in hieroglyphics.

Not far from the stairway, a large tent made of jute cloth has been erected to serve as a centre for study and cataloguing. Inside the tent, on a large worktable, is a sheet of glossy paper on which the hieroglyphic writing found on the wall has been copied. It is being studied by Professor Breasted, an academic with a passion for hieroglyphics, as well as by another specialist, Professor Gardner.

Carter is busy writing notes when Breasted says to him, in a satisfied tone, "Howard, we have managed to decipher this phrase. It was no easy matter finding the key to its meaning. That's why we needed six whole days".

Carter comes over to the table and looks at the writing. "Was it written as a puzzle?"

"No, but it was so complicated that it proved almost impossible to decipher. Look, it says: 'Nebkheperure, the King of Upper and Lower Egypt, spent his life making images of the goods, so that every day they would give him gifts of incense, along with libations and offerings'".

Carter pleasantly surprised, observes, "Nebkheperure was the ceremonial name of the Pharaoh TUTANKHAMUN".

Breasted and Gardner agree as to the importance of what has just been discovered.

Carter smiles, "Excellent, but don't let word get out to them," says Carter as he opens a tent-flap to take a look at the crowd of reporters being held back by Callender, Ali and the other workers. "We don't want them to know that the foremost experts of ancient Egyptian writing took six days to translate three lines!"

A certain distance from the tent, there are stands selling fruit, food and water. Groups of reporters and photographers are setting up tents, so that they can camp out in expectation of further news and events. Four armed guards stand by the stairs.

A group of reporters, seeing Carter leave the tent, rushes up to him, but before they can ask any questions, he announces, "Gentlemen, I'm sorry that you've gone to all this trouble, but, as

I keep trying to tell you, it may all turn out to be a huge disappointment".

Riding up on a mule comes a jolly, exuberant man who carries, tucked under one arm, a bundle of books and newspapers. Taking off his straw hat, he waves it to get Carter's attention. The man calls out in a heavy French accent, "Hallò Hallò! Howard!"

When Carter sees who it is, he smiles broadly. Making his way through the crowd of reporters, he reaches the man, who has dismounted from his donkey, and warmly shakes his hand. Then the two of them embrace.

"David!" exclaims Carter, "what a pleasure! So you've decided to come too? You're a most welcome guest!"

Carter, introducing the newcomer to young Callender, "Alan, this is my dear friend David La Fleur, a professor of English literature at the Sorbonne and an ardent connoisseur of archaeology!"

David agrees with the judgment, specifying, "Just think, at present I'm working on the Edwin Smith papyrus!"

Carter, his curiosity piqued, "Which topic in particular?"

"Principles of basic surgery," replies his friend in a satisfied tone, before smiling as he adds, "I could see from way off in the distance that you're dying from impatience. It's literally eating away at you. If the mythical Giovanni

Belzoni were in your place, he would have already knocked the door down and rushed right in, satisfying his curiosity completely".

The three laugh out loud. Then Carter sees Professor Maspero riding towards them on a horse, looking very upset.

"Howard! The people of Qurna are up in arms! They're protesting about the discovery of the tomb. They say it's a terrible sacrilege to disturb the pharaoh's sleep".

Carter, smiling sarcastically, "And to think that for centuries they've stolen more from the tombs than anyone!"

Night has fallen, and from the hundreds of caves and tombs dug over time in the hills of Qurna, the people of the town are pouring into the valley, carrying torches and letting out mournful laments. The different streams of protestors come together to form a procession led by Mohammed Hammed, the acknowledged head of Qurna, a stout man well along in years, but still possessed of a piercing, magnetic gaze.

The procession winds on, as thousands of blazing torches light the way. A number of women, ashes sprinkled on their heads and chests, wail in desperation. Off at a distance, on higher ground, Carter, La Fleur and Professor Maspero take in the spectacle of the lighted procession from horseback. Maspero is genuinely worried.

"They weep and moan, those eternal plunderers of tombs!" he comments. "Who's to say how many treasures aren't safely preserved in our museum, but hidden in the tunnels and secret chambers underneath those hills".

Carter smiles. "Still, there's no denying that in 1916 they helped me find the tomb of Queen Hatshepsut".

"Perhaps they fear only kings!" says Fleur in jest.

Maspero, looking increasingly concerned, "We'd better get more guards, perhaps call on the army for help. Look how many of them there are. And if they decide to plunder the tomb?"

Carter knows them all too well. "They are thieves, not idiots, and they certainly have no appetite for violence".

It is a lovely evening at Carter's home in Luxor. A light evening breeze, warmed by the heat of day, is blowing in from the desert, its ultimate destination the banks of the sacred river. The breeze lifts the curtains up, then they gently flop back into their original position, as if they were breathing in and out. Carter, Callender and La Fleur, the new arrival, are sitting at the dinner table, enjoying the meal served by Ali.

Professor La Fleur, sweating profusely, his shirt untucked, his appetite still fuelling his hearty eating, remarks to Carter, "You're a lucky man, Howard. If Lady Alina hadn't inherited all that money, you wouldn't be here today making history!"

Carter smiles as he sips the excellent French red wine that his friend has brought them and yells La Fleur, "There's no denying that yours is a nation of excellent winemakers".

Alan Callender, curious to know more about Lady Almina, "She inherited her money?"

David La Fleur, an inveterate gossip, is more than eager to let him know that, "Lady Almina was officially the daughter of a certain Marie Boyer and her husband Captain Frederick Charles Wombwell, though the good captain was often away on military duty, and so Lady Almina's real father is said to be Alfred de Rothschild, an extremely eligible bachelor, given his station as a member of the wealthy Rothschild family".

La Fleur continues, laughing to himself, "Alfred had a peculiar beard that puffed out in two thick clumps over his cheeks, like the wings of an airplane. When he died only a few years ago, in 1918, he left everything to his beloved Almina!"

An astonished Callender, "What luck! Both for her and for us, Howard!"

La Fleur pours himself some more wine, taking a healthy swallow before continuing, "Apparently Lord Carnarvon's financial situation was delicate, but then Lady Almina made everything right. She even restored the magnificent estate, including Highclere castle!"

A bemused Carter listens as La Fleur changes the subject, gazing into his glass of wine and observing, "The growing of grapes, both for fruit and to make wine, would seem to have begun with the Egyptians, dating from the pre-dynastic period, even if their favourite drink was beer!"

And with that La Fleur empties his glass.

"The scenes found on the walls of tombs," notes Carter, "show that the grapevines were often grown on bowers, while the grapes, once they had been harvested, were pressed by walking barefoot on top of them, in large tubs, just as was still done until very recently. Then the juice of the grapes was poured into jars and left to ferment. Once the jars were sealed, the wine's vintage and place of production was written on the outside".

A smiling La Fleur says to Callender, "Then please pour me another glass, as I believe this an excellent vintage!"

He takes a drink before moving on to yet another topic.

"It was madness to leave Paris at the start of the season, but that's just what I did! I saw the latest play by Sacha Guitry, with Sarah Bernhardt in the cast: 'Je t'aime!'"

Young Callender, "I adore Sara Bernhardt!"

La Fleur finds himself in agreement with the younger man

"Yes, you do well to adore her. But my admiration, every last bit of it, goes to Mistinguett! And let me add how jealous I am of that actor, the pretty boy who appears on stage with her. I would kill the fellow, if only I thought I could get away with it!

"That Maurice Chevalier! He gets to embrace her every evening, and I bet you anything that he doesn't limit his performances to the stage. The rascal!

"The last time I saw Mistinguette, she was appearing in 'Here I am ... Yours'. What a presence! What verve! What warmth! With Offenbach's spirited music to accompany her: Ta, ta, ta...taratatá...ta ta!..."

Unable to contain his enthusiasm, he gets to his feet and dances playfully, as if he were the tantalising Mistinguett, while Carter and Callender clap their amused approval.

Then Ali enters the room and hands Carter a calling card.

"Excuse me, Effendi," he explains, "but the gentleman has already called twice today, when you weren't here".

Carter reads the calling card and motions to Ali to bring the man in.

"We have a guest," he announces to the others as Professor Newman ethers the room while La Fleur hurriedly tucks his shirt back into his pants.

Carter walks up to him and shakes his hand.

"Let's go out on the terrace, Professor Newman. After you".

Newman, "Thank you, Professor Carter. I've brought a friend with me, Mrs. Olga Mittieri. She's an anthropologist".

Carter smiles as Olga enters the room, bowing to kiss her hand. Then he shows them the way to the terrace, saying, "Please follow me. It's lovely out here this evening".

Carter introduces his two friends, "This is Alan Callender, and this is my good friend David La Fleur. But please sit down. What can I do for you, Professor?"

Newman takes a letter from his briefcase and hands it to Carter, saying, "This is from a mutual friend of ours, Dr. Otto Gruber".

Carter takes the letter, asking, "How is Otto?"

"Fine", answers Newman. "He still hasn't settled down, in the sense that he's never gotten married. And yet I always see him out and about with beautiful women!"

La Fleur interjects, "Lucky man!"

As he reads the letter, Carter looks both engrossed and surprised. His face takes on a serious expression on his face and he glances over at Professor Newman only occasionally. Having finished the letter, he murmurs to himself, "Unbelievable!"

Callender looks at Carter, trying to figure out what is going on. La Fleur is curious too. Newman and Olga sit in silence. Carter folds up the letter and places it back on the table.

He says to Professor Newman, "I'm extremely interested to hear what you have to say, Professor Newman. But is it all right if my friends stay? If it's not a problem for you, Ma'am, I think they'd be interested too".

Newman turns to Olga, who signals her agreement with a smile.

"Of course," answers Newman. "We have nothing to hide. It will be our pleasure.

"What we are about to tell you, gentlemen," he begins, "may sound decidedly strange, quite possibly beyond the limits of all human experience, but it is the pure and simple truth".

Olga turns her eyes to Newman, who stops for a second, as if he realises how hard they will find it to believe what he's about to describe.

Newman resumes, "A young woman born and raised in Sudan is living a life that is not hers, in a time that is not her time. In other words, we are dealing with what would appear to be a case of 'reincarnation'".

His three listeners are visibly surprised.

Newman continues, "Yes Gentlemen, I said 'reincarnation', and I can understand your disbelief, but ..."

Carter, tapping the letter of introduction from their mutual friend, Dr. Otto Gruber, interrupts Newman. "But Professor, you teach an exact science in one of America's most esteemed universities. How can you believe in the kind of fantastical imagining that you've just alluded to?"

Olga, coming to the support of her friend Newman, "The Professor is talking about my daughter Elsa. She is the one who's experienced this".

Carter and La Fleur exchange glances filled with doubt, while Callender also appears unconvinced.

Newman once again starts explaining the case.

"As I was saying, this young woman claims that her mother is not 'her real mother'. She rejects the women who gave her birth".

"I should add," says Newman, "that at the age of twelve, she was travelling in the desert, when a sandstorm separated her and her father from the rest of their party. After the storm, she was found in a weakened, almost completely dehydrated state, but she was still clutching her father's hand, though he, tragically enough, had not survived.

"For a number of days, the young woman did not speak a word. Then, all of a sudden, she began talking in a language that no one knew. Respected philologists and psychiatrists were contacted, but none of them could help.

"Finally, after hearing the mother, Mrs. Mittieri, tell of a number of these episodes, I decided to carry out an experiment. I placed an ancient parchment from the time of the pharaohs in front of the girl, and to my great surprise, she told me that she understood what it meant. In fact, Elsa translated the text without the slightest problem.

"That led us to the only logical conclusion, gentlemen, and namely that the incomprehensible language which she had been speaking was ancient Egyptian".

Callender interjects, "But that would be extraordinary, given that no one has ever heard what that language even sounds like, much less how it is pronounced".

Newman continues, "We have taken her to meet with other scholars as well. The Director of the Staatliche Museum in Berlin insisted on meeting with her, and here is his report".

Professor Newman hands a letter to Carter, who briefly examined it and then passes the letter on to Callender and La Fleur. Olga clasps her hands, then relaxes them and squeezes them tight again, a nervous gesture she repeats more than once.

Newman takes another letter from his briefcase, "This is from the Director of the Department of Egyptology of the British Museum, and here are drawings that Elsa did in the presence of your illustrious colleague, the Egyptologist Elvin Shoukry. They show homes from ancient times, while this is an illustration that she drew from memory of the Temple of Karnak as it would have appeared back in the 18th dynasty. Of course we all know what condition that temple is in today.

"Elsa wanted me to show you the drawing of the temple. She said that the arrows trace the path taken by the sovereign, the one that you are searching for, on the day of his coronation".

Carter takes a close look at the drawings, as does Callender, peering over his shoulder. La Fleur joins them. The path taken by the procession is marked with absolute precision on Elsa's drawing.

Newman goes on. "When we heard of the discovery of the first step leading to the tomb, Elsa told us that you were in the exact right spot, seeing that the burial site of the sovereign whom you are looking for sits in front of the tomb of Ramses VI. At that point, she wanted to come here to see you in person, right away".

Carter says to La Fleur, with barely hidden irony, "Do you believe in 'reincarnation', Professor?"

La Fleur answers in an even more sceptical tone, "Reincarnation? That would simply be the least comprehensive synonym possible for metempsychosis".

With a smile, Carter turns to young Callender. "And do you believe in it, Alan?"

With the same sceptical tone as La Fleur, Callender asks, "Do you mean the transmission of the soul from one human body to another? In philosophical terms, that would naturally be a theory at odds with the Thomistic doctrine of the soul, or the substantial form of the body.

"This was the metaphysical and psychological principle that St. Thomas used to construct his general criticism of metempsychosis. As he saw it, each soul, though identical to all others, is suited in a manner specific for the body it was created to be inside of".

Newman shakes his head. Olga looks extremely disappointed.

La Fleur speaks up, "However, philosophical reflections from even further back in time viewed the soul as being separate from the body, which was seen as being nothing more than the soul's temporary dwelling place".

Newman slowly lifts a hand to interrupt the discussion.

"Gentlemen, these are merely metaphysical musings, and of no use to us at all. The subject of this marvellous, stupefying case is sitting right outside, waiting to meet you! May I bring her in?"

Carter is still not convinced. "Professor, it must be a particularly impressive case of clairvoyance, of extrasensory perception. That could be a one explanation".

Olga speaks. "Professor Carter, gentlemen, let me assure you that all this disturbs me just as much as it does you. Think of how I suffer as a mother? Elsa is not unbalanced or delusional. All my daughter wants is to understand who she really is, to discover her true self, and my hope is simply to see her less frightened, less anguished, if that will ever be possible".

Newman asks once again, "Would you like to meet Elsa, gentlemen?"

Carter answers as if he were forcing himself to be polite, out of consideration for Elsa's mother, "Yes, certainly. Bring her in".

Olga goes to get Elsa, leaving the four men sitting in silence. The shrill cry of an owl arrives from far off in the desert. The curtain rustle lazily in the wind. Then, stepping out of the dimness, the young woman of the 'reincarnation' appears.

She does not look much like her mother, having a distinctive, somewhat geometric face with large eyes. Carter greets her with a smile, while La Fleur, judging from his expression, finds her both attractive and intriguing. Callender, on the other hand, is staring at her with an astonished look, as if he had fallen under her spell.

Newman says to Elsa, "I want to introduce you to Professor Carter. And this is Mr. Callender, and Professor ..."

Unable to remember La Fleur's name, Newman is rescued by the professor himself.

"La Fleur, very pleased to meet you".

Professor Newman says to the three gentlemen, "This is Miss Elsa Mittieri".

The young woman adds, "Actually, that is not my real name, but please feel free to use it anyway".

She looks at her mother with a smile. "I like her very much, but I am not her daughter".

Carter, in an amused tone, "Can you tell us who you are?"

Elsa, smiles politely. "Who am I? Today it no longer means anything, so there is no point..."

Callender keeps staring at her, as if he had already seen that face, though he cannot remember where or when. But he is certain that he knows her. La Fleur finds the situation both enchanting and fascinating.

Carter decides to take a more direct approach. Indicating the sheets of paper, he asks Elsa, "You did these yourself? And what is this one?", he asks while pointing to the drawing of a home.

Elsa looks at the drawing and answers, "It is the home of the Vizier Nakht, located in Tell el-Amarna".

Carter, still with his undertone of scepticism and disbelief, "You did it very accurately".

Carter indicates a certain point on the layout drawing. "Here you even show where the harem would have been, and I must say, you put it in the right place, between the guest rooms and the main bedroom".

Elsa is grateful for the compliment. "That was the place where it would typically be found".

La Fleur smiles as Carter continues, "You even drew the layout of the Temple of Karnak".

Elsa corrects him, "Not Karnak. That building was known as the Temple of Ipet-isut, at least back in the 18th dynasty".

Elsa takes the drawing from Carter's hands and lays it on the table, as if to say, 'Enough with these games!'

"Gentlemen," she declares, "I am here to ask you: do you really want to interrupt the eternal sleep of that sovereign?"

Carter is beginning to lose his patience.

"Miss, the newspapers have made such a fuss about the whole thing that, even if we don't open the tomb, someone else will, and it might even be the thieves of Qurna. Besides, we are not completely sure that the tomb we have found is Tutankhamun's".

Callender has been staring at Elsa all this time, not even bothering to look at the drawing. La Fleur is watching her too.

Elsa answers emphatically, "That is his tomb".

Carter, once again sceptical, to the point of almost mocking her, "Well, seeing that Lord Carnarvon is taking his time to get here, and so I can't open the door yet, could you tell me what we will find inside?"

Suddenly inconsolable, Elsa murmurs, "Sadness, only sadness Professor. You must make sure that the door is never opened".

La Fleur makes a superstitious gesture, as if to ward off bad luck, and then knocks on wood for good measure. Callender is positively bewitched, gazing at Elsa's face with an increasingly puzzled look in his eyes.

Elsa herself catches sight of a bowl from the pharaoh's temple, as well as another, rather strange object, both of which sit on a sideboard filled with papers and drawings. Elsa draws closer and lightly runs her fingers over the two objects, staring at the one with the strange shape.

Noting the young woman's interest, Carter asks, "Would you like to know what that is?"

Elsa answers calmly, "Ankh! The symbol of life. And the raised characters on the handle, those are the names and titles of the king".

Her gaze immediately shifts to the bowl, which has something written on it in hieroglyphics.

Carter, hoping to put her in difficulty, "Should I tell you what's written there?"

Elsa takes a brief look and then reads out loud: "'Those who were poor will become rich, and he who is rich will be poor. He who understood nothing of the sound of the harp will now enjoy its harmony, and he to whom no one ever sang shall be beloved by the goddess of music ...'"

There is no mistaking the rapt interest on the faces of all those present. Elsa lowers the bowl but continues reciting: "'But by then all happiness shall have disappeared from the world, and no one shall ever laugh again'".

Carter looks at the young woman closely. Unseen by the others, Newman squeezes Olga's hand, while Olga herself appears visibly moved.

Elsa smiles, remembering, "It is taken from the lamentations of an Egyptian prophet by the name of Iper-wer, Professor. He lived in the age of the great Queen Hatshepsut, but he was not a very well-known poet".

Carter is increasingly sceptical, but also determined to sort things out.

"But were you familiar with the verses? The thing is, they were published a few years ago".

Elsa once again smiles, "I've 'known' those verses since long before that".

Callender searches among the papers he keeps in his large, battered briefcase, pulling out one that illustrates an ancient text. He hands it Elsa saying, "This is extremely difficult. It took a pair of noted philologists more than seven days to discover the key to its meaning. Please take it with you, study it, and then let us know what you think it means".

The idea of having a helper appears to amuse Carter. Elsa takes the sheet of paper and glances at it. The text is in cuneiform characters, overlaid with a transcription in hieratic script.

A supremely confident Elsa reports, "This comes from the Amarna correspondence. It is written in the cuneiform letters of Tel el-Amarna, with a transcription in hieratic letters from the year XIII".

This time everyone sits in silent astonishment, ready to listen to the young woman, though first she turns to Newman and asks, "This is another test, am I right, Professor?"

Newman nods to her to go ahead, and so she starts explaining, "As I was saying, it is written in the Akkadian language, using cuneiform characters. This was the language in which international affairs were conducted between Egypt and the principalities of the Orient. It was a diplomatic language, much like French in the world of today".

Elsa runs her eyes down the sheet of paper and starts reading, "My honoured brother, please control my gold in person before you send it to me. Because the gold you sent the last time, which had been chosen by your officials, was not pure".

Elsa hands the piece of paper back to Carter, who is at a loss for words. La Fleur also does not know what to say.

As for Callender, he is simply astonished. Unable to hide his bewilderment, he blurts out: "I've never seen anything like this!"

Carter, who is sceptical by nature, asks Elsa, "Where and for how long have you studied this?"

But Callender interrupts, "To read it straight through like that! Even after a lifetime of study, it simply can't be done".

Carter takes a piece of paper showing the seals and writing that they deciphered only a short time earlier, thanks to the considerable experience and knowledge of Breasted and Gardiner. He hands it to Elsa, who starts reading without a moment's hesitation.

"Nebkheperure, the King of Upper and Lower Egypt, spent his life making images of the goods, so that every day they would give him gifts of incense, libations and offerings".

She hands the paper back to Carter, who looks at her with an admiring but puzzled expression. Callender, who is clearly on the young woman's side, smiles.

Carter notes, "It took Breasted and Gardiner a week to decipher this text".

Professor Newman, realising that Elsa is fatigued, interjects, "Gentlemen, if you will excuse us, the trip was quite tiring".

Elsa gives a wan smile and takes her leave, together with her mother, as the men politely get to their feet to say goodbye.

Before walking out, Newman turns to Carter and says, "We are staying at the Winter Hotel". Then he too leaves.

After a moment or two of silence, Callender, still befuddled over what has happened, declares, "That face. That girl. I've seen her somewhere before! I know I have, but where?"

Carter, unable to lay aside his scepticism, "Maybe she is simply incredibly adept at studying languages? Or perhaps she is affected by a rare form of autism that allows her to decipher cuneiform. Certainly a most intriguing case."

An enthusiastic Callender, "But those texts are incredibly difficult to decipher, only for her it was like child's play!"

La Fleur looks shaken, but also eager to find out more. "Perhaps she has extra-sensorial powers?"

Callender, obviously eager to see her again, "Just think how she could help us, Howard, once we bring down that wall and go inside! We wouldn't have to lose any time translating or interpreting!"

Seeing his young assistant in such a state, Carter observes in a sardonic tone, "But Alan, you're so excited! I wouldn't want the girl to be too much of a distraction for you!"

They all have a hearty laugh.

CHAPTER VIII
Wonderful Things

The Luxor train station is a long, one-storey structure adorned with large windows set in white frames and an extended, covered veranda crowned by a crenellated trim of burnished steel, at the centre of which is a sign stating "Luxor Station E.S.R", together with the Arab translation of the title.

People are lined up at the "3rd Class Reservations", another sign obviously translated into Arabic for the convenience of local travellers. Outside the station, the usual hustle and bustle of people and horse-drawn carriages is in full swing, with local personnel dressed in white and wearing the traditional red fez on their heads assisting.

The locals wear black garments and white turbans as they sway atop mules they urge forward using branches as whips. Youngsters walk barefoot, their heads, unlike those of the adults, topped by close-fitting skullcaps, pulling carts from which they do their best to sell pistachios to the tourists.

Inside the station, all sorts of people come and go: European ladies protecting themselves from the sun with white lace parasols, British officers, people hauling suitcases with the aid of local porters. A whistle announces the arrival of a train, as a cloud of steam from the locomotive wafts along the platform, amidst the waiting travellers.

Lord Carnarvon and Lady Evelyn are among the passengers ready to get off the train, as is Field Marshal Lord Edmund Allenby, the High Commissioner for Egypt, as well as Lord Westbury and his son, Captain Richard Bethtell, plus other figures of note in Egypt, including Orsha Bey Hampi. There are also some ladies, a group of Lord Carvaron's friends, and Professor Maspero too. Lady Evelyn is accompanied by an older lady, Alice, while Walley, Lord Carnarvon's butler, is loaded down with quite a few bags.

Carter, accompanied by the Egyptian governor of the Region of Qurna, helps Lady Evelyn step down from the train, handing her a bouquet of flowers. Greetings are exchanged amidst the flash of photographers' bulbs and the lights of newsreel cameramen, as a swarm of journalists presses in to ask questions and take notes. Lord Carnarvon, whose mood is excellent, greets Howard Carter.

"My dear friend, congratulations! Your tenacity has been rewarded".

But Carter, not wanting to get his hopes too high, replies, "It remains to be seen to what degree, Lord Carnarvon".

Lady Evelyn joins the conversation.

"Howard, I'm so happy for you. These flowers are beautiful!"

"And I am happy for you, Lady Evelyn," responds Carter, taking her hand with a smile. "You were the first to share my enthusiasm, to believe in me... Let's only hope that we have found what we were looking for."

The two of them know that what they feel for each other is far more than friendship, though they dare not say as much, even if they would make a perfect couple.

Lord Carnarvon, speaking rather hesitantly, addresses Carter.

"I fear I may be interrupting, but Lord Westbury would like to ask you something, and he is a dear friend".

Lord Westbury, a cheery man, steps up, together with his son, a handsome young fellow, though a bit thin for a twenty-year old.

"Hello Carter! Allow me to introduce my only son, Richard Bethell. He would so like to be your secretary, or handle any other task you might wish to assign him.

"Well, we do need all the assistance we can get...," says Carter as he shakes Lord Westbury's hand.

Behind them, Dr. White, an Egyptologist, appears at the train door, together with his delightful wife. Helping them down, Carter exclaims, "You here too! My goodness, I hope you don't all wind up terribly disappointed".

"My dear," says Dr. White to his wife, "this is my old friend, Howard Carter".

They shake hands, and then Carter turns to introduce them to Lord Carnarvon and the others.

"My Lord, the two Doctors White are illustrious Egyptologists. We were all at school together, and...".

Dr. White interrupts, "... now we wish to place ourselves at your service, simply to satisfy our endless thirst for knowledge."

As they all laugh, Lord Carnarvon nudges Carter with an elbow. "We'd best not keep the Lord High Commissioner waiting".

"Now I know what being part of a circus is like," is Carter's ironic comment to Lady Evelyn.

Turning serious once again, he walks over to Field Marshal Lord Edmund Allenby, a figure with a great deal of political influence in Egypt.

It is early in the morning, and the temperature in the Valley of Kings is even hotter than usual. Carter, Lord Carnarvon, Lady Evelyn, Callender, Maspero, Lord Westbury and his son, as well as the Egyptologists, Dr. White and his wife, plus La Fleur and a number of other distinguished figures, including important Egyptians, have gathered in the Valley, across from the set of steps that, starting from dawn, have undergone a painstaking cleaning operation. Also present, but off to one side, are Professor Newman, Elsa and her mother Olga.

The photographers and the newsreel cameramen are kept at a distance by uniformed guards. Carter turns to Lord Carnarvon and points at the stairway, indicating that his Lordship should be the first to descend it. Lord Carnarvon smiles and shakes his head no, gesturing that Carter should have the honour.

Lady Evelyn places a hand on Carter's shoulder, gently pushing him to go ahead while whispering, "May your most ambitious hopes come true, dear Howard!"

He thanks her with a smile and begins to walk down the steps. A photographer and two newsreel cameramen, having managed to escape the attentions of the guards, scurry over to the top of the stairs and start taking pictures and filming, while two more cameramen set up their tripods and their equipment. Step by step, Carter begins slowly making his way down the stairs, as the two cameramen frenetically rotate the levers of their machines. Carter turns to them and smiles, in the midst of a silence broken only by the whirring of the camera levers.

Carter has almost reached the threshold. The look on Miss Elsa's face is one of anguish, as if she wished that none of this was happening. Coming down the stairs right after Carter is Lord Carnarvon, followed by Lady Evelyn, Callender, La Fleur and Dr. White.

Lord Carnarvon reaches Carter at the threshold, while the others stop on the stairs. In front of them is the sealed door, framed at the top by a sizeable wood lintel and blocked off at its base by stones whose plastered surfaces show traces of oval-shaped seals.

Carter, looking quite excited, uses a brush to remove an initial layer of dust before closely examining the wall. He sees something he had missed fifteen days earlier: seals of the royal necropolis on the upper portion of the wall. He shows them to Lord Carnarvon, who also manages to make out the seal of the necropolis further up on the wall, decorated with the jackal figure of the god Anubis, who is positioned above nine squatting figures who have had their hands tied behind their backs.

"Those are nine prisoners who were made slaves because they were enemies of Egypt," explains Carter before leaning over to look at the bottom portion, his forehead beaded with sweat.

He delicately brushes more dust from the wall, uncovering something that brings a satisfied smile to his lips. Among the many traces uncovered, there finally appears a seal bearing the name given to Tut-Ankh-Amun on the day of his coronation: Nebkheperure, and there is also no mistaking the black beetle.

"This is him! That's his beetle!"

But an instant later, Carter's smile vanishes. He points down to a portion of the entrance that appears to have been broken into, and then closed up again with the seal of the Necropolis.

"Someone must have profaned the site!"

Hushed murmurs can be heard behind him. Carter points to the seals on the upper portion of the door.

"These can tell us when the door was closed for the last time."

Callender comes to his side and examines them closely.

"It would seem that the thieves entered at some point during the 20th dynasty, or two centuries after the death of the king".

Lord Carnarvon, barely able to contain his impatience, "But why does the date matter? The important thing is what we find behind that door".

Carter signals to his photographers to take pictures of the door and the seals, something they do from every possible angle, making sure they capture even the smallest detail. Then a team of three workmen begin removing the door.

Across from the stairs, there is nothing but silence, as everyone waits in anxious expectation. The only sound is that of the workmen's chisels.

Not far off, sitting on the ground Egyptian style, next to some rocks, Elsa sobs in muted fashion. Her mother, seeing the girl cry, leans against Professor Newman's shoulder.

"Let's hope that something comes out of all this suffering".

Professor Newman, also gazing worriedly at the girl, puts a consoling arm around the mother's shoulders.

The door has been completely demolished. Behind it, at the level of the sixteenth step, begins a passageway, a corridor carved out of the rock and strewn, like the stairs, with stones, pottery fragments and pieces of wood. Among those looking on, a distinct sense of apprehension, mixed with disappointment, takes hold.

Carter has an oil lamp brought to him and, with Lord Carnarvon and Callender following close behind, he moves along the corridor, reaching a second door similar to the first one. Carter directs the light onto the debris scattered on the floor, exclaiming, "But why leave such a mess in the tomb? It's an offence, a sacrilege against a sovereign that they worshipped as a god".

Lord Carnarvon and Callender struggle to hide their disappointment. Professor Maspero appears at the doorway, his two "experts" in tow. The pair smiles in sardonic fashion. Carter, Carnarvon and Callender move closer to the second door, picking up pottery fragments that they examine closely. They seem disappointed.

Indicating the pottery, Carter says, "They have indented markings with the Names of a number of pharaohs: Echnaton, Sakere. Here is a beetle of Thutmose III", adds Carter, pointing at the fragments.

Callender picks one up. "This has another name on it: Amenophis III".

Carnarvon is downhearted. "All these royal names would make it seem that, contrary to our expectations, we find ourselves in the presence of another storehouse for royal mummies rather than the tomb of a single individual".

Professor Maspero shares Lord Carnarvon's opinion, as do the two "experts" following in his wake, but Carter is not about to give up.

"It is too early to say".

Lady Evelyn, who, in the meantime, has reached them in the corridor, notes in a calm, measured tone, "The final answer to your questions will only come once the second door is open, isn't that so, Howard?"

Carter, already on edge, barely manages to murmur, "That is right. Thank you, Lady Evelyn".

Then, his hands trembling, his forehead damp with sweat, he takes a crowbar that Callender hands to him and begins to make a small hole in the upper-left corner of the second door. The rest of the group walks down the last steps, entering the corridor in tense expectation. Lord Westbury hugs his son's shoulders, the boy smiles back at him.

Outside, the journalists and onlookers who have come from all around listen in religious silence as the blows of the crowbar pry open a piece of the second door. Elsa, hearing the noise, covers her head with a dark shawl that she gathers at her chest, pulling at the ends with her hands.

The heat, plus the number of people packed into the space of the stairs and the corridor, make the air unbreathable. When Carter pushes the crowbar through the opening, there is nothing behind the door to stop it. All that can be seen on the other side is darkness.

Carter makes the hole bigger, before testing to see if gas might be coming out.

Dr. White hands him a candle as Maspero murmurs, "The air may have been poisoned".

A gust from inside sets the candle's feeble flame to flickering, and then it goes out altogether.

"I doubt there's any poison," notes Carter, "simply a great deal of heat".

Everyone waits in anxious expectation as the hot air continues to flow out of the opening, causing the candle flames and the lamp lights to quiver. After a brief pause, Carter holds another candle up to the hole and, tense with expectation and curiosity, moves his face up to the hole to take a look inside.

He tries to focus, but at first can see nothing. Then, as his eyes become accustomed to the dim light of the candle, he is able to make out the first shapes, then shadows, and finally colours, all of which leave him spellbound, speechless, unable to move.

With all those present turning their anxious eyes and sweaty faces his way, Carter goes on gazing through the hole, standing perfectly still.

Lord Carnarvon, as if afraid that time were being lost, is unable to keep from asking, "Can you see anything, Howard?"

Carter turns around slowly, and in a tone of enchantment, with a voice that seems to come from the depths of his soul, answers, "Wondrous things!"

Carnarvon rushes up to take a look, and Callender joins him an instant later. They take turns gazing inside, astonished at what they see. Carter hands the candle to Lady Evelyn, who looks through the small opening, unsure of what awaits her. First she sees two figures, a pair of sentinels placed one facing the other, both in the form of black statues wearing aprons and sandals of gold. They hold long sticks, and their foreheads are adorned with glittering sacred snakes. Bizarre animal heads throw their elongated shadows on the walls, while a golden cobra stands bolt upright from one of the chests of objects.

Evelyn turns to the onlookers and exclaims in a thrilled voice, "It's marvellous, stupendous, unbelievable. Thank you Howard".

Carter smiles and, with the help of Callender and two of the labourers, continues to expand the opening in the door. No one takes their eyes off the spectacle, as if they were hypnotised by the extraordinary event, while assistants bring still more lights. Even Dr. White is unable to look elsewhere, having fallen under the spell of the many wonders.

Professor Maspero and his doubting experts stare in open-mouthed amazement, while Lord Westbury's young son stands transfixed by the gold cobra, which, caught in the full glow of the light, seems to pulse with a life of its own.

Chests of jewels are visible, along with ornate garments practically still intact, plus pieces from four gold carriages that had been dismantled and piled up to one side, along with exotic birds, staffs, weapons, papyri and ceramic works, as well as precious vases of alabaster. On the floor are other jewels, while off in a corner is a bodice whose pearls lie scattered on the ground, having been ripped off. Also on the ground is a set of jewels wrapped in a scarf, with two rings sticking out. Numerous prints of naked feet are visible on the ground.

"These must be the footprints of the thieves from three thousand years ago. What could have terrified them so badly?" wonders Carter, trying to imagine the scene.

Lady Evelyn has trouble picturing it too. "To leave behind so many treasures that were right there for the taking ..."

Carter continues her line of thought. "It wouldn't have been because the guards or the priests surprised them. Those were just normal, on-the-job hazards".

A puzzled Lady Evelyn, "What could have happened?"

Carter picks up an alabaster cup from the ground and begins translating its hieroglyphic inscription: "Long live his Ka. May you be given millions of years. You who love Thebes...As you face north and your eyes contemplate happiness".

Carter's hand brushes the feathers of a liturgical fan, pulverising them, when suddenly blood-curdling noises break out.

The wooden objects, sealed away for thousands of years in the extreme heat of the chamber, are undergoing sudden physical alterations, on account of the fresh air pouring in from outside. As the wood of the furniture adjusts to the new atmospheric conditions, it starts squeaking and screeching in a loud range of tones. Lady Evelyn puts her hands over her ears.

The Egyptologist Mace staggers backward in fright, covering his face with his hands as his wife steadies him on one side. The eyes of the son of Lord Westbury are filled with astonishment.

Carter takes in the scene, fearing that everything could fall apart at any moment. The sounds slowly fade away, leaving a deafening silence in their place.

Carter moves cautiously, adding in a low voice, "Don't touch anything, and don't make any sudden movements. Even a slight movement of the air could turn much of these treasures to dust".

Mace is staring at a life-like, polished eye that gazes back out at the intruders from among the various priceless objects: the white of the eye, which stays perfectly still, shines in the electric light directed onto it. Not feeling well, Dr. Mace turns unsteadily and heads for the exit, helped along by his wife.

Outside the tomb, the sun is about to set. The reporters rush up to get a photograph of Dr. Mace as he comes out of the tomb all pale and unsure of himself. He sits down on the steps with the aid of his wife, who dries the sweat off his forehead.

Seeing him in that condition, somebody asks, "What was it, Dr. Mace? Why did you come out? What did you see?"

Lord Westbury also emerges from the tomb, steadying his son, who regains his composure as soon as he has a chance to breath in some fresh air, at which point Lord Westbury sits down too.

"It was nothing. My son was simply overcome with excitement," explains Lord Westbury to the reporters. "Though I can assure that what we saw is capable of exciting all sorts of emotions".

A reporter asks what, in fact, they saw.

"Stupendous, incredible, extraordinary things! Except the heat is suffocating!" answers Lord Westbury.

Inside the tomb, Ali draws closes to Carter and signals that he has something to say. "Come and take a look ...", he murmurs, leading the way.

The two of them step carefully around the objects, followed by Callender, who carries a lamp. Carter and Ali reach a third door, which has been left ajar. Here too they find bare footprints left by a number of people.

Carter kneels to take a closer look. "Who's to say that we won't find the mummy?".

Callender and Ali open the door wide, as Callender lights the inside with his lamp, reporting, "It's another, smaller room, also filled with treasures".

In fact, there are chairs, couches, buffets, stools, cushions, baskets for fruit, stone jars, crates and chests, toys, lances, bows, arrows, shields, clothes and plates, all scattered in a disorderly mess, partly broken, torn, stepped on.

One chest is filled with myrrh, resin, rubber, antimony, gold and silver. There are bench chests packed with gloves, linen fabric, sandals, bracelets, necklaces of gold and pearls. On the ground are still more prints of barefoot thieves. Carter studies them in astonishment.

"They made it all the way in here!"

The flickering light of the lamps provides glimpses of large funeral biers inlaid with gold and styled as fantastical animals. Piled atop of them are coffers of jewellery, chairs and regal thrones totally covered in gold, with inlays of precious stones. There are also four gilded chariots that were dismantled and left in pieces, plus a giant fan of ostrich feathers.

Carter is unable to fathom the situation. "No sarcophagus, not the slightest trace of a mummy. Maybe they are right, and this is simply a hiding place."

"Or could the mummy have been spirited away?", suggests Callender.

Finally, Carter, along with the last of the witnesses to this great discovery, steps back outside the tomb, just as the setting sun is turning the sky a fiery red. The reporters, the photographers and the newsreel cameramen record the scene as best they can, popping their magnesium flash bulbs and turning on their portable lights.

The reporters and photographers crowd around Carter and Lord Carnarvon. His Lordship starts by solemnly announcing, "Today, November 25th, is the day of days, the most splendid I have ever experienced. A day like no other, unparalleled. We have made a discovery that exceeds our wildest expectations, providing us with unequalled quantities of extremely precious materials", concludes Lord Carnarvon, wiping the sweat from his brow with a handkerchief.

Carter adds a final phrase, "Today we have earned ourselves a very small piece of eternity".

Those present express their admiration with a round of applause, but immediately after, a reporter asks whether they have found a tomb, and if so, was there a mummy in it?

"We have not found either a sarcophagus nor a mummy," answers Carter. But the journalist insists, asking when the press will be able to see the site from the inside.

"In a couple of days. We must be very careful," cautions Carter.

A few hours later, in the Luxor telegraph office, a throng of reporters is occupying all the emergency telephone lines, yelling into them in a hectic babel of different languages.

An American reporter shouts, "With this unique find, 'A small piece of eternity earned!', thanks to one man, Howard Carter, backed by wealthy amateur archaeologist, Lord Carnarvon. They missed the tomb, in 1911, by only a few yards."

While an agitated French reporter dictates, "25 novembre 1922, une date historique! Une grande découverte archéologique, le tombeau de Tutankhamun roi d'Egypte," as a German journalist relays back home, "Unbezahlbare Schätze, unkalkulierbare Schätze wurden ans Licht gebracht", and an Italian reporter comments, "Tra tante meraviglie, la mummia del sovrano non è stata trovata. Dobbiamo pensare che sia andata perduta nei millenni passati o che qualcuno l'abbia trafugata?"

The scene is a massive hubbub of people writing, taking pictures, amidst the sound of countless voices in every imaginable language.

The Hotel Winter in Luxor, on the banks of the Nile, is also filled to capacity. Inside the extensive foyer, a din of voices is engaged in lively discussions in all sorts of languages. Lord Carnarvon, Lady Evelyn and Carter are surrounded by reporters and others bystanders who have flocked to offer their congratulations as the three of them try to make their way to the stairs that lead to the upper floors.

Elsa steps into the hotel through the main entrance, still cloaked in her dark shawl, together with Olga, her mother, and Professor Newman, none of whom expected to find such a crowd. But seeing that nobody pays them any mind, they take the stairs with out being bothered.

Only Lord Carnarvon, when he catches sight of the girl dressed in black, in the company of the more mature lady and the Professor, asks Carter in a whisper, "Is that her?"

Carter nods yes. Lord Carnarvon tries to get a better look at Elsa, and Evelyn is also curious, but the crowd keeps them from focussing on the girl, who is uses her shawl as a shield against prying eyes.

People are offering toasts at the bar, happy that they can say, in the future, that they were there.

In their hotel suite, Elsa puts aside the newspapers she was reading.

"If Carter is satisfied with what he's found in those two chambers, then he has no idea what still awaits him!" Elsa confides to Professor Newman.

"He still hasn't found the Pharaoh's body," answers Newman, after a brief moment of silence.

"Because he's only opened up two rooms," notes Elsa, after taking a lengthy pause.

Newman seems surprised. "You think there are more than two?"

A puzzled Elsa wonders out loud, as if she were talking to herself, "Did I say two?"

Olga joins the conversation, observing in a maternal tone, "Yes dear, you said 'two'! Wasn't that what you wanted to say?"

A bewildered Elsa answers, "I have no idea what I wanted to say. I talk without thinking".

Visibly worried, Olga turns anxiously to Newman, "Do you think it's a good idea for us to be here?"

Having overhear her mother, Elsa cuts in, stating unequivocally, "It most certainly is. And I am not leaving here. This is my home".

"Your home is in the Sudan, or rather Italy," shoots back Olga in a hurt voice. "You were born in Ondurman, where you live with me, your mother...".

Olga taps her own chest. "Because I am your mother!" she continues in tears. "I carried you in my womb for nine months, like any mother of this world".

Drawing closer to Olga, Elsa kneels down in front of her, takes her hands in hers and murmurs in a sweet, halting voice, almost a stutter, "You did give birth to me, and so yes, you are my mother. But I was also born somewhere else, in a different time. I have thoughts that are different, another soul, other memories."

Elsa points to her own head. "They come to me all on their own, whether I want them to or not. I have no idea whose memories they are, or whether they are real, but as you can see, they turn out to be right. I am afraid there is no solution to my existence, but I have to go on searching for one anyway. I have to try and understand..."

At the end of the phrase, her voice breaks. Her "mother" touches her face delicately, stroking her forehead with a finger while gently kissing her.

It is a lovely evening. The vivid glow of the waxing moon highlights ancient ruins in the vicinity of a village located between Luxor and the Valley of the Kings. A group of small homes, all of them built in rough-hewn fashion, with the exception of one that looks slightly more refined, are partially visible in the brooding blue light.

The house that looks better appointed than the others is the one Carter lives in when he wants to be near the valley, something he has also done during earlier digs. The silence is broken by the sound of the hoofs of the two horses pulling the carriage in which Lady Evelyn and her elderly governess are travelling.

The carriage stops in front of the first of the houses. Lady Evelyn gets out, takes a look at the surroundings and grimaces.

On joining her, the governess points out, "The homes here have no numbers. No signs".

Puzzled, the two women begin walking up and down the street, until Carter appears on a terrace and, seeing the carriage, he recognises them, calling out enthusiastically, "Evelyn, what a pleasant surprise! Please come in, through the door down below".

From inside the house, he calls for Ali, "Hurry, open the door for the ladies!"

Inside, the house is quite different from Carter's more comfortable quarters back in Luxor. This setting is Spartan, unadorned, with a very limited space for working, plus a fair-sized room with a bed placed off to one side and a table standing next to a wall, covered with plans and drawings, plus items of earthenware crockery bought at a local market.

There are maps posted on the walls, while a square table in the middle of the room is surrounded by four chairs on which everything a hard-working architect could need has been piled up.

Ali opens the front door, letting in the governess, followed by Lady Evelyn, who says, "I hope we are not disturbing you?"

"Far from it," replies Carter, visibly pleased by the surprise. "You've given me a wonderful excuse to stop working".

Ali asks, "Effendi, should I make drinks?"

Carter nods, before adding, "You might want to show Miss Alice the kitchen. Ali is quite the authority when it comes to making cocktails".

Evelyn smiles. "Sounds like an excellent idea!"

Ali bows to Lady Evelyn and ushers Miss Alice through the door of the small kitchen, which appears rudimental but functional.

Evelyn is glad to be left alone with Carter, who notes, and rather nervously, "I use this house, but only to be closer to the valley. The one in Luxor is far more comfortable, and it also has a lovely terrace that looks out onto the Nile".

Evelyn appears strangely ill at ease too.

"Forgive me for being so impulsive. Perhaps it was wrong to come out here and distract you from our work".

"No, I'm glad you came, Evelyn. It was one of those evenings when I couldn't get anything done anyway. I couldn't concentrate".

"Howard, your work is so fascinating," adds Evelyn in a tone of rapt admiration. "You have no idea how much I admire those people who discovered the immense temples that everybody is talking about, the ones buried in the

Cambodian jungle, but your work enthrals me in subtler ways. Searching in underground passages for royal dwellings buried more than three thousand years ago is something I find so adventurous, and your confidence is inspiring, Howard. My father says that, if there is anybody capable of finding the Pharaoh, you are the man ... I was always sure of it."

Carter, visibly moved by her compliments, points out, "It is not a matter of confidence, Evelyn. There is no enlightened guesswork involved. Nothing but a perfectly mathematical capacity to put together all the information in our possession. If our calculations are correct, then this portion of the valley should hold the tomb of the pharaoh."

"So the image that I have of the archaeologist as an explorer, always in search of new mysteries, is all wrong?", adds Evelyn, pretending to be disappointed.

Carter smiles. "Not completely. As you can see, I've brought in specialists to decipher the inscriptions, others to examine the artefacts, while I..." he concludes with a laugh, "have turned into a chief accountant charged with overseeing a sprawling dig-site".

Alice, in the meantime, has prepared two excellent cocktails: Ali brings out a box of dried fruit and places it on the table. Carter seems disheartened over how little he has to offer his guests.

As Alice and Ali go back to the kitchen, Evelyn returns to her conversation with Carter.

"I would say that, for an accountant, you have made an exceptional discovery."

Carter draws closer, whispering, "The accountant can wait...".

Just as the two of them are about to kiss, Alice comes back out of the kitchen, followed by Ali. But on catching sight of the scene in front of her, she stops short, causing Ali to run into her and then fall backwards in a clatter of pots and pans.

Lady Evelyn and Carter turn in the direction of the kitchen and, seeing Alice frantically signalling to Ali to be quiet, they break out in great peels of laugher.

At the Winter Palace Hotel in Luxor, Elsa and Professor Newman are having a conversation in the drawing room of Olga Mittieri's suite. On the other side of the Nile, the moon shines large, being in its waxing phase, so that it illuminates the room where the lamp has yet to be turned on.

Professor Newman is about to light his pipe, when suddenly he turns to Elsa to ask, "But you really didn't realize that you'd said: 'He's only opened up two rooms'?"

"No, Professor. I found myself saying it, but without having thought it. The truth is, that room is filled to overflowing with objects..."

She takes a lengthy pause before continuing.

" ... so yes, if there is a handprint on the white wall, between the two black statues, then that means that He is on the other side of the wall."

The next morning finds Professor Newman inside the tent where Carter and his staff are overseeing and recording, one by one, the artefacts that are then painstakingly wrapped in cotton and carefully packed away in large wood crates. Newman has come to ask for permission to enter the tomb with Elsa, a request that Carter at first seems inclined to deny. But Newman insists.

"We only want to see if there is a handprint on the wall. We won't touch anything".

Carter is unsure, but Callender gives him reason to reflect.

"Howard, the young lady might be able to help. How can it hurt?"

Carter lets himself be persuaded.

"But only if you go with them".

Newman would have preferred to have been the only one with Elsa when she visited the tomb, but having no choice, he accepts.

The three of them go down the steps, pass through the corridor and enter the tomb, were the stifling heat makes it hard to breath. On the white wall, between the two black statues, the handprint that Elsa spoke of is nowhere to be seen, though at the bottom of the wall, laid on the ground, is a wreath of flowers that dried out centuries ago. As Elsa gazes at it, her eyes fill with tears.

Professor Newman scans the portion of the wall between the two statues before moving closer to the girl.

"There doesn't seem to be any handprint. Could it be on another wall?" he asks Elsa in a hushed tone.

When Lady Evelyn enters the room, Callender motions to her to please wait in silence for a while. Elsa stares at the dried-out wreath for a moment, and then goes back to contemplating the white wall, a reverie interrupted by Ali, who has come to haul away, with the help of an archaeological assistant, the Pharaoh's folding bed, which will be subjected to a special chemical treatment.

Elsa goes back out to the corridor, where she finds Evelyn.

"Do you not feel well?" Evelyn asks gently.

"Only for a moment. It is terribly hot in here," answers Elsa, wiping her forehead with her hand before taking another look at the chamber and the wall.

"I knew who you are," continues Evelyn, in the same soothing tone as before.

Elsa stares at her, but Evelyn goes on. "We're actually quite a small community here."

"I am Professor Newman's assistant," says Elsa, telling a lie.

Not wanting to contradict her, Evelyn offers, "If that is so, then please excuse me. Otherwise, I hope we can become friends. I might be able to help you..."

"No one can help me," answers Elsa, staring at her.

"Carter said that there was supposed to be a handprint... I am sorry," concludes Evelyn politely.

Just then, Lord Carnarvon comes down the steps.

"You must be the young lady I've heard so much about?" he exclaims on seeing her.

Elsa gives a faint smile.

"Well, you have met my daughter," observes Lord Carnarvon. "Rest assured that you will always be welcome here."

"Thank you my Lordship. All of you have been most kind".

Lord Carnarvon goes on his way, reaching Professor Newman and Olga, who have stayed in the chamber, by the wall.

"We are most honoured by your invitation, My Lordship," declares Professor Newman. "Allow me to introduce Mrs. Olga Mittieri, Elsa's mother, who is an esteemed anthropologist in her own right."

"With great pleasure," says Lord Carnarvon, as he bows to Olga.

"I have heard a great deal about your daughter," he adds. "Perhaps she could help us with deciphering the inscriptions, which often prove to be exceedingly difficult. That would mean a great deal".

"Thank you," replies Olga, "I very much hope that she can."

Just then, Carter and La Fleur arrive, carrying special brushes able to remove dust in extremely delicate fashion.

"I want to see if there are any inscriptions on that wall, perhaps hidden beneath the dust," explains Carter. "But we have to work very delicately, David. Always move the brush in a downward direction, very slowly and lightly".

They begin passing the soft brushes over the wall with great care, always moving downward, sending the ancient dust falling to the ground. Carnarvon follows their movements. The brushes have already cleaned the upper portion of the wall and are now working further down.

"What is that?", calls out Carnarvon, his eyes focussed on one point.

Evelyn moves closer, so that she too can get a better look at the plaster, and Elsa follows her.

Carter tells La Fleur, "Let me see, David. Let's try one more time with the brushes, gently, slowly."

Olga purses her lips, to keep from exclaiming on account of the tension. Newman glances at Elsa, while Evelyn also looks at her in wonder. Elsa is staring at the handprint. Evelyn tries to say something to Elsa, who stands perfectly still.

Then the girl murmurs, "For a second I thought I was going to suffocate, it is so hot down here", her eyes never leaving the handprint on the wall.

Evelyn is astonished to see that it is there, just as Elsa had predicted it would be. Professor Newman is also hiding his surprise.

La Fleur examines the handprint. "Small, delicate fingers, possibly those of a women."

"It must have been made when the plaster was still wet," observes Callender, thrilled at the thought.

Evelyn also notes that smoke, back then, must have blackened a pot on the ceiling.

"A lamp would have made that mark. And the wreath left there on the ground. The handprint looks so fresh, so well-defined. It all seems like it happened only yesterday. I feel like an intruder".

Carter is surprised too. Then he sees something on the wall that had escaped his attention.

"Look over there," he points it out to La Fleur. "That could very well be a seal of the necropolis!"

Gently removing the dust from the spot, he shows it to La Fleur, who wonders, "But what does that mean? Why is there a seal stamped on the wall?"

Carter smiles, "It means that this is more than just a mere wall!"

"It means," adds an excited Lord Carnarvon, "that there are more rooms behind this wall."

Carter taps on the wall with the tip of the brush, producing a muted sound that shows there may be an empty space on the other side, probably another room.

"At least one. And let's hope it holds the sarcophagus," ventures Carter.

"But why only one?!" exclaims an enthusiastic Lord Carnarvon. "There could be any number. Perhaps there's a corridor laid out around it. The funeral room could be far away"

Professor Newman listens in silence before throwing a doubtful glance in Elsa's direction.

"There are two more rooms, only two," murmurs the young woman. "And in one of them, behind that wall, is He!".

Everyone's eyes turn towards Elsa, who has an indecipherable expression on her face.

"Ah...Mon Dieu!!" mumbles La Fleur, before passing the brush over one side of the wall, where he brings to light signs of a hole that has been closed up again and bears a seal in its upper portion: a seal of the necropolis.

"Damn them!", exclaims Carter in exasperation.

"What does this mean?" wonders Lord Carnarvon.

"That the robbers reached this spot too," replies Carter. "Look, it was closed up again with the seals of the necropolis. Who can say if the sarcophagus is still in there. Let's hope it wasn't spirited away."

"The robbers were here, but then they ran off, leaving these precious objects on the ground. What could have scared them away?" wonders an astonished Callender.

"The only way to find out," declares Lord Carnarvon resolutely, "is to knock down that wall."

Carter seems hesitant.

"I'm tempted to do just that, but for now, we can't. A lot of these objects have to undergo special treatments before they can be touched, otherwise we risk destroying them. They need to be reinforced, and that will take a good deal of time. We don't went to lose all these priceless treasures, do we?"

On New York's Fifth Avenue, people pass by the majestic Metropolitan Museum, with its broad stairway and its fountains, as they hurry to work. Inside, in the department devoted to ancient Egypt, a prominent sign on an office door says: "ALBERT M. LYTHGOE – DIRECTOR EGYPTIAN DEPARTMENT".

A window of the office looks out on Central Park, on the other side of which stand the buildings of the West Side of the great metropolis. Lythgoe, the Director of the Egyptian Department, is giving some final instructions to photographer Harry Burton, who has just laid his bulky photographic equipment on the ground.

"They have found a new wall, Mr. Burton, probably the one behind which they will eventually find the mummy. They will only open it up once they have catalogued all the valuable relics discovered to date. They are waiting for you, so you should leave immediately," says the Director as he hands Burton his tickets. "This very evening, if you can make it on time. The steamship leaves at a quarter to seven."

Burton is a passionate traveller, and the idea of being able to take part in this extraordinary adventure strikes him as the ideal assignment.

"Excellent, Mr. Director. I'll be on my way."

Before leaving the room, Burton shakes the hand of the Director, who calls out to his secretary, "Please send this telegram to Prof. Howard Carter, in Luxor, Egypt.

"As always, delighted to provide any assistance possible. Feel free to use the services of Harry Burton, plus any other member of our organisation, as you see fit. Congratulations."

In Carter's home, the one he keeps in the village, to be closer to the dig, there is a ton of mail. Both the worktable and the floor are covered with stacks of letters and newspapers from all over the world. Ali is saying goodbye to a pair of postman who have delivered still more.

Inside the study are Professor La Fleur, who appears to have recovered from the moment of ill health he suffered at the tomb, and Callender, who is leafing through the telegrams his friend Carter has received.

Carter says to Callender, who has just finished reading Lythgoe's telegram to him, "Please thank Professor Lythgoe. Tell him that we eagerly await Burton's arrival."

La Fleur informs Carter, "George Bènedite, the Head Curator of the Department of Egyptian Antiquities at the Louvre Museum is about to leave to be at your side."

Callender, reads from another telegram.

"This is from the Egyptian government: 'The Government of Egypt expresses its gratitude for the success you have achieved, as well as its wish to play an active role in your invaluable work by providing you with whatever support you may need".

The offer draws Carter's sarcastic response of, "Endless thanks!"

Callender picks up one of the telegrams, as of it were just another of the countless messages, but for this one he gets to his feet and hands it to Carter.

"It's from His Majesty, the King of England".

Carter takes the telegram and reads it out loud: "'All glory to Carter e Carnarvon!' Signed: King George".

"But how does one respond to a telegram from the King?" Carter reflects for a moment.

"Should I thank him and say that I'm most grateful? What do you think?"

An oversized moon shines in all its splendour above Luxor. The great River Nile flows slowly, solemnly, through the night, sparkling in the moonlight. The waves break gently on its banks, making sounds that resemble faint murmurs.

Not far from one of the banks, a lone woman can be seen. It is Elsa, who is staring at the waters flowing in front of her, spellbound.

As she walks along, her anguished face is reflected in the water by the bank. Elsa kneels down and cups her hands, filling them with water that she then plunges her face into. She looks up, her face shiny with dripping water, towards the moon, which tirelessly continues its interplay of dazzling light.

Above her, the sky is filled with stars. A short distance away, sticking out from the sand, is the silhouette of the giant, half-buried head of Ozymandias, wearing the royal crown of ancient Egypt. Nearby is the statue's pedestal, still attached to its broken-off legs and bearing a hieroglyphic inscription on its border. Elsa reads it in a whisper.

"My name is Ozymandias, king of kings. Look at my works, ye mighty, and despair, though you may be destined to live millions of years".

Elsa's reflection breaks up and disappears. Not far from her, Professor Newman is looking for the girl, with the help of Muna, who lights the way with a lamp. The Professor spots Elsa and calls out, but she keeps moving towards the ruins of the ancient complex of Karnak, on the right bank of the Nile.

The moon casts its light on the massive complex, providing glimpses of the writings and designs that adorn its impressively proportioned colonnade. Newman finally catches up to Elsa, who has almost reached the temple. Owl hoots travel through the night air, and further off a jackal howls from time to time.

At last, Elsa, Professor Newman and Muna the governess, guided by Muna's lamp, arrive at the temple, where they can see the twin colossal statues of Ramses II. They look at the first face, then at the second, the twin version.

"There are gaps in my memory that keep me from recollecting things. I often find myself unable to connect one piece of life with another," observes Elsa while contemplating the statues.

"You made a good impression on Carter", Newman responds in a measured tone. "He likes you, but he's a man of science and believes only in what can be proven. I act that way too, though I often forget to when I'm with you..."

They move on, with Numa out in front, leading the way with the lamp, like a tiny firefly flickering along, amidst the massive statues.

"The French archaeologists are doing a fine job of restoring as much as they can," states Newman, impressed by the extraordinary spectacle to be had at night.

"Does this temple, or what's left of it, help you remember anything?"

"On the day of the coronation," says Elsa with a smile, "there were also signs of restoration work that was supposed to cover up more than a thousand years of neglect and deterioration".

She squeezes Newman's arm as her mind returns to the realm of memory. "The coronation of TUTANKHAMUN was held in this very spot, right here where we are walking".

She goes on, but as if she were talking to herself, a pained expression on her face.

"It was a political act, to show to the powerful clerics of Thebes that the dynasty had surrendered, that it was returning to Thebes in defeat. He was only a frightened little boy, unsure of himself...".

Elsa keeps walking, her steps lit by the lantern, as her memories carry her back to the distant past.

"It was daytime, the sun was shining in a clear blue sky. He was a child of roughly ten. I can see his face, his frightened eyes as he gazed at the sumptuous trappings of the ceremony at the Temple of Karnak..."

The priests take turns chanting a mournful lament. The incense gives the procession a magical, unreal, deeply spiritual atmosphere. Waiting inside the large courtyard of the portico are the priests, arrayed both to the right and the left of the colonnade, together with the court dignitaries, the vizier and other officials, these last stationed in front of the entrance to the temple.

Tutankhamun was still just a boy. He moved forward slowly, in a confused, awkward manner, even though he had been given all the instructions on how to preside over the ceremony. But he looked bewildered, his eyes wide open but empty, even though he did seem to grasp the importance of his role.

Just a step behind him was his tutor, the "Divine Father Ay", and then the head of the army, General Horemheb, followed by Tutankhamun's faithful friend and squire Thumose, as well as the great prophet Amon, plus the royal scribe and the scribe of the temple, along with four sem priests and, at the tail end of the procession, the royal princes.

Tutankhamun still wears his hair in a braid that falls alongside one temple, a style typical of young children. He is dressed in a thong and walks barefoot. All those present bow their heads as the boy slowly crosses the courtyard under the blinding sun. The silence is broken only by the low, ponderous beating of a drum.

Not until then does the young prince note that, beneath the portico, between two columns, is a statue hidden by a mat, standing alongside another statue of a sovereign whose face has been chiseleld away. The divine father Ay lays a hand on the prince's cheek, turning his head so that his eyes look forward, away from the statue.

The procession finally reaches the façade of the portico. The muted drumbeat fades, giving way to the slow, subdued reading of the psalms.

"You are in peace! You come in peace, into the dwelling of Amun. You come in peace, sent by your father Amun, who loves you."

The boy continues, going from the glare of the sunlit courtyard to the murky shade of the pillared hall. A priest steps out from the shadows, wearing white sandals, the traditional thong and a falcon's mask. He takes the prince by the hand and solemnly leads him inside the temple.

There he finds another priest, this one meant to resemble Amun, as shown by the two-feathered crown on his head, his gilded face and the white sandals and thong he wears.

This second priest takes Tutankhamun's hand and, together with the first, leads the boy to a chapel, in order to begin the Royal Ascent. At the centre of the chapel is a tub with a border on which four priests stand, positioned at spots that correspond to the cardinal points of the compass. They too wear white sandals and traditional thongs. The face of each priest is covered with a mask: the first wears the mask of Thoth (an Ibis), the second the mask of Seth (a dog with a long nose, rectangular ears that stick straight up and a tail in the form of an arrow), while the third has on the mask of Horus of Behdet (a hawk), and the fourth wears that of Duamutef (a falcon).

All these sacred figures hold gold pitchers. Tutankhamun steps into the tub, where the water laps at his calves. The four priests pour purifying water from their jars onto the boy's hands and arms, which he holds straight out from his sides, the palms pointing up. The priests begin pronouncing the rite.

"Now you have been purified! You are pure!"

Tutankhamun exclaims, "Now I am purified, I am pure".

The four priests lead him beyond the door, towards the inner colonnade. They walk close to the wall, until they reach another, larger chapel. Roughly three-quarters of the way through it, sit scale models of the archaic sanctuaries of the north and the south.

From the back of the hall, the priest Imhotep moves forward, arriving from the sanctuary of the south, followed by ten priests wearing long vestments and white sandals. They carry six imperial crowns and two sceptres, the flaying whip and the pastoral staff, along with the royal sandals and the giraffe's tail.

Imhotep, followed by the sandal bearer, steps up to Tutankhamun and cuts his braid. Then he takes the sandals, whose soles are decorated with images of the enemies of Egypt, and laces them onto the Prince's feet, pronouncing the fateful words: "Your Majesty's war cry echoes in all foreign nations. Your enemies fall beneath your sandals, because you have been given all the earth as your domain."

Next the priest puts the white belt around the Prince's waste, so that the giraffe's tail attached to it hangs behind him. Now Imhotep leads Tutankhamun to the throne in the north sanctuary, where the Prince sits as the priest places two sceptres in his hands: the Heka crook and the Nekhakha flail. The boy receives both of them while assuming the ritual position, as Imhotep continues pronouncing the rite.

"Now you are destined to reign millions of years! You sit on the throne of Osiris, holding his sceptre in your hand. You give orders to all living things."

As the ceremony proceeds, assistant priests bring forth the objects needed for the function. Imhotep places the red crown of lower Egypt on Tutankhamun's head while continuing to recite: "You reign over lower Egypt! The doors to the horizon open up for you! Its shutters are flung wide open! The red crown comes to you."

The young prince responds, "How beautiful you are when new, when brand-new".

"A god brought it," continues Imhotep. "The father of the gods. Here is the King. It comes to you, who are rendered powerful by magic."

Imhotep takes the red crown off Tutankhamun's head and hands it back to the assistant priest. Tutankhamun steps down from the throne, then from the platform, still holding the two sceptres, as called for under the ritual.

He leaves the sanctuary of the north and climbs the stairs to that of the south.

Suddenly a cobra's shrill hiss is heard, amplified by a special instrument.

The "Great Magic" slithers along the floor, in the guise of a cobra snake. Other priests accompany the dance, agitating the instrument that imitates the snake's high-pitched hiss. When Tutankhamun enters, the "Great Magic" rears up and stares at him. Then, in a gesture both solemn and symbolic, it wraps him in its coils, as of they were an immense cloak.

The expression on young Tutankhamun's face is calm, detached.

"Oh Great Magic, Wadjet the fiery snake! May all my enemies fear me as they fear you! May I govern and guide my people!"

The "Great Magic" slithers back into the shadows. Imhotep leads the King to the throne and places the white crown of Upper Egypt on his head.

"You are the King of Upper Egypt! You sit on the throne of Horus, as his successor! You have the power and wear his crown!"

Tutankhamun leaves the pavilion of Upper Egypt and sits on the throne placed between the two sanctuaries.

"Now you are the King of both Upper and Lower Egypt," exclaims Imhotep, placing a red crown on top of the white crown already on the boy's head.

"You are the father and mother of your people. You are welcomed and acclaimed by all! Give your people law and guidance. Now it is you who lead them."

Tutankhamun keeps his arms crossed, the two sceptres resting against his chest. He is wearing a white skirt, the royal sandals and the two crowns on his head. He gets up slowly and then walks swiftly pace around the perimeter of both sanctuaries, before sitting back down on the throne found midway between the two.

The royal scribe and the temple scribe walk up to the young prince, they crouch down and begin writing the titles that Imhotep pronounces, in keeping with the rite.

"Golden Horus, King of Upper and Lower Egypt, son of the King, Nebkheperure Tutankhamun".

Once the scribes have finished writing down the names of the young king, he gets up from the throne. Imhotep takes the double crown off his head and replaces it with the Atef crown.

"You have appeared on the throne of Horus. You guide all living things. You shall be glorious, in eternity."

Imhotep removes the Atef crown from his head and puts on the Khepresh.

"I give you strength and energy against all foreign countries".

Tutankhamun, with the Khepresh on his head and the sceptres in his hands, walks along a portion of the colonnade and enters the small chapel of Amun. The court stays outside: only the young king can enter.

Standing in the temple, with an imposing air, is a priest whom wears the crown of Amun and has his face painted gold. Tutankhamun lets go off the sceptres and takes two cups, half spheres with holes, that contain milk. He offers them to the god, laying them at the feet of the tabernacle. Then he turns around, away from the priest, but instead of leaving, he kneels down, leaning forward as the priest of Amun proclaims, "You are my son, King of Upper and Lower Egypt, Nebkheperure Tutankhamun".

The young sovereign gets back on his feet and proceeds to an unadorned chapel, in the middle of which is an archaic throne that he sits down on. To one side of him is a symbolic pillar with "unite" written on it in hieroglyphics. Four more priests step forward, wearing masks of the spirits of the Nile. With bulging stomachs and breasts that hang heavy, as if to evoke the fertilising function of the river, they intertwine around the pillar the seal and the papyrus, symbolising the union of the two lands.

"May he dominate his enemies. May he make offerings to the gods. May Upper and Lower

Egypt both be under his power", announce the four priests.

The King stands up again and retraces the route that brought him there. Waiting for him at the door of the first chapel, the one where the purification took place, is Ankhesenamun, his thirteen year-old bride, and also his half-sister, seeing that she too is a child of Akhenaten, though her mother is Nefertiti. The beautiful girl bows as he passes, while the royal princesses who accompany her prostrate themselves at the sight of the King.

"The Bride of God," exclaim the four priests. "The Mother of God, the Grand Royal Consort, the Lady of Upper and Lower Egypt, Ankhesenamun."

The King continues towards the exit, leaving behind the glaring sunlight of the courtyard surrounded by the porticos. The priestly college and the court are both located under the porticos, together. Followed by the head priests and the royal princes, as well as his young queen and the princesses of the realm, the King reaches the courtyard and walks down one-quarter of its length.

The royal scribes go up to the Vizier, who places his seal on the four papyri, which are rolled up and put inside leather holders closed at the top by belts. Next, the four scribes go up to four horsemen, one posted at each of the four corners of the courtyard, and present them with the cases, which the horsemen sling across their shoulders.

The young King is wearing the Khepresh. One of the royal princes serves as his charioteer. The great temple gates open wide. Outside, the expectant crowd fills the air with acclamations and best wishes. One after the other, the four horsemen carrying the leather cases begin galloping away, crying out, "Nebkheperure Tutankhamun: long life, strength and health to the King of Upper and Lower Egypt!"

The King's chariot starts off, leaving behind the gates of the temple. A group of high-ranking officials follow the royal chariot on horseback, then come two carriages, one carrying the Divine Father Ay, the other General Horemheb, along with their mounted escorts, all as the people's cries of praise for the new sovereign are heard far and wide.

It is almost dawn, and Elsa is still recounting her memories, as Professor Newman attentively takes notes.

"The Divine Father Ay and Horemheb had won the first battle, because the coronation of the young pharaoh amounted to recognition of Thebes as the sacred capital, restoring the clerics of Amun to the position of power they had lost during the reign of Tutankhamun's father, Akhenaten, who had moved the sacred capital north, to Thebes, where it stayed for twenty years, along the river that flows through the desert, which is where he had Akhetaten built."

"Akhetaten?", asks Newman, intrigued.

"It means horizon of the Aten," explains Elsa. Today it is known as Amarna, but even then, no one dared speak the name of Akhetaten, because it been built by Tutankhamun's heretical father, any sign of whose works was immediately erased".

CHAPTER IX
The Disagreement

The light of dawn reveals the desert sand stretching majestically off into the distance, as a carriage makes its way along an unpaved path in the midst of gently sloping dunes, all beneath a sky tinged with red. Inside the carriage are Lord Carnarvon, Evelyn and Carter, on their way back to the Valley of Kings. Lord Carnarvon appears to be in excellent spirits.

"I couldn't be happier, my dear Howard!"

"I'm glad to hear it, My Lord," answers Carter sleepily.

Lord Carnarvon sings the first few notes of an English ditty, stopping to observe, "A hundred years ago, Lord Elgin's efforts led to priceless treasures of Greek art finding their way to the British Museum, and people were still talking about it long after, but when I bring my rightful share of these unmatched wonders back to London, Lord Elgin's star will be eclipsed!"

Carter turns to Lord Carnarvon, who is sitting beside him, with an astonished look.

"What we have found, and whatever else we shall find, must remain here, in this country, my Lord!"

"Professor Carter!", exclaims Carnarvon, looking straight back at him, "I hope you speak in jest, as otherwise your words are quite ill chosen! It is my express wish that everyone in London admire the share of our discoveries that rightfully belongs to me, as stated under paragraphs 8, 9 and 10 of the concession for the dig".

"My Lord!", Carter responds crossly, "Paragraphs 8, 9 and 10 of the concession, and especially paragraph 8, state that all materials discovered, and held to be of 'primary importance', belong to Egypt's Office of the Superintendent of Antiquities. And everything found so far falls precisely under the clauses of that paragraph".

"Mr. Carter", retorts Lord Carnarvon icely, "you are forgetting the clause under which the Superintendent's Office, in the case of sepulchres 'that have not been violated', reserves the right of ownership over all objects held to be of importance to the history of archaeology, "with the exception" of mummies and sarcophagi. As for whatever else is discovered, the holder of the concession will 'also' have a share".

Carter cannot believe what he is hearing.

"The mummy, if we actually find one, will be considered 'of primary importance', and so, under article 8, it is the property of the Egyptian State, which I feel is only right".

Carnarvon stubbornly insists, "But it is also right that anybody who invests and risks his money to finance almost six years of exploration should receive something in return!"

Carter motions with his walking stick for the carriage to stop and gets out. Turning to Lord Carnarvon he notes, "But you are a patron, not a merchant!"

With a restrained bow, he adds, "Lady Evelyn, My Lord!", and walks away at a brisk pace, moving ahead of the carriage.

Evelyn, who has observed the argument with increasing concern, hoped to calm the two of them down, but never had the chance. Lord Carnarvon motions to the driver to catch up to Carter, who continues walking at the same swift pace.

Lord Carnarvon says to Carter, though without actually looking at him, "Tomorrow, Mr. Carter, my daughter and I shall be returning to England for the Christmas holidays. When you decide to bring down that wall, would you kindly let me know in advance."

Carter continues briskly walking straight ahead, as the carriage moves past him, raising a cloud of dust and sand.

At the Luxor station, the train prepares for its departure, letting off steam. Lord Carnarvon's servants are carrying on the last pieces of luggage, as his Lordship himself boards the train, preceded by Evelyn, and closes the door behind him.

The stationmaster, accustomed to blowing his horn to signal that the train should depart, but only once his Lordship has tipped his hat in Carter's direction, is at a loss, given that no one has leaned out from the window of Lord Carnarvon's car. The puzzled stationmaster finally blows the horn, the train pulls away, and just then Carter arrives on the station platform, panting and out of breath... only to find that the train is already off in the distance.

Inside the tomb, three archaeologists, Dr. Mace, along with the Frenchmen Benedite and La Fleur, are helping Carter painstakingly pack a number of small statues of the pharaoh into a crate lined with cotton padding.

Outside, in the valley, the first packing crates are being loaded onto the cars of a Decauville train, a small-gauge railway used to transport goods down to the banks of the Nile. A swarm of tourists has filled the valley, attempting to get a closer look at the excavation, or even peek inside the tomb.

In England, Evelyn and Alice are finishing the Christmas decorations in the drawing room. Laid out on the table next to the fireplace are coloured drawings done by Carter, depicting some of the objects found in the tomb. There is also a photograph of Carter and Lord Carnarvon shaking hands, both smiling, with the outside of the tomb appearing in the background.

Glancing at the photograph, Evelyn asks, "Alice, have you seen my father this morning? His dog hasn't been around either."

Alice, perched on a step stool, risks losings her balance.

"I think he went out for a walk with Mayor".

Outside, the castle is cloaked in a fresh coat of snow. The day is cold, and the grounds are also covered with snow. Lord Carnarvon stands with one hand resting on a wooden gate. A fatigued look on his face, he seems to have aged.

By his side, his faithful boxer hound Mayor lets out a whimper while gazing inquisitively towards his master.

Lord Carnarvon returns the dog's glance, telling him, "It's nothing Mayor. Just a shadow that passed over my grave. Let's go."

His Lordship moves on, the dog following him at a trot, barking at the birds off in the distance.

Unlike the weather in England, the city of Cairo is enjoying a day of bright sunshine, though not enough to bring light to the lowermost floors of the city's museum, where the lamp of a native guide leads Elsa and Professor Newman through the underground portion of the large institution.

At a certain point, the lamp reveals the imposing, and quite unsettling, mummy of Seqenenre Tao, his head bearing the marks of a number of blows. His expression, frozen in the moment of death, is frightful.

Elsa looks at the face with undisguised distress, as the guide explains, "A great king of the 18th dynasty..."

"Actually, the 17th dynasty," Prof. Newman corrects him, "that of the Pharaoh Seqenenre Tao, known as "the Brave".

"Yes, precisely," answers the guide before continuing.

"His head still displays the wounds from his last battle".

Elsa listens, but she clearly wants to move on to something else. They reach another mummy with a serious, solemn, handsome face.

"Ramses II", explains the guide, "one of the greatest sovereigns history has ever known. Perhaps the greatest ever. The prophet Moses grew up in his court..."

Professor Newman again corrects the guide, "Moses may have grown up there".

The guide seems offended that there should be any doubt, while Professor Newman adds confidently, "His father Seti was the founder of the 19th dynasty..."

But before he can finish, Elsa has moved on to another mummy with a very young, attractive face.

"Thutmose?", ventures the guide in an uncertain tone.

"Yes, Thutmose III", answers Professor Newman with a smile. "The greatest, the most handsome pharaoh of all time. He who extended the borders of Egypt beyond present-day Khartoum, through central Africa, as far as the Euphrates River in Mesopotamia".

The guide bows even further down before this pharaoh, and then moves on.

Professor Newman identifies the next mummy directly, observing, "Ahmose, who drove out the

Hyksos, after they had dominated Egypt for a century and a half".

The guide, having given up his role, simply lights the way, continuing on to one of the most intriguing mummies yet.

Professor Newman reads his names aloud, "Menmaatre... Seti I, father of Ramesses...".

The lamp shines on still another sovereign, causing Elsa to show a certain agitation, until her expression once again turns impenetrable.

"Amenophis III, the father of Akhenaten", offers Professor Newman.

The guide moves on. Professor Newman follows, only to turn around at a certain point and find, to his astonishment, that Elsa has prostrated herself on the ground, in a sign of deep respect for the sovereign.

The lamp shakes in the trembling hands of the guide, who calls out, probably more taken aback than the Professor, "Memsahib!"

Professor Newman moves towards Elsa, to help her get back up, but she has returned to her feet before he can reach her. Stepping closer to the mummy, she states in a calm, unperturbed voice, "The King of both upper and lower Egypt, the son of Ra-Ne Mare Amenemhat... and of the Great Royal Wife "Tiye", he too married his own daughter, Sitamon, in order to make her divine!"

Professor Newman takes a long look at Elsa, before letting his eyes return to the sovereign's face, as the guide timidly observes, "In the reigning dynasties of the time, it was not uncommon for brothers to marry sisters, or for fathers to marry their own daughters. It happened on occasion."

"No other woman was ever worthy to be the bride of a god and king," declares Elsa as she heads for the door leading out of the hall of the mummies.

Professor Newman looks at her in amazement. The guide is at a loss for words.

"Thank you," Professor Newman says to him, "I think we have seen enough. The museum is truly exceptional."

The guide bows and leads them out.

"You must be wondering," Elsa whispers to the Professor, though without looking him in the eye, "why I threw myself down in such dramatic fashion."

"Not even I know the answer," she goes on, "but I did it naturally, without thinking, even if it was nothing more than the respect that everyone should show to the sovereign."

The three have almost reached the door, at which point the young lady light-heartedly observes, her spirits having picked up considerably, "But I imagine I would have little idea of how to bow before your Queen Mary."

Evening has come to Highclere Castle, and it is snowing outside. The Carnarvon family is gathered around the Christmas table, including Lady Almina and the Carnarvon's' son, Lord Porchester, as well as Aubrey Herbert, half-brother to Lord Carnarvon, and Lady Elisabeth, his Lordship's sister, plus two officers of the Guards, along with an elderly gentleman accompanying the Duchess of Wembley and the head of the Clan of the Macleans, dressed in traditional Scottish garb.

Next to the fireplace, a pair of pipers, also dressed in the Scottish tradition, play Christmas carols on their bagpipes.

As soon as Lord Carnarvon takes his seat, the music stops. He bows his head in prayer, and the others do the same, maintaining a solemn silence.

When Lord Carnarvon finally lifts his eyes again, he exclaims, "Merry Christmas, dear friends and family," and the footmen, under the direction of Walter, the head butler, begin to serve the Christmas dinner.

"Father, I read in this morning's Times that Howard has decided to pull down that damnable wall on February 17th," notes Lord Porchester.

"I myself have been told of no such development," states Lord Carnarvon in a dark, annoyed tone.

"They are saying that the ceremony will begin precisely at two o'clock in the afternoon," adds

Maclean. "It should be an exceptional event! People will be there from all over the world".

Evelyn would very much like to change the subject, but her father replies, "Now that I have been informed, though not by Carter, I shall be there on that very day, and at that hour, though only to bring back the Pharaoh's mummy, if we find it, or whatever else is rightfully mine. And we shall see who dares to stand in my way!"

"But Father," adds his son, "consider how many scholars and individuals of note from all over the world have visited the tomb in the last two weeks, leading to an extraordinary increase in the number of tourists."

"Which can certainly do no harm to the finances of Egypt!", notes Maclean.

"Humph.." snorts Lord Carnarvon, unconvinced by their reasoning.

For her part, Evelyn attempts to win him over with guile.

"But Father, just think, If you had already taken everything you're entitled to and brought it to London, then all those important people, all those tourists, would be obliged to come all the way over here to see the rest of the treasures, leaving the wonderfully mild climate of Egypt for London's fog. Can you imagine how many colds they would have come down with?!"

The butler allows himself a fleeting smile, while Maclean adds, "And they would have to spend a great deal more money, a matter of no small concern to a tourist!"

Even Lord Carnarvon is unable to hide a hint of a grin as Evelyn insists, "So with all due respect, and despite my immense admiration for my father, I must say that perhaps Carter is right. That maybe the treasures should all be kept in the same spot."

"Yes indeed... here in England!" concludes Lord Carnarvon, looking straight at his daughter.

The "Sudan Steamer", the elegant steamboat that departs from Cairo, taking well-heeled tourists on cruises along the Nile, is reaching its docking point under a bright sun. Recently repainted a creamy white, the ship flies a series of flags from all over the world. Waiting on the dock are Carter, together with the key members of his team. Also on hand is the Qadi, the local Islamic magistrate, as well as the mayor of Luxor, plus various other local figures of note.

The boat arrives at the wharf while a band plays in the background. The ship's lines are secured to the docking bollards, the passengers disembark. The first to come off is Queen Elizabeth of Belgium, accompanied by Prince Alexander. Lord Allenby, the High Commissioner, follows with his wife, and then come the officials of the Egyptian government, those of the British government and, finally, a distinguished gentleman who turns out to be none other than Gustavus Adolphus, the King of Sweden.

Carter steps forward and bows to the Queen of Belgium.

"It is an immense honour, Your Majesty, to welcome you to Luxor".

"Thank you, Mr. Carter," Queen Elizabeth answers cordially. "You have no idea how happy it makes me to be with you for this historic moment."

"Your Majesty, may I introduce some of the key members of my expedition?", asks Carter, once he has completed his bow.

Elisabeth smiles, nodding in assent.

"This is my assistant, Mr. Callender, and these are Professor Breasted of Chicago, Professor Bénédicte of the Louvre, Dr. Mace and Mr. Burton of the Metropolitan Museum of New York, and finally, Professor La Fleur of the Sorbonne".

"Congratulations to all of you, Gentlemen. Mr. Carter, my son and I hope you will be able to dine with us tonight".

"I will be honoured," answers Carter, bowing once again.

Prince Alexander shakes Carter's hand. The Qadi and the Egyptian officials wait impatiently.

"Your Majesty," exclaims the Qadi as he bows.

Smiling, the Queen moves towards them, together with her son. The photographers take pictures, the crowd voices its acclamation.

Lord Allenby walks up to Carter and shakes his hand. "Well done, Carter. This is a great thrill for everyone."

"Thank you, your Lordship," answers Carter, clearly gratified.

The landing is crowded with people exchanging official greetings. Carter catches sight of King Gustavus Adolphus standing off to one side.

"My goodness! I had no idea he was coming," he remarks in a tone of pleasant surprise.

"Who is he?," asks La Fleur.

"The King of Sweden, Gustavus Adolphus," answers Carter under his breath.

"Why my dear friend," exclaims La Fleur in a tone of admiration, "you know everyone."

"Your Majesty," says Carter, walking up to the King.

Gustavus Adolphus smiles and shakes Carter's hand, asking, "I hope you don't mind, Mr. Carter, but I couldn't resist the idea of joining the others."

"We are delighted to have you, though it comes as a complete surprise."

"I was travelling incognito," explains the King, "though I am flattered that you remember me".

"We met after the war, at the home of the Duke of Northumberland. How could I forget?" answers Carter with a smile.

"But you've met so many kings in your time, including some that have been dead for centuries," observes Gustavus Adolphus in jest.

"And today," he adds with a smile, "We shall see if you meet another".

In the valley, near the stairs that lead down to the tomb, Burton is organising a group photograph. Carter, Callender and La Fleur, who leans on his cane, looking quite fatigued, have taken their places alongside the other members of the team, including Breasted, Gardiner, Bénédicte, Mace and Lythgoe, along with other illustrious archaeologists.

Seated in front of them are Queen Elisabeth of Belgium and King Gustavus Adolphus, along with Prince Alexander and his Excellency the Minister Abd El Hlinr Pasha, as well as Lord Allenby and his wife. Other officials and their spouses have also made it into the picture.

"Please look this way!" announces Burton, standing alongside his tripod.

The group focuses on the old-fashioned box camera, ready to smile all at once. The camera makes its click. The date is February 17, 1923. The subjects of the photo go back to socialising.

"A great day, Howard," Callender congratulates Carter.

The other reporters and photographers, along with the crowd of curious onlookers, are being kept at a distance by the police, when Lord Carnarvon appears in a carriage that pulls up from behind the throng.

"Lord Carnarvon has come," observes a pleasantly surprised Callender. "Did you know he was arriving today?"

"On the one o'clock train," answers Carter with a nod.

"And you weren't there to meet him?", asks a puzzled Callender.

Carter stays silent, but there is no mistaking his discomfort.

Upon noting Lord Carnarvon's arrival, the reporters begin mumbling among themselves.

La Fleur comes up to Carter and asks, "Why has the press turned against him?"

Callender explains, "They are angry because he has sold the exclusive rights to the story to the Times of London."

"He was right to do so. At least that keeps them out of our way", notes Carter with satisfaction.

The carriage, carrying Lord Carnarvon, Evelyn and a distinguished elderly gentleman, passes in front of the crowd. Lord Carnarvon offers the assembled press a patronising nod, while Lady Evelyn, looking far more worried over the fact that she can see Carter waiting for them, ignores everyone else.

The carriage stops. Lord Carnarvon gets out and helps Lady Evelyn step down. The elderly gentleman follows them.

They walk by Carter. Lord Carnarvon ignores him, but Carter steps forward, saying, "Lady Evelyn, Lord Carnarvon, welcome back."

"I did not expect to have to learn the date on which you plan to open the chamber from the papers," replies Lord Carnarvon coldly.

"We had a lot to do..." answers Carter.

"Allow me," Lord Carnarvon adds in a haughty tone, "to introduce Sir Henry Holloway, a professor of international law".

The older man gives a bow.

"Mark my words, if we find the mummy, I shall take it back to London with me," states His Lordship as he leaves Carter to greet the royalty in attendance.

Evelyn hesitates, offers a pained smile and then follows her father. Lord Carnarvon is kissing the hand of the Queen of Belgium.

A magnificent tent has been set up in the desert, complete with lighted globes as lamps. The richly adorned shelter looks out on the splendid panorama of the desert. The Queen of Belgium and the King of Sweden sit at the places of honour at the table, surrounded by the other guests. Also on hand are the leading authorities from Cairo, including the Qadi, who is dressed in white, a red fez on his head.

Carnarvon is seated to the left of the King of Sweden, and Carter to the right of the Queen of Belgium, who is saying something to him with a smile.

Evelyn is speaking to the King of Sweden, while the servants, dressed in white tunics secured with green and red cloth sashes, pour champagne.

The Qadi asks politely, "Would your majesties mind if I speak with the wise Professor Carter?"

The Queen and King smile, nodding to show they have no objection.

"Almost a century ago, a fellow countryman of yours, Dr. Loyard, was talking, just as we are now, with Sheik Abd el Raham. The Assyrian city of Nineveh had been discovered, and the Sheik, may Allah keep his glory undiminished, said to the Englishman: 'My father, and the father of my father, pitched their tents here before I did. For twelve centuries my ancestors have lived as true believers, blessed with the far-seeing wisdom that has allowed them, Allah be praised, to settle and thrive in this area. But none of them had any idea that there was a palace beneath their feet'."

He has everyone's rapt attention.

"'And then behold! A Frangi arrives from a land that lies many days' journey away, and he goes right to the spot. He takes a stick and traces a line on one side, a line on the other, and says, "Here is the door", and he shows us what has been right under our feet our entire lives, without any of us having the slightest idea.'

"Whereas you, Professor, have come and uncovered not an entire city, which would actually be easier, given its size, but a tomb no larger than a single home.

"An extraordinary accomplishment! Stupendous! Did you learn to do this from books, with magic, or did your prophets tell you? Oh Bey, please reveal the secret of your wisdom!"

Though he finds the Qadi quite amusing, Carter makes every effort not to offend him.

"God alone holds the key to any wisdom I may have received," observes Carter. "We archaeologists study, we use our imaginations, we follow our hunches, but most importantly, we are patient".

After an enthusiastic round of applause, the servants pour everyone champagne, except for the Qadi, who raises a cup of coffee to make his toast.

"Here is to study, imagination, hunches and patience!"

The next day, the two chambers of the tomb have finally been cleared of all the precious artefacts, freeing up a space for those eager to witness first-hand the event that everyone has been waiting for.

Rows of chairs have been arranged, with each bearing the name of the individual for whom it is reserved. Callender escorts the guests who have just arrived on the steamship to their places. Queen Elisabeth of Belgium and Prince Alexander, King Gustavus Adolphus of Sweden, Lord Carnarvon and Lady Evelyn all take their seats.

Only then does Lady Evelyn realise that Miss Elsa is among those present.

"If you like, you can sit here," she says to the young woman, indicating a seat next to her.

The portion of the wall around the door has been completely uncovered, so that both the entrance and the seal of the necropolis found in its central portion are visible. Further down is a handprint that was left in the plaster.

Professor Newman and Olga are seated to the rear. As Carter walks by, Professor Newman says to him gratefully, "Thank you so very much for the invitation, Professor."

Carter smiles. "It is well deserved, Professor. By any chance is Miss Mittieri here too?"

Professor Newman points towards the spot where Evelyn is sitting.

"Yes, up there."

Evelyn is keeping a close eye on the emotions that pass across Elsa's face as she gazes around her, at first without showing much of a reaction, until she sees the handprint on the wall, which clearly moves her.

Evelyn takes her hand and holds it tight.

As the others look on in silence, Carter makes his way up the steps of a stool specially designed for working on the wall.

Professors Mace and Callender are by his side, ready to serve as his assistants, though Callender also takes the opportunity to steal a fleeting glance in Elsa's direction.

Lord Carnarvon and his son, Lord Porchester, sit alongside one another. Young Lord Westbury waits in eager anticipation, though he seems bothered by some barely concealed sentiment. All eyes are Carter as he pries open a small hole in the upper portion of the wall.

"Your Majesties, My Lords, Ladies and Gentlemen, we know for a fact that the thieves entered, and then left, through the same area where you are sitting. And these same robbers may violated this wall too, gaining access to whatever we will find on the other side. The seal is the same as that of the royal necropolis."

"In a moment," he adds, "time will lose all meaning, as we find ourselves breathing in air that has been sealed off for centuries, after it was first breathed in by those who may have placed the sovereign here, in this site, while accompanying him to his eternal rest."

There is tremendous expectation on the faces of those present. Some take out their pocket-watches to note the exact time, while others wipe the beads of perspiration from their upper lips with a handkerchief, and still others tap their fingers nervously.

La Fleur slowly, ceaselessly rotates the pommel of his walking stick as Carter tells those assembled: "To keep portions of the wall from falling off on the other side, and damaging what might be found there, I shall proceed with the utmost caution."

Mace and Callender assist Carter attentively, as he works on the initial opening in the upper portion of the wall. Meanwhile, the handprint found further below remains untouched. Miss Elsa is finding it hard to control her emotions, something Evelyn notes discretely, but with no little concern. Carter signals to Callender to hand him an electric light tied to a cord. As he inserts it inside the opening, a muffled whispering begins.

Carter takes a second look at a spectacle more wondrous than anybody had expected. For what strikes his eye, momentarily defying all understanding, is a glittering wall whose size is impossible to determine, seeing that it blocks the entire entryway, from one side to the other.

Carter pushes the light as far inside the opening as it will go, but the massive gold wall still appears limitless.

"Astounding, mind-boggling. Help me make the opening bigger..."

With the help of Callender and Mace, Carter removes more stones, giving everyone a chance to marvel at the splendour of the gold surface.

Tears fill Elsa's eyes, as Evelyn holds the girls in her arms, wishing she could do something to help with whatever makes Elsa so sad. Meanwhile Lord Carnarvon sits in astonishment, prisoner to a whirlwind of emotions has left him bewitched.

One by one the stones are removed, slowly enlarging the visible portion of the gold wall. The excitement of the spectators is palpable, their murmuring becomes a steady hum.

As Carter, Mace and Callender lean over the opening and peer into the chamber, their faces beaded with sweat, they realise that wall they have been admiring is actually just one side of the largest, most magnificent casket that mankind has ever laid eyes on, in the form of an enormous shrine of cedar gilded with two decorative motifs that repeat themselves in relief against a blue background: the "Tyet", a knotted amulet of Isis, and the "Djed", a ritual symbol of coupled pillars.

Carter enlarges the opening even further, spotting by the threshold the pearls of a necklace that must have split off and scattered when dropped by the plunderers.

In the sand, amidst the pearls, are the same sort of bare footprints found in the portions of the tomb already discovered.

"Whatever frightened them must have been terrifying indeed, to keep them from snatching up these pearls!", exclaims Carter in disbelief. "I can't imagine what sent them scurrying away in such haste."

Whereas Carter, bringing to bear all the patience of a true archaeologist, takes the time to gather the pearls up one by one.

The patience of everyone else on hand is nearing its breaking point as Carter finally moves the light inside the chamber wall and steps inside the space that separates it from the gilded wall of the shrine.

The entire sepulchral chamber is only a metre deeper than the antechamber, while the passageway between the side of the shrine and the chamber wall is barely sixty-five centimetres wide.

Carter ventures inside cautiously, with Callender and Mace following close behind, only to stop at the sight of eleven wooden oars laid out on the ground, set horizontally.

"The oars were to be used to propel the Pharaoh's boat during its voyage to the great beyond," observes Carter before turning around, retracing his steps and saying to Lord

Carnarvon, "My Lordship, would you do us the honour of being the first to go ahead?".

Lord Carnarvon gets to his feet, as Evelyn shows relief over the gesture on the part of Carter, who follows right after her father, with Callender and Mace bringing up the rear.

Lord Carnarvon, face to face with the massive gilded shrine covered with mysterious hieroglyphic inscriptions, is at a loss for words. Finally he manages to murmur, "Simply amazing!"

Young Westbury cannot take his eyes off an engraving of Osiris, the divinity of the great beyond, who is kneeling in expectation of meeting Tutankhamun during his journey that follows death. The walls of the shrine are covered with gold and lapis lazuli, while the blue maiolica tiles inlaid along its sides are decorated with magical motifs, with the two eyes of Horus playing a particularly prominent role. The edges are adorned with the sacred snake, while a winged sun sits atop the door.

Taking a closer look, Carter realises that the two halves of the door on the eastern wall of the shrine are closed with a bar but not sealed. With trembling hands, he pulls the bar back and the door comes creaking open. Behind it is a second shrine, another splendid cabinet, this one also made of stuccoed, gilded wood, its doors secured with an ivory latch.

The bas-relief figure on the left half of the door shows the Pharaoh in the presence of Osiris, the god of the dead, while the goddess Isis, both wife and sister of Osiris, appears behind Tutankhamun. A large linen cloth, a funeral shroud decorated with a series of gilded bronze rosettes, covers a portion of this second case. The rings holding the bar bear a seal, that of the sovereign, and it is still intact!

"The seal ... it is unbroken! Thank goodness!," exclaims a thrilled Carter.

Carnarvon, Callender and Mace allow themselves a lengthy sigh of relief, while Carter observes, "Up until now, the robbers have always arrived before us, but the thieves never made it through this door."

"Shall we continue?..." asks Carnarvon, a hand on Carter's shoulder.

"First we need to take photographs of the seal," answers Carter after a moment of reflection. "This is the first one to have ever been found intact."

The photographer takes the picture, as the magnesium whiff of the flash draws coughs from those on hand.

Carter finally removes the seal and opens the door. Inside the shrine is yet another shrine, the third so far. Though gilded like the others, this one is covered with religious writings, including phrases taken from the "Book of the Dead", meant to help the Pharaoh find his way amidst the dangers of the afterlife.

Carter removes the latch and opens the doors, which reveal a fourth gilded shrine. Engraved on the right half of the door of this cabinet is an image of the goddess Isis, the heroine of the Osiris myth, according to which the goddess brought her husband, the divine Osiris, back to life after he had been assassinated. The myth underlay the belief that she could help the deceased return from the afterlife, just as she had done for Osiris.

Pictured on the left side of the door is Nephthys, Isis's sister, worshipped as the goddess who protects mummies and, therefore, by association, a divinity of death and the afterlife. Also depicted on this portion of the door is Nut, the goddess of the sky, together with Horus, the son of Isis, pictured with his traditional falcon's head, both of whom look towards the sky.

Carter opens the fourth shrine as well. Inside he finally discovers the ark of Tutankhamun, a sarcophagus carved out of an enormous block of quartzite, a variety of sandstone. Waiting for them inside the ark, within the massive sarcophagus, should be the coffin, but to remove its heavy cover, they must first dismantle all the surrounding shrines, a job that will take quite a few days of work.

Callender, who has continued down the corridor, disappearing behind the corner of the first shrine, calls out in excitement, "Come here! There's another room full of treasures."

Lord Carnarvon and Mace head off to join Callender, as Carter closes the two halves of the gilded door.

Back in the antechamber, where everyone is sitting in silence, reflections from the luxuriant gold of the wall, as lit by the electric lamps, play over their faces, creating a moment of extraordinary magic.

From one of the back rows, Professor Newman and Olga keep an eye on Elsa, who is sitting motionless. Evelyn is watching the girl too, well aware of the veil of sadness that has fallen over her gaze.

Carter returns, stopping at the threshold to say, "Ladies and gentlemen, one at a time please".

Addressing the Queen of Belgium and the King of Sweden, "Your Majesties..."

Evelyn lays a hand on Elsa's shoulder, encouraging her to enter the chamber.

"Shall the two of us go together?"

"I already know... there's no need for me to go with you..." she answers, drying a tear.

Elsa stays behind, not entering the chamber, but she does walk up to the entrance and what is left of the freshly demolished wall. Kneeling down, she slowly lines her hand up with the handprint on the wall. A perfect fit: the fingers, the palm, the shape of the hand, everything is identical.

Her mother, who has been watching her, is shaken, on the verge of fainting away, if Professor Newman were not there to aid her.

"I need air. Please, a little air".

Professor Newman helps her outside. Evelyn turns and sees them leaving, then she notices that Elsa is kneeling on the ground, her hand fitting perfectly inside the handprint. The girl leans her head against the wall, as if praying, and Evelyn is forced to wipe a tear from her own cheek. She turns back, letting her emotions get the best of her, and kneels alongside Elsa, who points to a clay brick bearing a hieroglyphic inscription.

Shining the light of a lamp on the brick, Elsa reads the text, her lips barely moving, "Death, with its wings, will strike whomever disturbs the Pharaoh's repose."

Elsa tells Evelyn, "Now we can go in, if you want..."

Lowering her head, Elsa enters the chamber, with Lady Evelyn following her, after a moment's hesitation, along the passageway between the painted walls and the enormous gold shrine with the inlaid decorations.

Elsa lets her fingertips brush against the shrine, as if to caress it. Then, together with Evelyn, she reaches the room discovered by Callender, where the most impressive of the sepulchre's treasures are to be found. At the centre of the room is a statue of the god Anubis, the protector of the dead. He is shown kneeling, with the head of a jackal, his traditional.

Behind him, a large gold tabernacle is all aglow, though its splendour pales in comparison with the grace, the natural vigour, of the four goddesses who embrace it, as if determined to protect its contents.

"They seem to be asking for pity, and mercy too," exclaims Lady Evelyn, sounding very moved.

"But there was no pity, Lady Evelyn," notes Elsa, "no mercy either."

"These four goddesses were to protect the canopic jars found inside the cabinet," she explains. "Isis, Nephthys, Selket and Neith embrace the jars to defend the treasures found therein: the vital organs of the deceased, which he needed for his rebirth."

Elsa takes Lady Evelyn's hand and places it on her own heart.

"I beg of you, see to it that his place of rest remains here, where he was buried!" a tearful Elsa beseeches Evelyn.

Overcome by a tumult of emotions, Evelyn catches her breath as a shudder of sympathy gets the best of her her. "I promise... Most certainly, I promise".

All around them are boxes of jewels and other precious items. Lord Carnarvon has been left speechless. A gold statue depicts the pharaoh striding forward with a flaying whip in one hand, a pastoral staff that he uses as a walking stick in the other. Off in a corner is an elongated box holding a frame shaped like a mummy of the god Osiris.

"They filled it with silt from the Nile," murmurs Carter as he sticks a finger into the soil in the frame, pulling out a grain that has germinated.

"This is wheat," Carter notes with surprise, pointing to the moss-like growth atop the dried-out clay.

"The grain was left to germinate, so that the image of Osiris, a symbol of resurrection, would be green. The sprouting of the wheat was meant to trigger the sovereign's resurrection."

As Lord Carnarvon looks on in fascination, something else catches his eye: a lock of hair in a gold box.

Elsa is gazing at it dreamily, as if thinking back to the boy from whose head that same lock of hair was cut during the ceremony at the temple of Karnak.

Meanwhile, Carter's attention is drawn to another object: a systrum.

"It looks like a rattle," he says as he picks it up. After a moment's hesitation he shakes it, causing the instrument to give off a shrill, startling, high-pitched sound that breaks the silence of the tomb.

A bewildered Elsa covers her ears, as everyone's eyes turn to the unseen source of the sound, somewhere off beyond the glittering gold wall.

Carter carefully puts the instrument back where he found it. Then, followed by Lord Carnarvon and Professor Mace, he retraces his steps, walking back alongside the massive gold shrine.

Among those admiring the treasures is La Fleur, who has stopped to take a closer look at the engravings on the massive gilded cabinet. His attention is drawn, in particular, to the sculpture of the great Udjat, or eye of Horus, done in lapis lazuli and glaze. La Fleur appears entranced by the mysterious eye and the many facets of its appearance. The myth behind it tells of Horus, the son of Osiris, challenging his uncle Seth, a usurper and an assassin, to a duel. Only Seth pulls Horus's eyes out, breaking them into sixty-four pieces. At this point, the most learned of the gods of Egypt, Thoth, a divinity connected with the moon, wisdom and magic, uses his knowledge, and his familiarity with the esoteric side of existence, to put the blind god's eyes back together, leaving Horus, the solar hawk, with eyesight even sharper than before, which allows him, once the duel resumes, to come away victorious.

And so the light of Horus once again sets the Nile valley aglow, while Seth slinks back to the parched, arid desert. For Horus had listened to the sound advice of his mother, Isis, who told him not to kill Seth, not to seek vengeance, though the ways of "Maat" always justify revenge, but Horus would be wiser to keep good and evil in a perfect balance, as otherwise chaos would hold sway.

Meanwhile the others who have visited the tomb, perspiring but contented, return along the corridor, brushing against one another as they make their way back to the antechamber, where the air is easier to breath and they can sit down in the chairs.

Those still waiting to enter note the emotion that sets the eyes of those returning aglow, the way they move their hands about, trying to express, though words fail them, the wonders they have seen.

In the antechamber to the tomb, on a makeshift counter set up in a corner of the room, a number of waiters wearing white gloves are opening bottles of champagne, while others pour it into glasses of crystal arranged on large silver platters.

Professor Maspero takes the first glass and hands it to Lord Carnarvon.

"To Their Majesties, and to His Lordship, the Earl of Carnarvon, who has tied his name forever, in the annals of archaeology, to that of the sovereign who waited thirty-five centuries to be brought to light".

"Are you quite certain," says Lord Carnarvon in a voice betraying doubt, "that the Pharaoh was so anxious to be brought to light? I rather doubt it ..."

"In any event," he adds with a smile, passing the first glass of champagne to Carter, "It is Mr. Carter who deserves all the praise".

Lady Evelyn is visibly content. Those present, expressing their best wishes, clink their glasses together, as Lord Carnarvon proposes a toast: "To study, imagination, hunches and patience!"

Everybody applauds before drinking their champagne.

"I don't see La Fleur. Where is David?", Carter asks Callender in a puzzled tone.

"He must have stayed inside," answers Callender.

Indeed, La Fleur has remained in the corridor where the cases are, his eyes glued to the Udat, which would almost seem to be staring back at him.

Callender arrives, bringing a glass of champagne forn La Fleur.

"David!"

"Oh Alan," says La Fleur, sounding somewhat unnerved. "It's the strangest thing, but for just an instant... I thought I saw signs of life in that eye, as of it were a real live human glance."

"David, it had to be the light playing tricks," answers Callender in an amusement. "Perhaps the reflections of the different facets. And to think that you haven't had anything to drink yet! Come along..."

"But I'm serious," answers La Fleur in a sombre tone, not moving from where he stands. "It was just a fraction of a second, but it left me feeling terribly uneasy, a sort of gnawing anguish."

"Well here's to the swift return of your good humour," says Callender, passing him the extra glass of champagne while raising his own in a toast. But La Fleur seems not to hear him.

"David!", insists Callender, until he finally manages to interrupt La Fleur's trance.

"Oh yes... to your health, Alan".

At the Hotel Winter in Luxor, Elsa sits by the window of the drawing room in their apartment, watching as the waters of the Nile flow by, glittering in the moonlight. A sad, singsong voice arrives from afar, off in the direction of the river, carrying the sound of a traditional tune that tells of how "The mandrake is a fruit of love".

Professor Newman is leading the doctor out of the apartment, while Olga stays in an armchair, alongside Muna, who hands her a hot cup of herbal tea. As soon as the doctor has left, Professor walks over to Elsa.

"The next few days will be unforgettable. Did you see the looks on everyone's face? They were ecstatic, bewitched. Carter was impatient... but he hasn't opened it yet," says the professor, smiling at the memory.

Elsa continues to gaze out at the Nile.

"He held himself back to make sure everything was done properly, but he will open it, sadly enough... He will not leave that poor child in peace."

Moving her head slowly, to the tune of the song that arrives from the riverbank, she observes, "It is a sad melody from ancient times, when the mandrake was thought to be the "knob of love", on account of its properties as an aphrodisiac and for treating sterility... Professor, no matter what happens, promise me you will always stay by mother's side," Elsa beseeches him in a low voice.

Taken aback, Professor Newman, who certainly was not expecting such a request, answers, "Of course Elsa. You know how I feel about your mother... But what could possibly happen?"

Elsa smiles and kisses him on the cheek, "That is what I needed to hear, Professor. And you know I feel the same way too."

Trying to change the subject, Professor Newman shows her the headlines on the newspapers.

"A few months ago, no one had any idea who Tutankhamun was. Now the whole world is talking about him."

"His name," points out Elsa, "means 'the living image of Amun', or 'the splendour of Amun', because his real name, until his father, Akhenaten, died, was 'Tut-Ankh-Aten', or 'image of the sun'. Afterwards, he was forbidden to use that name, as it was changed from Aten to Amun".

"But forbidden by whom, if he was the king, the pharaoh?!" asks a puzzled Newman.

"He was just a child. The real power was in the hands of the Vizier Ay, his tutor." answers Elsa gently.

"Ay was the brother of Tiye, the Great Royal Wife of Tutankhamun's grandfather Amenhotep III. For many years, Ay was a counsellor to Akhenaten, Tutankhamun's father, and when Akhenaten died, Ay took Tutankhamun under his care. He was known as 'The Divine Father' and was respected, but he was also very elderly."

"Who can say if Tutankhamun was ever able to enjoy being pharaoh?", wonders Newman calmly while taking notes and lighting his pipe.

"No," says Elsa, shaking her head with bitter regret. "At the age of seventeen, he still had no idea who his father was, or how he had wound up on the throne. So he went to see the most beautiful of the Queens of Egypt, but also the saddest, the Royal Wife Nefertiti, who had been married to his father, but was not his mother..."

The sound of the song starts to drift away, and the outline of the window looking out on the Nile slowly loses its form, as Elsa's recollections turn the drawing room into a large, majestic hall: that of Queen Nefertiti.

The bench on which she sits, a piece of furniture decorated with precious inlays, has a high, thin backrest. Around her neck is a gold necklace that holds glittering stones. She is posing, so that a sculptor by the name of Bek can mould a plaster bust of her.

Off to one side, the elderly Ay eats from a bunch of grapes, picking them off one by one while watching the sculptor at work.

Though she is beautiful beyond any imagining, Nefertiti says to the sculptor, "Bek, don't make my nose any longer."

"I shall do my best to show it in its natural state, my Divine Queen: perfection."

"Well now," observes Nefertiti with a smile, "you have become not only a great sculptor, but also an expert courtesan. You once told me that you sought to reproduce life only as you saw it."

"That was back when truth was everywhere," says Bek with a smile. "Now it can only be found here, inside these walls, where we can paint and sculpt what we truly see and not the false, ritualised landscapes that the priests impose."

Ay speaks up: "Religion is the guiding light that keeps our country together! We can do without artists, dear Bek, but not without the clergy, not without priests. Always keep that in mind!"

A female slave walks up to the Queen and tells her something that grabs her attention, leaving her with a look of expectation, until finally Tutankhamun arrives, followed by his Chief Squire, plus a helper who bears the royal standard, along with four court officials.

The Pharaoh is seventeen years old, healthy and noble in appearance, with delicate features, gentle eyes and arms that appear well proportioned but also strong.

Nefertiti bows, the elderly Ay offers a deeper bow. The sculptor has already gone down to his knees.

Tutankhamun steps forward, as those escorting him recede into the background.

"Why do I need so many counsellors?" he asks the Queen. "Is it that difficult for me to make a decision?"

"The Counsellors are there to examine matters, as it is humbly advised that they do," she answers in a respectful tone.

"When will I be allowed to rule?" asks the youngster in a pleading tone.

"You are too young. The present political situation is too delicate," observes Ay. "The strengths of youth do not include patience and prudence."

"You were my father's Great Royal Wife," the boy says to Nefertiti. "Tell me why the name of a great king was cancelled from all the records. Why am I not allowed to know anything about my father?"

"In the royal dynasty, you follow Amenhotep III," answers Nefertiti gently, though her gaze remains impenetrable.

"Which leaves out my father, Akhenaten, or Amenhotep IV, as you call him, as if he had never existed!"

Nefertiti, her expression still giving away nothing, glances at the noble Ay. "It is best that the Pharaoh be the son of a great sovereign!" she says, her gaze turning cold and inscrutable.

The young man's resentful eyes look straight into hers. Realising that she will say no more, he addresses the elderly Ay.

"Nobel Ay, Chief of the Royal Council! You were close to my father. He made you a Divine Father, you were the brother of his Royal Wife Tiye. Tell me about him. What did he do that was so wrong?"

"It is best that the pharaoh be the son of a great sovereign!" answers Ay, using the exact same words as Nefertiti.

The sculptor is still kneeling. Tutankhamun walks to his side and helps him get to his feet.

"Oh Bek, your father was a great sculptor, but you are even greater, because for the first time, urged on by my father, you dared to show faces displaying their actual feelings. You had the good fortune to create works that resemble the way life really is. You were allowed to set aside romantic, idealised art and be true to reality, presenting it without sentimental embellishment."

"Do you see" adds the boy sadly, "how they've chiselled the name of my father off all the monuments of Egypt? They've cancelled the pharaoh they call 'accursed', the 'heretic', and yet no one would dare ask you to return to the false, traditional style. And so your works may very well live longer than the names of the pharaohs. Tell me what he did that was so wrong!"

"Divine Master, he did no wrong. It was just that he..." the sculptor starts to answer, his head bowed.

"... he never existed!" Neferirti interrupts him harshly.

"... that is right Master, he... never existed!" murmurs the sculptor, gazing downwards in confusion.

The sad lament of the song being sung by the banks of the Nile starts up again. Elsa's memories fade away, replaced by the hotel room in Luxor, where the plaintive notes of that tune from the distant past still fill the air.

Professor Newman waits for Elsa, who has fallen silent, to resume her account.

"You see Professor, Nefertiti was the wife of Tutankhamun's father, but she was not his mother. He was born of a second marriage, and so he went with no small amount of hope to see the princess whom he had always considered to be the most intelligent, the most loving of them all: Sitamun, the eldest of the four daughters of his grandfather Amenhotep III. Following her marriage to his father, the Pharaoh, she lived in his palace..."

A room in the palace of Sitamun slowly takes shape. The song sung by the river is replaced by another delicate sound, as the elegant, finely tapered hands of Princess Sitamun flit across the strings of a harp.

Wearing a precious ring on one finger, the Princess is accompanying a melody played on another harp by a young, sightless, male musician. Other princesses are listening to the music, some sitting, some standing, including Nubian princesses of exceptional beauty.

Some wear diadems, others have flowers in their hair. Female slaves are gathered at the doors to the room, motionless, as Sitamun's hands continue to draw harmonies from the strings.

One of the doors opens and a female slave enters, bowing before the Princess before whispering something in her ear.

Tutankhamun has paused at the threshold. Sitamun bows, as the other princesses have already done.

The blind musician, with the help of a male slave, bows in the direction of the Pharaoh.

"Paheri, your music is always so lovely, so comforting."

The musician bows again and then leaves, accompanied by the slave.

"He is blind from birth," notes Sitamun, "and that has sharpened his other senses."

The Princess, wearing an exquisitely crafted diadem on her head, motions for the young man to sit down.

"That old song is so sad," she says, "and yet it soothes me."

The young man smiles, drawing closer to her. "You are more beautiful than ever, Sitamun."

"And you have become stronger, more handsome even than before," she notes with a smile, her eyes lowered.

"It has been some months since you last came to see me," she adds. "And I, unlike you, have become older. Yesterday I turned twenty-nine years old."

Tutankhamun draws still closer, softly kissing her lips and taking her hands.

"If you look in my eyes, you can see how I suffer," he says to her in an intense but gentle tone. "Twenty years are missing from the history of Egypt, and I will be the first sovereign following that empty period. Let me talk to you, my favourite Princess. You were my father's sister..."

Tutankhamun pauses. She gives him a soft caress. He kisses the palm of her hand.

"Hear me out, you who have known me since I was born, whose young hands gave me food and gifts. Do you remember the ivory bracelet you put here?" he asks, pointing to his arm.

"Do you remember the other one, which I refused, because it showed me killing a lion when I was only a baby. But what baby boy can kill a lion?"

A smiling Sitamun nods in agreement before lowering her eyes, looking slightly intimidated.

"You were the first to introduce me to the joy of love, the pleasures of the flesh, my very first time," the young man insists.

"You, the favourite royal princess, cannot lie to me," he implores her, gently lifting her face back up. "What terrible things did my father do?"

Turning serious, the Princess hesitates for a moment. "For many, your father was not a good ruler," she answers the young man in a gentle tone, looking him straight in the eyes.

"He gave too much power to the governors of the provinces, and he neglected the princes, who reacted with arrogance. But he was a great man who wished to be both the father and mother of all Egyptians."

Finally satisfied, Tutankhamun asks, "But what did he do that was so terrible?".

After a long pause, the scene turns back into that of Elsa's drawing room. Just as Sitamun did, she lifts her sad, melancholy eyes.

Returning to her telling of history, she explains: "The most serious accusation against him, the one for which he was never forgiven, was closing the temples, relegating the gods to the darkness of the sanctuaries and proclaiming that there was only one god, the sun, which gave wealth and well-being to all men through the Pharaoh."

Professor Newman and Olga listen to her every word with rapt attention.

"The other terrible misdeed they accused him of was holding that all men, no matter what their race, were created equal. He preached love and peace, he freed the slaves. He wanted to end one era and begin a new one, in which people everywhere would treat each other as brothers and live in truth and justice."

Professor Newman and Elsa's mother, intrigued by the girl's account, are unable to take their eyes off her.

"He overturned two thousand years of Egyptian religion and beliefs. The priests, fearing for their future, reacted furiously when he made it known that they would no longer receive royal donations or slaves. He moved the capital away from the poisoned atmosphere of Thebes, seeking peace and tranquillity in the new city whose construction he had ordered. Everyone was happy in Akhetaten, only they forgot, lulled into a sense of safety by its massive walls, about the princes to the east, about the soldiers and the generals. Increasingly alone, Akhenaten was certain that he was right, but the priests who were plotting to keep his dreams from coming true had him assassinated."

Olga is visibly shaken, speechless.

"By whose hand was he killed?" asks Professor Newman, caught up in the tale.

"There were many," answers Elsa in a mournful tone.

"The high priests had lost all their power, along with their wealth. They pretended to believe in the new truth. They invited him to the temple built to worship it. They celebrated his visit and gave him a gold chalice holding a powerful poison meant to kill him slowly. But he still had time, in the throes of his illness, to elevate his wife Nefertiti to the position of co-regent, just as his father, Amenhotep III, had allowed his wife, the Great Royal Spouse Tiye, to play a role of considerable importance. In fact, she became so powerful that she took an active part in setting policy. After her husband's death, her influence was significant, even in the early years of the reign of her son Amenhotep IV, or Amenophis, as he was called before he changed his name to Akhenaten".

"What you say about the political importance of Queen Tiye is confirmed," observes Professor Newman, who has stopped taking notes, "by a letter discovered at the archaeological dig in Amarna. It was sent by Tushratta, the sovereign of Mitanni, who asked Tiye to speak to her son and remind him of the excellent relations that Tushratta had enjoyed with his father, Amenhotep III. But please continue."

"When he was taken ill," resumes Elsa in a sorrowful tone, "Akhenaten had Nefertiti's name changed to Ankheperura Neferneferuaton. He did this for political reasons, so that his subjects would know that he had elevated his wife to the position of co-regent, which meant that she could sit on the throne as his equal and deal with questions of both politics and religion. Following Akhenaten's death, in the sixteenth year of his reign, Nefertiti was left to rule the two lands all by herself. The clergy were up in arms, the generals grew bolder, while the princes in the conquered territories sought their independence. Nefertiti took the advice of the elderly Vizier Ay, sending a signal to the people by removing the word "ATEN" from her name, and from that of her young son Tutankhaten, the heir to the throne.

"Aten, the solar disk, the sun god, was losing importance. The clergy were pushing for a return to the old ways, to the original gods, with the capital move back to Thebes. Nefertiti changed her name to Ankheperura Smenkhkare, and her son's name to Tutankhamun. Akhenaten, the great visionary king, was reviled as a heretic and cancelled from all written records. Even the poor forgot him, while the slaves he had freed cursed him, because if they no longer had any work, what good was their freedom? The false gods were seen once more on statues and in the temples. Nefertiti, the Great Royal Wife, also turned her back on Aten, forsaking him as the only god. No one has ever discovered where Akhenaten's body was laid to rest"

Elsa closes her eyes.

"He wrote a poem dedicated to the sun, which for him was the one true god: 'Splendid you rise with the powerful dawn/Aten creator of life/And when you set in the west/The darkness of death descends upon the world/The lions venture out from their dens/The snakes bite..."

The eyes of Olga, Elsa's mother, are filled with tears of astonishment. The song coming from the direction of the river has grown fainter, more distant.

"He was ahead of his time, a founder of modern religion," exclaims Professor Newman, taken aback by the realisation. "He was the first of the monotheists, not Moses, as everyone has always believed."

"People were not ready, his momentous project was never understood," observes Elsa.

Professor Newman ventures another question: "Elsa, you seem to be slowly putting your memories back together? As if, that is, they were starting to make some sense."

"At times it all seems so clear, but then I'm overwhelmed by confusion again. Small rays of light break through now and then, only to fade away."

Someone knocks at the door. Elsa's mother clears her throat and calls out, "Come in please, the door is open."

Callender enters, carrying one of the wooden boxes used to hold the artefacts from the dig.

"Please forgive the intrusion... perhaps this is not the right moment," he observes with discretion, noting how pensive they all look following Elsa's account.

"No trouble at all, Professor Callender. Please come in and have a seat. Are there any new developments?"

"I wanted to show Miss Elsa something we found, assuming it's no problem," answers Callender, placing the box on a table.

"Are you here on behalf of Professor Carter?," asks Professor Newman.

"Actually, I was hoping to satisfy a curiosity of my own," says Callender hesitantly.

Elsa smiles her approval and Callender opens the box. Inside, snugly packed amidst wads of cotton, is a riding crop.

"We have managed to decipher the inscription you can see here..."

Elsa interrupts Callender with a smile, as if she already knows what he is getting at.

"This is the riding crop of Tuthmose, which is why the inscription says: 'TUTHMOSE, Captain of the Guards'".

Callender turns to Professor Newman in surprise.

"That's absolutely right," Callender says to the Professor, sounding impressed.

"But I was wondering why the riding crop of a simple captain would be in the tomb of a king. Would you have any idea?..." he asks Elsa.

"He was a prince," says Elsa, smiling fondly at the memory.

"He was very handsome, and Tutankhamun's trusted squire, as well as a dear and loyal friend.

The riding crop was the Pharaoh's gift to Tuthmose upon his appointment as 'Captain of the Guard'. May I?" asks Elsa, reaching to pick up the object.

"Very gently please," says Callender in a worried tone.

And indeed, as soon as Elsa picks up the riding crop, she is practically overcome by a flood of memories, hectic, violent, confused scenes, with the strong hand of a man driving a chariot frantically whipping a galloping horse. The wheels fly through the undergrowth, the legs of other men are seen fleeing through a marsh. The riding crop urges the horse on, until a spear strikes another man in the back, brutally passing straight through him.

Elsa cries out, terrified by her violent recollections, which include the blood-spattered hands and white garment of a woman, triggering memories of the nightmare the girl suffered through some years earlier. Desperately wiping her own hands on her clothes, she throws the riding crop to the floor, only to fall suddenly calm, her eyes shut, even if she is still trembling.

Her dismayed mother wets a handkerchief in a pitcher of water and, cradling her daughter in her arms, pats the girl's forehead and her lips. Elsa stops trembling. Callender looks on, petrified by what he has seen.

"Fortunately," observes Professor Newman, handing the riding crop back to Callender, "it isn't broken."

"I am so sorry," answers a mortified Callender. "I had no idea... please forgive me."

"It is not your fault," says Professor Newman as he walks Callender to the door.

"The same thing has already happened, and more than once. But as soon as the attacks caused by these sudden, violent memories pass, she normally finds some relief, almost as if she were seeing glimpses of light after centuries of darkness. We should probably leave them alone".

The two men exit the suite.

The moon sets the Valley of the Kings aglow under the night sky. Lanterns can be seen scattered here and there, shining like gold stars set against a great blue cloth. A group of guards assembled near a wall made of large stones is having tea, while others sleep, waiting for their turn on duty.

Inside the tomb, the golden wall makes for a brilliant site, despite the darkness. Spread out on a wooden table is a large mechanical drawing of the elaborate device needed to lift the heavy cover, once the four shrines have been dismantled. Carter, Mace and La Fleur, together with the carpenters responsible for building the mechanism, examine the designs, which include renderings of winches and beams.

"How long will it take to put it in operation?" Carter asks the master carpenter.

"At least a couple of weeks."

Carter had hoped it would be ready sooner.

"All right, but make sure it's strong. I don't want anything to break. Let's get to work."

The equipment makers take their leave. The professors are about to remove their working aprons and gowns, when Ali walks in.

"Effendi, there is a strange Arab who wants to see you. He says he was your friend, that you worked together between the Tigris and the Euphrates."

Ali's words leave Carter perplexed. "Could it be?..." he says, a curious light flickering in his eyes.

"Bring him in!", he tells Ali, who hurries off as Carter walks towards the corridor that leads to the stairs at the entryway. A figure dressed in Arab garb, all in white, complete with a turban, comes out of the corridor. He removes the turban, showing his face and putting an end to Carter's puzzlement.

"Thomas, what a pleasant surprise! How long has it been?"

"God is great, Howard!"

The two men embrace warmly.

"May I let these illustrious friends and colleagues of mine know who you are?" asks Carter, indicating the other archaeologists in the room.

Saying 'yes' with a smile, the Arab guest adds, "I can only stay this evening. Then I must disappear again."

"My friends, we have the honour of a visit from a very special colleague," Carter proudly announces to the others. "He is known throughout the world as Lawrence of Arabia."

"To keep from being recognised," explains Lawrence, "I have donned these garments that I favoured for so many years, putting them on one last time."

They all crowd around him, eager for the honour of shaking his hand.

Carter asks, "I heard that you refused a knighthood, and after the Cairo Conference you gave up your officer's commission! You practically disappeared. Why?"

"I betrayed the Arab people," answers Lawrence, his voice tinged with sadness.

"I was persuaded to make promises that were never going to be kept. The Arabs believe in individuals, not in institutions, and I naively promised that they would receive their just reward: a united Arab world. They followed me with this dream in their hearts, performing acts of exceptional courage..."

Everybody listens to him attentively, in absolute silence.

"I too was betrayed by my people, by the politicians, the bankers. They made me believe that, if the Arabs were led to victory, they would be given a position of privilege in the future. But once the Turks were defeated, those promises were broken and the black gold was taken from Mesopotamia."

"I have spent the last two years," he adds, "writing an account of those times..."

"That should set the whole world straight as to how things are," Carter encourages him.

"Perhaps, I hope so, though who can say..." answers Lawrence with a melancholy smile.

"The wounds are deep, my friends," he admits. "But let me have a look at your treasures, the magnificent success that the whole world is talking about."

Carter leads the way, holding a lamp that that throws light on the massive gold shrine. An astonished Lawrence delicately runs his fingers along the wall, including the seal. His thrilled expression sums up the momentous nature of the find.

Standing guard on the outer surfaces of the doors, knives in hand, are relief carvings of infernal genies.

"You've deciphered this?" asks Lawrence, indicating an inscription on the lower portion of the door.

"The hand of vengeance will reach out in the night and kill those who dare profane the resting place," answers Carter, jokingly pretending to tremble with fear. "This second inscription runs along the same lines: death shall swiftly descend upon any who disturb the sleep of the Pharaoh."

Carter continues to point out details, including a torch carved alongside the double doors at the entrance to the large gold shrine.

"The flame of this torch was supposed to drive away the night and its evil spirits," Carter explains to Lawrence before showing him the treasure chamber, whose gold tabernacle, placed under the protection of the four goddesses positioned above the snakes sculpted on the frame, is topped off by the disk of the sun.

Pointing to the four goddesses, Lawrence observes, "Magnificent! This would be Iris, of course. And here we have Nephthys, and then Neith and Selket. Am I remembering right?"

Carter gives an approving smile.

"Its touching how earnestly they guard the cabinet holding the treasures," adds Lawrence. "How that one face there is turned to the side, to make it look even more vigilant."

Next to the cabinet is an alabaster chest adorned with hieroglyphics. Goddesses are stationed at each of the four corners, holding out their arms to protect the contents.

The chest is covered in linen. Inside are four compartments, each holding an alabaster vase whose lid is adorned with a head of Tutankhamun wearing the nemes, a vulture and a cobra displayed on his forehead.

Carter removes the lids, with their human features, revealing a set of small sarcophagi glazed in gold, one for each compartment.

"These hold the ruler's vital organs, his liver, lungs and stomach. The heart was left in the mummy. Each vase was placed under the protection of a female divinity, while a male god stands guard over each lid."

"Have you found the Pharaoh's 'Book of the Dead'?" asks Lawrence, who has been paying close attention.

"I'm afraid there was nothing of the sort in the tomb," replies Carter.

Off in a corner is a long chest that holds a frame shaped like a mummy of the god Osiris.

"In here is mud deposited by the flooding of the Nile," says Carter, using a finger to pull out a grain of wheat that has sprouted.

"They planted the wheat in a pattern, so that, when it sprouted," he points to the fuzzy deposit on the dry mud, "it would produce a verdant image of Osiris, who symbolises resurrection. The growing wheat was m eat to trigger the ruler's resurrection".

"Because the Egyptians," notes Lawrence in a fascinated tone, "held that the sun, after spending the day giving off its heat, replenished its thermal energy at night from the bodies of the gods, and in the same way the Pharaoh, upon reaching the world of the dead, would receive the renewed strength he needed to be reborn, to achieve resurrection".

Gathered together alone one wall are the gold coaches, the arrows, the bows and the weapons.

"The sovereign was thought to need these to fight the hordes of corrupt beings that inhabit the shadows," remarks Carter, "while Shed, the god of youth and the hunt, was called upon to protect against evil spirits. Riding out in those light hunting chariots, he would kill all the demons."

Something catches Lawrence's eye: a lock of hair in a gold box.

"How intriguing!"

"It might have belonged to Queen Tije," says Carter, "or perhaps to the young pharaoh himself. We don't know."

Carter points to a small statue, "This is Amenophis III, the Pharaoh's father".

"Actually, that may not be the case," interjects Callender with a smile.

"Well perhaps not," responds Carter with surprise. "Everything about that period is rather confused. But what makes you say so?"

"It's something Miss Elsa told Professor Newman," admits Callender after a moment's hesitation".

"Not her again!" blurts out a bemused Carter.

"Actually, a few weeks ago," continues Callender warily, "she gave a truly fascinating account of the coronation of this ruler. The ceremony could very well have taken place just as she described it, with all the various historic figures she mentioned taking part. The lock of hair would have been cut from the boy during the procession."

Carter smiles in amusement as Callender adds, "If you're interested, she gave Professor Newman another account that was even more fascinatingly poetic." Pointing at the casket, Callender goes on, "Even as a boy, this pharaoh was in search of his father, the ruler who had been erased from history, the greatest mystic to have ever lived: Amenophis IV, Akhenaten, also known as the Heretic."

Carter notes, as if he were trying to get Callender to reason, "Nothing is absolutely certain, he could very well be the father, but who is Miss Elsa to tell us as much?".

"Is Miss Elsa an archaeologist?" asks Lawrence, whose interest has clearly been piqued.

"Nothing of the sort," answers Carter in a dismissive tone. "She's an unbalanced young woman who claims to be the reincarnation of some personage from the eighteenth dynasty. It may be a case of autism."

Carter points to the riding whip with the silver handle adorned with arabesques. On the back of the handle is an inscription.

"We have already deciphered this inscription," he notes as he translates it out loud:

'TUTHMOSE Captain of the Guards'. Ask your Miss Elsa if she can explain what this was doing in the Pharaoh's tomb, and who this Tuthmose might be? I have yet to hear of anybody by that name. It might open up a whole new chapter of history," he adds ironically.

"He was a prince, Howard" responds Callender hesitantly. "A friend of the Pharaoh, a sort of squire and bodyguard. He received the riding crop from the Pharaoh himself on the day he was named Captain of the Guard."

Carter shakes his head.

"And Miss Elsa told you all this? But when do you meet with her?"

"I remember once in Arabia," remarks Lawrence, "in a place where there was nothing but sun and sand, and yet there was a Bedouin girl who could neither read nor write the language of our times. Still, she amazed everybody by reading effortlessly from the oldest copy of the sacred book of Islam, a text written on a gazelle skin and kept in the library in Medina. The world is filled with mystery, dear Howard. Who's to say what is true and what is not?"

CHAPTER X

The Runaway

It is still night, as a silhouetted figure moves about in the murky darkness of Olga's bedroom. Were it not for the glow of the moon, nothing would be visible. Draped in an elegant cloak, Elsa draws close to her mother, who is sleeping, but restlessly, and gently kisses her hair. Then, suitcase in hand, she leaves.

Dawn's rays illuminate the Nile. A number of small skiffs are already out on the water. Birds fly by, skimming the surface, seeming to play as they frenetically chirp to one another while falling into formation, as if for a dance. A carriage pulled by two horses arrives from a small road along the riverbank. When the carriage stoops, Elsa unfastens the elegant cloak and lets it fall onto the seat cushion. Underneath she is wearing a "Uamaayas", a traditional garment of the people of Qurna, while her head and shoulders are covered by a long shawl. She opens the suitcase, places it next to the cloak, on the carriage seat, and removes a bundle.

Getting out, she pays the driver and walks towards the ferry. Once there, she boards the vessel, mixing in with the crowd of local people carrying baskets, packages and bundles of their own, plus various types of animals. The ferry is unadorned but roomy, filled to overflowing. Elsa takes her place among the other passengers, as dawn continues to rise, giving way to the light of morning. The boat heads for the opposite bank, passing alongside a skiff decked out with flowers and carrying an entire family that sings to the accompaniment of a "darabouka", a goatskin tambourine. They may be on their way to celebrate a country wedding. Elsa watches with a smile as the festive skiff moves off into the distance.

The rising sun brings forth a marvellous array of colours. The air is filled with the sun's orange-tinted rays, though the temperature is still tepid. Accompanied by the ferryman, Elsa walks up the great hill of Qurna, which is filled with caves and tunnels dug over thousands of years of time.

"This is the sacred, 'smiling' land of treasures where our illustrious ancestors lie in rest," says the ferryman, stamping his foot on the dusty ground.

The rough, uninviting path rises steeply, amidst ruins that date back to other millennia. A gust of warm air blows on Elsa's face.

"Did you feel that?" she asks. "What was it?"

The ferryman hesitates before continuing on with a troubled look.

"This is the land of the dead of Thebes, Miss. The Valley of the Queens".

They come to a cavern around which phrases dedicated to a local goddess have been inscribed. Elsa can see that the writing is in ancient cuneiform.

"Martseger, she who is loved by the Lord of Silence."

The ferryman is dumbfounded to hear her make out the inscription. Then she continues.

"Here was the abode of the 'Serpent Goddess', she who loved the 'Lord of Silence'... and ruled over the 'sacred mountain'", says Elsa, talking to herself.

"Miss, I have done what you have asked of me. This is Qurna," says the ferryman, clearly frightened. "Up there, at the end of the trail, you should ask for Mohammad Hammad."

The young woman holds out money, but the man has already hurried off. Walking up to the entrance to the cavern, she sees a boy seated atop a waterwheel, gently coaxing two donkeys with a whip, as his own rough, nasal chanting accompanies the creaking parts of the wheel. Next to the entrance is a woman dressed entirely in black, including a veil that shows only her piercing eyes.

"Who are you looking for?" she asks.

"Mohammed Hammad", answers Elsa.

The woman motions for Elsa to follow her inside, where they move among cells and tunnels that make the hill seem like a termite mound. Many of the cells are connected with one another, with their paths frequently disappearing, only to make their way back up to the surface again. Starting from the early-morning hours, an aroma of spices fills the ancient, chapel-like spaces where a group of women are busy cooking. So engrossed are they in their work, that they appear not to notice the two women who pass right by them, on their way to an underground cavern connected to other tombs.

The woman shows Elsa the direction she should take.

"That is where you want to go!"

Elsa enters a low-ceilinged passageway, moving slowly to get past the tight, twisting spots along the way. Finally she arrives at a larger, better-lit space where daylight enters through the bars on the window openings that face outwards. Mats and pillows are spread out on the floor, a table holds some statuettes, vases and shards of pottery, while a pair of benches that double as storage chests sit nearby, both of them closed. Elsa walks up to the table, takes one of the statuettes and examines it.

Somebody else appears, possibly the man she is looking for. Visibly overweight, he seems to be between 60 and 65 years old, with a beard, a moustache, and sly eyes.

The man bows. "It is I that you are looking for, Miss! Mohammed Hammad, honest and respected trader, especially when it comes to the authenticity of my wares. Please have a seat."

Elsa takes a seat, while the heavyset man notices the statuette she is holding.

"That gem in your hands dates from the 7ᵗʰ dynasty. Excellently crafted, it even bears an ancient inscription. We found it in the tomb of a very important figure from the past. It is priceless, and I have no wish to sell it. I would rather keep it jealously for myself."

"It's a fake! Sell it to some unsuspecting tourist," says Elsa with a smile.

Mohammed pretends to be taken aback.

"What do you say? A fake?"

She points to the 'ancient inscription'.

"This writing means nothing. The letters were put together at random, without any logical connection".

The man is genuinely astonished.

"How can you read them? That takes years of study! But the statue is real, that I know for sure! As for the letters, you're right, a friend of mine did them without any idea of what they meant".

He rushes over to the table, picks up another statue and comes back to Elsa to show it to her.

"Is this real or fake? It's an 'ushabti', and it also has writing on it."

Elsa seems amused.

"Fake! Every 'ushabti' has a verse from the "Book of the Dead" engraved on it. What's written here is something else altogether."

"But there is something there to read?!"

Elsa finds the larger-than-life fellow strangely endearing.

"Yes, but it is not the standard phrase engraved on an 'ushabti'"

"The imbecile!" grumbles the man. "What did they used to write on 'ushabti'?"

"'When you are called, get up and answer: 'I am coming'. An ushabti was a servant who offered to work in the place of the deceased ...'"

The man expresses his contempt for the friend who wrote the phrases: "What did that moron copy instead?"

"Vintage year III," answers Elsa, reading the phrase. "Wine from his Majesty's vineyards on the right bank".

Mohammed breaks into hearty laugher.

"So they drank back then too, wherever this was written!"

Elsa watches him, clearly enjoying the spectacle.

Mohammed walks quickly to the storage chest that also serves as a bench, opens it, rummages around inside and returns with something cupped between his hands. He holds them out to the young lady, finally revealing a small, delicately crafted box. Elsa takes a closer look.

"Fake or real?"

"Real," she answers in a pleased tone, leaving him visibly satisfied.

"We found it next to a young woman, possibly a princess of the 6th dynasty. That was 4,300 years ago."

"It's a cosmetics holder," says Elsa, recognising the object.

He cannot help adding, while pointing to a hard substance which, at first glance, is not easily identifiable: "That's some leftover lipstick! Even back then our women were vain! I had a sample examined, and they told me it was lipstick made with antimony. What does the writing say?"

"Helmsman Knemhotep", she reads. "Who journeyed to Punt. Expeditions were organised to the Land of Punt, on the Red Sea, to bring back antimony, incense and myrrh plants."

"If you want it, you must pay a lot!" says Mohammed with a cunning tone.

Elsa places the object back on the table. "Thank you, but I'm not interested."

She takes out some money nonetheless and offers it to Mohammed, who takes it with a disappointed look. Sitting down, he grumbles, "I've never been given money without having to provide something in exchange. This just isn't like me. I have to give you something".

He watches her silently, his expression revealing the scheming behind his silence. Elsa seems willing to play along.

"Who are you?" he asks. "Who sent you? Why are you here, if you obviously have no wish to buy anything? What do you really want?"

"To live here!" she says frankly.

An astonished Mohammed replies, "May Allah forgive me! What did you say? You want to live here?"

Scratching his side, he thinks the matter over.

"With everything you know, I could certainly use you. But no! We live in filth here, the police always have their eye on us. There are scorpions and poisonous snakes everywhere".

Elsa tries to reassure him: "I know the ancients formulas against scorpions and snakes."

Despite his misgivings, Mohammed decides to put her to the test.

"Pairs of cobras raised respectfully as pets are a tradition dating back thousands of years in these parts, done in the ancient way. Back then, children were taught 'the language of the snakes'."

Mohammed watches the girl closely, to see how she reacts, but she calmly relies, "I am not afraid."

Pointing to a basket over in a corner, he warns her, "You could die."

She nods for him to continue and waits, as Mohammed goes over to the basket and removes its cover with a stick. He moves to one side, against the wall. Elsa follows the scene with interest, but without any show of concern. First the heads of two cobras appear from inside the basket, then their bodies.

Elsa remains calm and collected. Only her eyelids give a slight shudder. The cobras begin slithering along the ground, moving closer.

Perhaps Mohammed would have been better off not carrying out this test, but he is paying close attention, ready to step in with the stick.

The cobras have almost reached Elsa, who stays perfectly still, her lips sealed tight. Suddenly the snakes rise and puff themselves up, making the hissing noise that typically proceeds an attack. Mohammed, his forehead beaded with sweat, holds the stick tight, ready to take action, when Elsa's lips begin to utter incomprehensible sounds.

"Matey matey mottey motey, hy-nw mutef mitey mitey hrs-wtr".

Elsa lets her hands softly slide onto one another, tapping her fingertips together as she does so. She moves her face even closer to the cobras, whose heads begin to vibrate as they puff up. She keeps murmuring her incomprehensible words and sounds.

"Mitey mitey...hrs...wtr..."

Then she lifts her open hand and moves it towards the reptiles, who bend and stretch themselves out on the ground before slowly returning to where they came from.

Mohammed wipes the sweat from his forehead while staring in astonishment at the girl. Her eyes are closed, her face perfectly still.

"We too know the formulas for 'charming' snakes," he says, "but they are in Arabic. What language were you speaking?"

Elsa opens her eyes again, at first with a bizarre, faraway look, before her smile finally returns.

"The words date from so far back that even the ancient Egyptians, though they knew that the formula worked, considered the language to be incomprehensible."

Mohammed closes the basket back up, taking extreme care. Then, after a moment's hesitation, he reaches into his pocket, pulls out the money Elsa gave him and gives it back to her.

"I don't want your money."

In Luxor, on the terrace of his comfortably appointed home, Carter is finishing his breakfast. Alì brings Dr. Servet, Lord Carnarvon's personal physician, out to see him.

"Good morning, Dr. Servet. Any new developments?" asks Carter, getting to his feet.

The physician, a worried look on his face, answers, "I have a message for you, Mr. Carter: Lord Carnarvon has left for Cairo".

"Left?"

"Yes, I advised him to, after examining his shoulder, which I found to be quite inflamed."

"He was bitten by an insect," says Carter in a concerned tone.

"Yes, that could be the cause, but he cannot receive the proper treatment here, so I advised him to see a specialist."

"Of course. Did Lady Evelyn leave too?"

"Yes".

In a grave, preoccupied tone Carter observes, "Almost half my team is suffering from some sort of affliction: Mace, La Fleur, young Bethell".

The physician's voice also reveals considerable concern, "I have yet to understand what ails them, though Mr. Bethell's condition definitely falls outside of the realm of internal medicine."

"What does he have ..."

"The answer would appear quite simple, at least as illustrated in texts on mental health: he suffers from an emotional disturbance bordering on depression, with attacks of panic and anxiety. And although many have cast doubt on the therapeutic benefits of psychoanalysis, an Austrian neurologist and psychoanalyst, Dr. Sigmund Freud, has recently developed a theory that unconscious psychic processes can have noteworthy repercussions on human behaviour and thought, as is in the case of young Bethell. According to Freud, there is a link between unconscious visions, which are nothing more or less than symbolic representations of actual mental processes, and the mind's complex structures. Psychoanalysis is a field that we have barely begun to explore, and which surely reserves any number of advances currently unknown to us physicians as well".

The doctor is about to leave, then he pauses.

"Would you like a drink?" asks Carter.

"Some other time, thank you. You have reminded me that I have patients to attend to."

Richard Bethell sits in an armchair in a magnificent suite of the Hotel Winter in Luxor. The bedroom window offers a view of the trees of the finely manicured grounds, even though Bethell appears to see nothing. He sits pale, motionless, barely present. The nurse sitting alongside the door gets to her feet when Lord Westbury and Dr. Servet arrive.

"Is he still afraid of the dark?" Dr. Servet asks Lord Westbury.

"Yes," comes the anguished answer. "It's only in the dark that he gives some small, almost imperceptible signs of life, as if he were afraid of something, except I can't understand what. We have to leave all the lights on, and we can never leave him alone."

Servet nods, as if to acknowledge that the situation defies understanding.

"Doctor, what should we do? What do you recommend?"

Clearly troubled, the physician replies, "My only advice, Lord Westbury, and it is the same recommendation I made to Lord Carnarvon, is to go to Cairo, where he can receive more suitable treatment, or better yet London."

"Can he travel?" asks a worried Lord Westbury.

"Always keep an eye on him. But a change of setting might do him good, a return to his familiar habits".

In the same hotel, two floors further down, Olga is sitting in an armchair in the drawing room, in the company of Professor Newman. Olga looks anguished, marked by fatigue and tension, but still doing her best to carry on.

"Why has she disappeared like this?"

"I have no idea, Olga. We did everything we could for her."

Olga has no more tears to cry.

"Why didn't she tell me where she was going?"

"I don't know, but we have looked everywhere."

Olga sits down again, exhausted. She tries to pull herself together, hesitating before going on, "For eleven years now she has kept saying that I am not her mother. And I have suffered, but never have I held it against her. Instead, I have tried to understand, to help her. I felt guilty over my husband's death. If he had not followed me for my work... When will this torment end?"

Newman does his best to comfort her.

"It was not your fault, Olga. It was an accident. Of course your husband was going to follow you, just as we are here for her. We've searched every district of Egypt without finding any answers, just instants and fragments of exceptional memories. But you are the same strong, exceptional woman as always. This is no time to give up. You'll see: we'll either find her, or she will come back to us."

Professor Newman seems to be carrying a great weight. He takes Olga's hand and says, "Elsa is a considerate, sensible girl. Whatever she does, she does it for a reason. We simply have to give her time".

Looking a little less downhearted, Olga hugs him.

"What would I have done without you all these years? But I've made up my mind: when we find her, we are going home, to the Sudan. There is nothing left for us here!"

She looks him in the eyes.

"Carl, I hope you will decide to come with us..."

Working up his courage, Newman gives her a gentle caress, followed by a kiss. The two look deep into each other's eyes. Then she kisses him still more passion. They embrace, they touch each other, swept up by feelings that they have held back for far too long.

She shudders, he holds her tight, exploring her garments, inside and out. Her nails press into his back. The two of them frantically remove each other's clothes, losing all control between the sheets.

Seen in the moonlight, the Qurna hillside resembles a Christmas tree aglow with the fires that sparkle in the countless niches and caves dug into the rock. Elsa and Mohammed are sitting on the ground, eating a typical local dish, a stew flavoured with a variety of cabbage and other aromas.

Elsa is fond of the local cuisine, but at the moment her attention is drawn to a ring Mohammed is wearing. It has a seal adorned with hieroglyphic characters. Taking his hand, Elsa examines the ring closely.

Though he knows full well it is authentic, he craftily asks her, "Is the writing real or fake?"

"If you found it in the tomb of Queen Nefertiti, then it is real. Her name is written here: Nefer-Neferu Aton".

"What does that mean?" asks Mohammed.

"The beautiful one has arrived. It is the name she was given when her husband, Akhenaton, died. Nefertiti was her first name..."

"Was it a ceremonial ring?" he asks with interest.

"No, a funeral ring, the kind placed on the fingers of mummies. But how could you have come across it," she asks, once she gets over her surprise, "if the body has never been found?"

"If you can keep a secret," says Mohammed with an air of mystery, "I will show you something the likes of which you would never imagine."

He takes a lamp and leads Elsa further down into the hill, through tunnels lit only by the ghostly lamplight, until they reach an even lower zone where further passageways appear, forming what amounts to an underground labyrinth.

Mohammed chuckles, "It is worse than a maze down here. Two policemen got lost once and were never heard from again. Who knows what became of them... but here we are..."

They arrive at a very large cave, where Mohammed leads Elsa along one side, until they reach an enormous table that stands on an antique carpet covered by a cloth. Mohammed lifts the cloth, revealing a large trapdoor beneath the carpet.

"This is proof of how much I trust you, because now you, and you alone, know where to find my treasure chest!"

With a great deal of effort, Mohammed finally gets the trapdoor open, and the two of them climb down into what seems to be a hiding place.

He lights another lamp, bringing into view a space that holds any number of objects stolen over the years from various tombs, including statuettes, 'ushabtis', ointment jars, jewellery cases, alabaster lamps, cups for libations, rings, bracelets, tabernacles, scribes' easels, earrings, fragments of papyrus and much more.

Mohammad, unabashedly proud of his cache, declares: "The treasure of the people of Qurna!"

Elsa is too astonished for words, but of all the vast array of objects, one spot draws her attention.

Over in a dimly lit area where only flickers of the lamplight arrive, there would appear to be quite a few mummies. Grabbing the lamp from Mohammed's hands, Elsa sets off in that direction. The light reveals an untold quantity of mummies all jumbled together, their faces immersed in the grave, dramatic solemnity of deaths that occurred thousands of years ago to these women, priestesses and noble ladies, some of them young, others less so; some placed in coffins, others simply lying on the floor or set against a wall.

Elsa, her face frozen in apparent disbelief, stares at Mohammad.

"They aren't even any signs as to who they were. And as you know, bodies without names can never have eternal life."

"Burying the dead with their treasures was probably a mistake," he offers as a justification. "Even back then, it must have made for too much of a temptation. They would hire us to dig, but quite often they wound up not paying, so what were we supposed to do?"

The lamplight reveals other mummies of princes, priests, plus more women. Mohammed trips on the mummy of a young woman who is completely wrapped up and laid out in a sarcophagus. Elsa draws closer, trying to read the hieroglyphics that appear on the feet, but her heart skips a beat when the mummy's hand moves.

Then Elsa, already petrified, sees the mummy's head and chest slowly start to rise. She steps back, as the mummy continues to lift itself up. Suddenly, from behind the trunk of the mummy, which has reached a sitting opposition, the head and body of a massive snake, an albino python, pop out. The reptile slowly lowers itself to the ground before slithering off into the darkness, amidst the sarcophagi, while the mummy of the young woman falls back into the coffin with a loud thud.

Elsa, unable to stifle a convulsive tremor, brings her hands to her face in horror.

Mohammed smiles and says, "We run into him every once and awhile, and then he'll disappear for quite some time. No one knows where he goes or why he comes back. For us, he's sacred."

Elsa, her hands still pressed against her face, gives a nervous shudder. Mohammed signals that they should keep going. Elsa moves forward, brushing past mummies and sarcophagi until she sees, in a space set apart, leaning against a wall, a wooden sarcophagus that, having been opened, holds the mummified body of Queen Nefertiti, covered in torn, tattered bandages. There are no jewels, no sign of royal rank, only her unforgettably beautiful face.

Elsa draws closer. Without touching it, she runs her hand along the face blackened by the acids. Then, with infinite sadness, a tear sliding down her cheek, she slips the ring with the seal onto the mummy's finger and murmurs in a muffled voice: "Nefer Neferu- Aton".

Mohammed comes closer.

"I was still small when she was brought here, probably no more than five years old. All the wild talking and shouting woke me up. I remember it was a moonless night, and there were torches to light the way for a group of men from Qurna. There were shouts, orders, endless cursing, as they pushed a sled carrying the priceless coffin. It was windy that night..."

Mohammed as a young boy, hidden amidst the mummies, watches what is going on. He sees a host of hands, arms and faces lift the Queen's body from the casket and lay her on the large table. The scene leaves the boy practically indifferent, being like so many he has seen before, though the mummy brought in that night is especially important for all of them.

Hurried hands unwrap the bandages, grabbing at whatever jewels they find, each piece more precious than the next, both outside and below the garments. The theft goes on for quite a few minutes. Hands with dirt under their nails remove rings from fingers, bracelets from wrists, ankles and feet. There is even a diadem, a true marvel of gold craftsmanship, together with a necklace that glows in the light of the lanterns.

The boy notices that a ring has fallen to the ground in the fury of the sacrilege, escaping the attention of the plunderers. He reaches out and grabs it, as the men hammer away at the exquisite sarcophagus, using the pieces to feed a fire which lights the entire scene.

"A short time later, my father became rich. He took three new wives, all of them much younger than my mother, and left us here to our fate. Many years after that, I came to know that the tomb was found in the region of Amarna, where it was discovered by chance, following a rockslide caused by torrential rains in the month of July".

Elsa is terribly sad. "It was a huge mistake to take her away from there".

Mohammed glances at the mummy and asks with conviction, "Should we take her to a museum, where everyone can see her?"

"No, that would only make things worse. She's better off here," concludes Elsa in a despondent tone.

Cairo's Grand Continental Savoy looks out onto the elegant Opera Square. Atop the massive, richly adorned hotel fly three large red flags bearing the half-moon and the Ottoman star. The building takes up an entire block of the city's downtown. Its ample lounges and rooms have frequently had the privilege of hosting celebrated individuals, dignitaries and leading political figures.

Today, as always, any number of well-dressed people enter and exit the establishment. Carriages and automobiles line up in front of its entrance, delivering the guests to the care of the 'houseboys', who dutifully open the doors of the vehicles and help the visitors out. From there, the cars and carriages continue along a tree-lined drive, circling a handsome fountain before dispersing into the neighbouring streets.

A trolley passes by the hotel, stopping a little further on, at the corner, in front of the Gran Café. A Bedouin on a mule leads the way for some companions who have convinced a number of tourists to ride through the streets of the city for a few drachmas.

Carter arrives in one of the carriages and walks straight into the hotel, amidst the greetings of the doormen who respectfully open the large doors for him. He moves through the luxuriant lounges embellished with immense crystal chandeliers and fine carpets before hurrying up the stairs and crossing the second-floor landing, where a group of Lord Carnarvon's friends has gathered.

He knocks on a door that has been left ajar at the entrance to a corridor, and a nurse lets him in, leading him through a room equipped as an infirmary, and from there into the bedroom.

Lord Carnarvon is lying in bed, being comforted by his wife, Lady Almina, who has just arrived from London, together with her sister, and her daughter Evelyn. Two doctors are also in attendance at the sickbed.

Lord Carnarvon turns his eyes towards Csrter, and his face comes alive. One of the doctors motions for Carter to come closer.

"How are you feeling today, Sir George?"

Lord Carnarvon, clearly worn down, answers: "Dear Howard, I feel poorly, very poorly. But you, please, continue with the wonderful work you've done so far."

"Sir George..." replies Carter, his voice betraying his emotion.

"Howard, everything that we have found... and that you shall find in the future, must stay in Egypt."

A smile comes to Carter's face.

"Thank you, Sir George..."

"I have already given my attorneys instructions... to this effect. For whatever else you need, you can depend on my daughter Evelyn."

Seeing the old lion in such a diminished state, Carter is unable to keep his feelings in check.

"Sir George, you speak as if..."

"What difference does it make to have a year more, a year less, to live ...".

Evelyn, shaking with a sob, hugs her mother tight. Turning to Lady Almina, Lord Carnarvon motions for her to draw near, saying: "I wish to be buried in England, beneath the grass, at the top of Beacon Hill, facing our home ...".

The Countess nods yes, before she too is unable to stifle her tears. Lord Carnarvon's gaze goes empty, showing just how weak he has become. The doctor motions for everyone to leave him and the nurse alone with the patient.

In the small sitting room outside, Carter rubs his forehead, failing to grasp how such a drama could occur.

"It is devastating! What could be happening!"

"The root cause of the illness is obviously the infection, but now the lungs have become congested", says the most senior physician.

"Will he pull through?" asks Carter in a shaken tone.

"Quite unlikely. It would be a miracle."

Servants dressed in immaculate white livery turn on the lights in the entryway as Lord Porchester, Lord Carnarvon's son, enters the hotel lobby.

The nurse, seated on a small armchair in Lord Carnarvon's room, turns towards Lord Porchester as he walks in. With the ticking of the clock clearly audible, he goes to his father, who has yet to recognise him.

"It is awfully hot. Would you please open the windows," Lord Porchester asks the nurse.

She does as he requested, letting a slight breath of air enter the room. Outside the city shines with the glow of thousands of lights.

Night has fallen. The nurse is alone in the room, sitting silently on the small armchair as she listens to the patient's troubled breathing. The large windows frame the spectacle of the city lights at night. The clock says 1:43 am. The nurse seems strangely anxious, as if fearful that something might happen at any moment.

Appearing from behind the upper portion of the dresser, a black beetle similar to the one depicted on the seal found on the tomb door makes its way along the upper surface of the dresser. The nurse spots it and places a glass on top of the beetle, keeping it from going any further. Intrigued by the insect, she observes it, until suddenly Lord Carnarvon's laboured breathing falls silent.

The nurse goes to his side. Lord Carnarvon whispers: "I hear beating wings, two large wings. Now he can leave the tomb and go wherever he likes. He is back there," he declares, pointing at the window.

The nurse reassures him, "There's nothing there, Sir. Just the wind, a light breeze."

But Lord Carnarvon insists. "No, I heard the wings, and his heated, restless breathing."

With the little strength he has left, His Lordship tries to unbutton his pyjamas, as if in need of air, while continuing to stare at the window, his anguished eyes wide-open.

The clock keeps ticking away. The time is 1:50 am. A sudden gust of wind throws the window wide open, blowing in a cloud of dust. A whistling similar to a human shout fills the room, as the long white curtains flap across it. The sound of the beating wings grows louder, increasingly real.

The nurse covers her face with her hands, as if to protect herself from something that has passed close to her. Suddenly she realises that the beetle has disappeared from underneath the glass.

The lights go off, first in the room, then in the entire city of Cairo stretching out beyond the wide-open window. The nurse screams and leaves the room, yelling for help in the hallway, which has also gone dark.

Hearing the nurse's cries, Carter, the family of Lord Carnarvon, and the other guests of the hotel come running from their rooms. Lord Carnarvon's son leans over the stairway banister, shouting: "A light! Bring candles! A lamp, quickly, please!"

Inside the bedroom, lit only by the glow of the moon, the curtains return to their original positions. The wind has calmed, and the shrill whistle that came with it can no longer be heard. The tick-tock of the clock echoes in the silent room. The nurse, accompanied by Lady Almina, returns to it by the light of the candle she holds in her trembling hands.

Lord Carnarvon is dead, his eyes still open, gazing towards the window. Lady Almina's hand mercifully lowers his eyelids, while Lady Evelyn flings herself on top of her father's body, crying desperately. The clock strikes 2:00 in the morning. Lady Almina stops its pendulum, and the domestics enter, together with servants carrying candelabra.

Carter, off by himself, unable keep his emotions in check, finds himself crying softly.

Highclere is surrounded by the dark of night. Lord Carnarvon's dog, Mayor, howls forlornly on the castle grounds, not heeding the servant who tries to calm him, but yowling in desperation, his head lifted to the sky… then, after a final groan, he collapses. A servant with a candelabra walks up to the dog and delicately touches his unmoving chest, taking note of the animal's apparently inexplicable death.

The news of Lord Carnarvon's passing is the only topic of conversation in the main lobby of the Hotel Winter. Dr. Servet struggles to free himself from the group of journalists who have surround him on all sides.

"Doctor, do you really believe it was a mosquito?"

Dr. Servet is in a foul mood.

"I know nothing. I believe nothing!"

But the journalists keep after him.

"They say that even the worst bites cause just a few days' fever. What about that, Dr. Servet?"

The doctor responds ironically, "If you say so, then it must be true!"

The reporters refuse to give up.

"But what is your opinion?"

Dr. Servet answers firmly, "I have no opinion."

"Doesn't this illness that's going around seem strange? Or have you, like Lord Carnarvon, sold the exclusive rights to your story to the Times?!"

Dr. Servet pronounces, as he struggles to make his way through the crowd, "The world is one big mystery."

"But then ..." the journalists simply do not know when to stop.

The doctor blurts out angrily, "Leave me alone, will you?!"

But the reporters keep hounding him.

"A doctor should know these things!"

Dr. Servet gives his final word: "When it comes to the mind, a doctor has no idea what is going on!"

In the Office of Antiquities in Cairo, Professor Maspero and his two "in-house" experts are meeting with Carter, as well as an Egyptian politician by the name of Morcos Bey Hanna and, finally, seated behind his desk, the General Director of the Office, Pierre Lacau.

Carter appears nervous.

"Mr. Lacau, the concession for the dig should have been automatically renewed in favour of Lady Almina Carnarvon. When Professor Maspero was still in charge, consideration was also given to that unfortunate possibility."

Carter turns to Maspero. "As Professor Maspero himself can confirm."

Maspero speaks up, "It's true, the terms of the concession also took that possibility into account."

The Egyptian politician joins in, "But the idea of giving the exclusive to the Times was not in the terms, and our government was never even consulted."

Pierre Lacau, the Director, calmly observes, "Professor Carter, your point is well taken, but put yourself in the place of our government. You have achieved a discovery of universal importance, but it still took place in Egyptian territory".

Becoming increasingly agitated, Carter replies, "But with the proper concession and following a very sizeable investment!"

Morcos Bey Hanna counters, "This is an unquestionable case of discrimination! Do you really think such news should be kept from the local publications?!"

Naturally, Carter understands the political implications, but he wants to stay true to his patron's wishes.

"The decision was taken by Lord Carnarvon, without whom, let me remind you, there would be no reason for any of us to be discussing the matter".

The new Director, who has just taken office, and so has no wish to make enemies, state firmly: "Very well then. Professor Carter, it seems only fair that the concession be granted to Lord Carnarvon's widow, but to be perfectly clear, from this point forward, if one journalist is allowed onto the site, then they all are."

In the Valley of the Kings, the reporters flock around Carter and Callender, who are not far from the entrance to the tomb. The newsmen are looking for scoops to boost the circulation of their respective publications.

"Do you still intend to open the sarcophagus?"

"Of course," answers Carter forthrightly.

"What do you expect to find inside?"

Carter begins walking faster. "The sarcophagus".

From the back of the pack, another reporter shouts out: "Aren't you afraid of the 'Curse of the Pharaoh'?"

Carter refuses to dignify the question with an answer, but he does look with disgust towards the bookmaker's tent, which is flying the British flag.

The bookmaker hammers on his table, urging the public to bet by reading off the items on his poster board: "WAGERS ACCEPTED ON: 1) The date on which the sarcophagus is opened. 2) Is there a mummy inside or not? 3) Is the mummy intact or not? 4) After Lord Carnarvon, who will be the next victim?"

Carter, with the journalists at his heels, begins walking even faster, finally reaching the entrance to a tomb not far from that of Tutankhamun. The guards keep out the journalists, who slowly drift away. The Valley of the Kings seems to have become an amusement park. There are vendors selling drinks and kebab, along with photographers ready to take pictures that the tourists will take back with them overseas.

Inside the other tomb, which has graciously provided as a work area, Mace and his wife are busy cataloguing the finds. A tired-looking La Fleur is there too, seated next to Mr. Merton, the correspondent for the Times.

"I am sorry, Mr. Merton," Carter tells him in a regretful but final tone, "but as a journalist and correspondent of the Times, you will no longer be able to enter the tomb, simply because I don't want it filling up with reporters".

An astonished Merton exclaims, "But I don't understand! We have an agreement. You had better talk to..."

Carter cuts him off.

"I officially appoint you a working member of the team, in the position of assistant cataloguer. If you decide to pass on some news to your paper, then that's your own private concern, of which I wish to know absolutely nothing."

Carter hands him some sheets of paper. "Now please begin cataloguing!"

Callender gives a satisfied smile.

Mace and his wife seem worried. "Are they turning this into a political question?"

Carter, sounding clearly annoyed, states, "Politics should have nothing to do with science! Have you seen that fellow out there?" he continues heatedly, "the one taking bets on us!

And with the Union Jack flying over his tent.
Incredible!"

CHAPTER XI

Lord Westbury

It is the middle of the night in England.

Lord Westbury's estate includes an old manor house built by the family's illustrious ancestors. Inside, the fireplace that heats the large main room, combined with the light from a table lamp, creates a striking pattern of shadows. A moaning wind whips around the house, setting the panes of the large windows to shaking.

Richard Bethell is sitting by the free. His face looks pinched, high-strung. He shivers, gets to his feet and puts more wood on the fire to heat the room. The wind, after calming down for a while, goes back to blowing more forcefully. Drawn to something, but without knowing exactly what, Richard walks up to the large window and stands there, listening to the wailing of the wind as it slips in and around the cornices and the towers of the castle.

Then the wind picks up still more strength, its lament growing even shriller. Richard opens the curtain a crack and looks out the window, beyond which is nothing but darkness. Lord

Westbury enters the room and, seeing his son by the window, calls out, "Ah, there you are, Richard! I imagined you had gone to bed. It's late."

His words draw no reaction from Richard. Lord Westbury walks over to the sideboard where drinks are prepared.

"Can I get you something?"

Richard shakes his head, but barely. He seems wary, haunted. The father pours a glass for himself and one for his son.

"Here, let's have one last brandy. It's an ugly night."

Richard, continuing to stare outside, says, "The wind. There is no sky, no clouds either."

Doing his best not to contradict him, Lord Westbury replies, "That's right, you can't see the sky and the clouds because of the trees."

But Richard, like a lost soul, exclaims, "It is a wind that brings death."

The wind turns even more tempestuous. Richard recoils in fright, letting the curtain close back up again. Lord Westbury does his best to reassure him.

"There's no reason to be afraid. It's only the wind, just like we've heard so many times before."

But Richard shakes his head, as the wind continues its wailing. "These are shouts of deaths and death," he murmurs.

Lord Westbury pours him a glass of brandy, but he will not take it. The father leaves it on the table and begins sipping at his own.

"Is it death that's coming to get me? From outside? From the darkness? Is this the night?"

Lord Westbury sits down on the couch, letting himself sink into the cushions.

"Try to stay calm, my boy. Come here, sit down next to me. It's warmer by the fire,"

Richard keeps staring into space. Then he lifts his arm, as if to protect himself from something. He staggers back and bumps into the table, knocking a glass to the floor and breaking it.

He keeps moving backwards, terror filling his eyes. "Do you hear it? It's here, right now, in this room."

Lord Westbury looks all around him, but sees nothing, only the shadows flickering on the wall.

"There's nobody here. It's just the shadows from the fire. We're all alone!"

Suddenly, the wind stops, leaving only the sound of the wood crackling in the fireplace. Then, from outside, a shrill whistling sound is heard. Lord Westbury turns to Richard, who continues moving backwards, towards the wall, until finally his shoulders are pressed up against it.

Richard is staring in terror at a corner of the room. In the grip of a hallucination, he sees something take form in the shadow, possibly a human body. Lord Westbury looks in the same direction but sees nothing. Richard tries to speak or shout, his eyes open wide with fright, but no sound comes out. In the murky shadow he sees a human body with the head of a cobra, identical to the one engraved on the side of the gold sarcophagus. It starts moving towards him. Meanwhile the wind has picked up strength again.

The pulsating head of the cobra is still coming for him, as Richard stays plastered against the wall, terror in his eyes.

Lord Westbury runs to the door, opens it and shouts out: "Renton! Jackson! Come quickly!"

Richard, his back against the wall, his arms hanging limply by his sides, his eyes and mouth wide open, lets out a barely perceptible moan. The cobra's head strikes. Richard collapses onto the floor, as Lord Westbury runs to his side,

The butler and the servants appear. Richard's face is locked in anguish, his eyes are open in an empty stare. His heart has given out, duped by his mind into dying of fright.

That same evening, many kilometres away, in the sacred hills of Qurna, Professor Newman, Alì, a houseboy from the hotel, the ferryman and Mrs. Mittieri, lanterns in hand, all move up the steep path flanked by the caves used as homes, the unreal silence of the scene broken only by the cries of the birds of the night.

Every now and then, Alì pushes aside one of the rags that serve as the doors to the caves and sticks his head inside, speaking a word or two in Arabic.

Now, as he moves on, he asks the ferryman, "Are you sure you brought her here?"

The jumpy ferryman looks around. "Yes. She read that inscription there. She spoke of the serpent and the sacred mountain. How could I forget?"

Finally, having reached the entrance to a cave that leads further inside the hill, Alì walks up to a woman wearing the traditional niqab, the same lady whom Elsa spoke to when she visited, and says something to her in Arabic. The woman shakes her head no, though she is lying.

Mrs. Mittieri's eyes drop dejectedly. Then she takes some money and offers it to the lady, who refuses it, retreating inside the cave.

A disheartened Alì tries to explain the woman's behaviour.

"Ma'am, it is strange that anyone who lives in Qurna would act like that, refusing to take money. Miss Elsa must have been here, but everybody feels that they need to hide what they know. I am sorry."

Feeling faint, Mrs. Mittieri leans against the cave wall. Professor Newman immediately comes to her aid.

"Olga what is it? Should we stop?"

Olga vomits. Professor Newman gives her his handkerchief.

"Take this, wait. Let me help you". He hands her his canteen. "We should go back. You are not feeling well my dear".

But she pulls herself together. "No, let's keep looking for her."

The group continues searching in the massive hills of Qurna, where the home fires burning in the caves speckle the nocturnal landscape. Seen from a distance, the wandering group, with their lanterns, resembles a meteorite following a path through the stars.

In the sun-baked Valley of the Kings, the journalists crowd around Howard Carter to get his reaction to the headlines announcing the death of Richard Westbury.

"Now do you believe in the 'curse of the Pharaoh'?"

Carter naturally answers as a man of science.

"These ridiculous notions are spread by people of scarce intelligence. Sad to say, in terms of ethical integrity, mankind has made very little progress."

A reporter with a French accent asks him, "Professor Carter, did you know that Lord Carnarvon's nurse is being cared for in a clinic for the mentally ill?"

"I am truly sorry."

"And what can you tell us about the inexplicable death of Richard Westbury?" insists yet another reporter. "Doesn't it all strike you as highly unusual?!"

Visibly saddened, Carter replies, "He was very sick."

"Be sincere! Professor Carter!"

Carter tries to break away.

"I have nothing else to say."

The reporters continue their siege.

"Papers all over the world are talking about a 'curse', saying that the pharaoh is taking 'revenge'!"

Carter stops in his tracks.

"Gentlemen! Please! I am the one most responsible for opening the tomb, and I am still alive! And so are my chief assistants. All the workers who spend time in the tomb every day are still alive. You run the risk of appearing ridiculous!"

A voice shouts out from the back of the crowd, "Is it true that your bird, the one who knew all the different languages, died on the day of the discovery?!"

After pausing for an instant, Carter moves away quickly, passing in front of the betting stand where the English operator yells to the people crowded around him, "Nobody has won yet, because nobody bet on Westbury! I accept bets on everybody and everything! Step up and place your wagers!"

Pointing to a gentleman sitting with a rather haughty air at the betting table, the bookmaker adds, "Ladies and gentlemen, we have our own notary public here! He can guarantee winnings you wish to send abroad! So place your bets ... Anybody can become a winner."

"I bet five pounds on Dr. Mace," calls out an emboldened tourist. The notary writes down the name.

"Three pounds on Professor La Fleur!" shouts somebody else.

Disgusted by the bookmaker's impudence, Carter mutters to himself, "Jackal!" and moves on, shaking his head disdainfully.

On reaching the entrance to the tomb, he sees that a military tent has been set up as a bivouac for some soldiers, while two others have been posted at the entrance to the sepulchre.

He goes inside, where the archaeologist Arthur Mace, along with Archibald Douglas Reid and the French Egyptologist Georges Bénédite, are preparing large scale crates. The beams and winches have been assembled, and are almost ready for the task of removing the sarcophagus, as the archaeologists and the mechanical experts busy themselves with the equipment. In short, the work is progressing smoothly.

Off to one side, Maspero, together with Callender, have been waiting for Carter to arrive. When he does, he immediately asks

Maspero, "What is all this about?! What are the guards for?"

"Howard, the idea of pretending that the reporter for the Times was part of the research team has led to a great deal of controversy," says Maspero in a pained tone.

"Lacau is under enormous pressure from Morcos Bay Hanna, who, as if there weren't enough problems, has just been appointed the Minister of Public Works. Try to understand..."

Carter interrupts him.

"Dear Maspero, we are all under pressure, and this outburst of nationalism on the part of the new minister won't do anyone any good!"

Maspero's tone remains cordial, "Maybe you should speak with the journalists and explain ..."

But Carter retorts, "There's nothing to explain! It's a matter of principle. Lord Carnarvon made an agreement with the Times, and I intend to respect it!"

Maspero is sincerely troubled.

"I am here due to my ties of friendship with Lord Carnarvon, and my respect for you, but you are making it very hard for me to help. I am afraid I must tell you that, by order of Lacau, militiamen are on their way, with instructions not to let any reporters in, and that includes Mr. Barton ..."

A furious Carter cannot believe what he is hearing.

"Well if that's the way they want it, we'll see who wins! Stop working right now, all of you. Everybody out," he says to the mechanical experts and the labourers.

"Arthur, can you write something down for me?"

Mace takes a blank sheet of paper and gets ready to take notes. Instead, Carter starts dictating: "Due to the unacceptable restrictions and interference placed upon us by the Egyptian Department of the Ministry of Public Works and the Antiquities Service, all of my team, in protest over the situation, refuse to continue our research efforts inside the tomb".

To Maspero he declares, "This should be posted at the entrance of the Hotel Winter."

Then, speaking to the rest of the group: "Gentlemen, for the first time ever, we archaeologists are going to go on strike too!"

In front of the Hotel Winter, while two members of the staff post the notice regarding the striking archaeologists, a carriage pulls up. The hotel's houseboy opens the carriage door and Olga Mittieri gets out. Just then, a woman wearing a chador over her head (the veil that leaves only the face visible) comes up to Olga and says in a firm voice, "If I tell you about white girl, you give me baksheesh?"

Startled, Olga says, "You know about my daughter?"

The veiled woman answers, "Go to Qurna..."

A disappointed Olga replies, "I've already been there."

The woman insists, "Go back. Ask questions. You must talk with Mohammed Hammed. He knows... Tell people that you come to buy antiques. He is the expert. He will never let a customer get away."

Professor Newman gives the woman a handful of banknotes. She grabs them and hurries off.

Mohammed Hammed is sitting in his cave in Qurna, twisting and turning the traditional "tasbeeh", or Muslim rosary beads, in his hands. Suddenly, Mrs. Mittieri appears, her silhouette outlined in the doorway. Professor Newman is with her.

Mohammed jumps to his feet, humbly observing, "If you have come to Mohammed to buy, you will not be disappointed. Everybody knows that Mohammed is the only one who does not cheat the tourists, like the shopkeepers of Luxor do. Thieves every last one of them. Never to be trusted."

Olga looks him straight in the eye.

"I am the mother of a young lady whom you know. Can you help me find her?"

She takes a roll of banknotes from her purse and holds them out to Mohammad. But though he looks sorely tempted, he politely refuses the money, moving her hand away.

"This is the second time that I give money back. It is not a good thing. It rarely happens to Mohammed."

He smiles before turning serious and stating, "I do not want your money, because I have nothing to sell. I do not know where your daughter is. Does this seem like the kind of place were a nice girl would stay?"

Olga sits down on a bench, though Mohammed has yet to offer her a seat. Her mind is made up.

"I know that you're a cheat, as sly as a fox, though everyone in Qurna respects you. I am here because a woman told me that you met my daughter..."

Mohammed cuts her off. "And she asked you for money. And you gave it to her."

Olga is taken aback. "... How did you know?"

Mohammed answers craftily, "There are people who make a living deceiving tourists."

Olga shoots back, "I had never seen that woman before. And there are only a few of us who know of Elsa's disappearance."

Mohammad gets up, obviously intending to say goodbye.

"I swear to you, Ma'am, I know nothing. But I promise, should I hear anything, I'll come right away to tell you."

A desperate Olga keeps after him.

"I shall be forced to go to the police, something I was hoping not to have to do, because Elsa would not like it. But I have no choice, and god only knows what will happen then!"

Mohammed sits himself back down and says, in a measured tone, "Listen, I did see your daughter, but only once. She wanted to purchase some ancient objects. We spoke, and then she went away. But I think you are ill advised to go to the police. They will simply turn everything upside down and come up with nothing. Maybe the girl wants to be alone for a while. She is troubled, looking for something that is very important to her. You will see, she will come back. Why would a pretty, smart, well-off girl, somebody used to eating well and sleeping in a soft, comfortable bed, choose to simply disappear?"

Mohammed gets to his feet and heads for his storage space in the back, a cramped little room with a slew of objects for tourists. But when he turns around, he finds, to his astonishment, that Mrs. Mittieri has followed him.

Standing there, in the doorway, she looks very determined.

"I'll call the police and the consulate! It will be an international scandal!"

Realizing that the woman means business, and that persuading her to let the matter drop will not be easy, Mohammed offers, "Let us make a deal, Ma'am. You do not stir things up, you avoid going to the police. I will find your daughter and tell her that you are looking for her. I will say that you are very fearful over what has become of her. But you should leave her alone. I have seen her eyes, I spoke with her, and she is fine. Maybe she is looking for something. When she finds it, she will come back to you."

The man's words seem to sooth Olga.

"Thank you Mohammed. You know where she is, I can tell, and maybe you also know what she is looking for."

"This I have not figured out yet, Ma'am, what your daughter is looking for. But if I can help her, I will gladly do it."

The desert offers a splendid landscape, with the dunes lit by the moon on a still night. Carter and Callender are in Carter's home in Luxor. On the table are newspapers with titles like "SURPRISE IN LUXOR: tomb closed, all work stops", another says: "THE TOMB IS NOT HIS", and yet another: "TOMB IN LUXOR: authorisation of Carnarvon's widow revoked".

Callender reads one of the front page headlines out loud: "GOVERNMENT ULTIMATUM FOR MR. CARTER". With a worried look, he reports, "If the work does not start up again within two days, the Department of Antiquities will assign the project to another team of archaeologists. The rogues!"

Carter is sad and fatigued. He sees a letter sent by Lady Evelyn, from Highclere. Opening it, he reads out loud: "Dear Howard, my mother and I want you to know that we are exceedingly proud of you. We wish we could be there with you, but there are a number of matters that keep us in England. Rest assured that our attorneys have initiated legal actions in your support".

Carter gives a satisfied smile, as Callender begins reading another article. Suddenly a mournful sound echoes in the air, as if a whole lot of violins were playing, producing a bizarre song that fills the air. Callender looks up in surprise, turning to Carter with a quizzical expression.

The two of them go out on the terrace, beyond which stretch the dunes, bathed in moonlight. The mournful sounds is coming from those dunes, and then spreading among them, some closer, some further away, eventually reaching another part of the desert, where the riders of a caravan stop to listen to the sounds in fright, until one of them screams and runs away in terror, quickly followed by the others.

Out on the terrace, Carter and Callender listen as the sounds slowly dissolve. Carter smiles, glad to have finally found something to take his mind off the news stories.

"It happens from time to time at night, when the air temperature reaches a certain level. As the grains of sand cool off, they slide down the dunes, producing these sounds. The camel drivers believe it is spirits singing."

Suddenly, the voice of Mohammed Hammed can be heard from somewhere outside the home.

"Professor Carter, it is me, Mohammed."

Carter exclaims in surprise, "Mohammed who?"

The voice answers back, "The honest, the just one, Professor."

Carter smiles, "Get up here, you unholy thief!"

The tapping of the hoofs of the donkey carrying Mohammed on its back echo in the house as Carter whispers to Callender, "This is a character whom you absolutely must meet. As the most respected and popular thief in Qurna, he can be quite useful."

The two of them go back into the drawing room, where they see Mohammed standing in the doorway, though rather than come forward, he steps aside to let a lady wearing a niqab walk toward them. The woman uncovers her face, and both men recognise her as Miss Elsa.

They get to their feet in surprise. Carter offers her a seat while saying in a tone of wonder, "Mohammed, you're working as Miss Elsa's guide?"

Mohammed answers humbly, "I am only a servant, Professor, without the proper knowledge!"

Turning to the young woman, Carter says, "At last, Miss Elsa. Professor Carter and your mother have been looking for you everywhere. They are worried sick."

Elsa answers in a sweet, muted tone, "I am sorry. I know that they are looking for me. I will return to them tomorrow.

Throwing Mohammed a knowing look, Carter asks him, "How is business these days, Mohammed?"

The man sits down in a spot behind the young woman.

"Not good, Professor, not good at all... sales are down. Original pieces can no longer to be found. Since your discovery, the good times are over. And to think of all the times I stepped on that very same spot where you uncovered the first step. For let me tell you," he observes to Callender and Elsa, "that I dutifully served the Professor at the time of the discovery of the tombs of Thutmose IV and Queen Hatshepsut, both of them, sadly ... empty."

"Yes," exclaims Carter with amusement, "And when I first came across him, he was rummaging around in a modest tomb that, by then, was already half-empty, except in that case, it was he who had made the discovery!"

"In all humility, I am the furthest thing possible from an archaeologist," observes Mohammed with a smile.

Meanwhile, Callender has continued to stare at Elsa. Feeling herself observed, she asks him, "Why do you look at me that way, Professor?"

"Excuse me," answers Callender in a chastened tone. "I keep trying to remember where I have seen you before, because I am certain that I have."

"In Sudan, or Jeddah?... perhaps Cairo," wonders Elsa.

Callender keeps nodding no. Ali brings some oranges. Mohammed grabs one and starts to peel it.

"Professor," he ventures boldly, "Everybody is talking about the 'curse of the Pharaoh!'"

Carter gets up with an amused look and goes to pour himself a brandy.

"Even you Mohammed? Someone who has visited more tombs than an ancient undertaker! You who have trifled with the resting place of every last mummy in Egypt want to bring up this fanciful tale?"

Mohammed swallows the fragrant orange in his hands and continues, "Still, there must be something behind to it. Once, when I was only a boy," he says, glancing briefly at Elsa, "a tomb of great value was discovered... worth more than you could ever imagine. Ten men entered that tomb, and within a year's time, eight of them had died from an inexplicable illness of which no one ever managed to understand anything. But perhaps Miss Elsa has more to say on the subject."

His hands still wet with the juice of the orange, Mohammed motions for Elsa to speak. After taking a second to gather her thoughts, she says, "During the reign of Queen Hatshepsut, a grey substance was found in the gold mines of Umn-Garayat. Whoever touched it wasted away, and ultimately died."

Carter listens to the story with a sceptical air, while Callender seems enthralled.

Elsa continues, "Death latched on to whomever entered the mine, coming into contact with this substance, whose flow, or so it was said, was never-ending. In the dark, it glowed with a dim light. Given the name 'weapon of the spirit of death', it was placed in the grain left in the tomb of Ahmose I, in order to protect the tomb from plunderers."

Callender notes with surprise, "This would mean that, even back then, they were able to recognise toxic materials!"

Carter ponders the question for a second and then observes, "Gold and uranium are found in the same mineral, together with other compounds of radioactive material, such as thorium. The Egyptians, who used large quantities of gold, may have found traces of uranium in it. For that matter, uranium, to an even greater extent than thorium, remains active for a number of millennia. So yes, they may have recognised it as toxic, seeing that uranium, once it disintegrates, gives off radiation."

Callender continues Carter's train of thought: "... That would also explain why the robbers hurried away from the tomb. They may have seen the dim glow given off by the substance."

Carter still seems unconvinced. "Then we would have seen the same glow," he points out.

But Callender is ready with his reply, "The glow effect could have been exhausted, after the robbers fled, whereas the radiation would be capable of killing a man even today, especially someone already in poor health. Howard, this could be the solution to the 'curse'!"

"Alan, there is no curse! Don't you start too! This is absolutely absurd!"

Meanwhile, Elsa takes a section of orange that Mohammed has offered her and observes, "People have died, others have fallen dreadfully ill and can only await for death to arrive, without anyone being able to understand what they are suffering from, not even your doctors."

At that very moment, the sound of Dr. Servet's walking stick banging against Carter's door can be heard.

"Professor CARTER! Professor CARTER!"

Callender rushes to the door to let Dr. Servet in.

"Pardon the intrusion, Professor, but your friend Arthur Mace is in a bad way. You should come immediately!"

The final instants of Arthur Mace's life are slipping away in one of the bedrooms of the Hotel Winter in Luxor. His gaunt face looks wasted, pinched tight with fear and anxiety. He is sitting in an armchair by the window, looking out at the Nile. Sitting next to him, overcome with sorrow, is his wife Winifred.

Carter and Dr. Servet enter. The doctor goes straight to the sick man, while Carter goes to the wife's side.

"Winifred, how are you doing?"

"He hasn't spoken for three days," comes her anguished reply.

"Three days! Why didn't you let me know?"

"He is extremely weak," notes Dr. Servet, shaking his head while feeling the patient's pulse.

"I had no idea it was this serious," explains Mrs. Mace.

The physician's face shows his consternation over the slow death he is witnessing. Mace twitches nervously, as the moon rises outside the window, adding its light to the night sky.

"To simply wait for death in silence, a ridiculous way to have to go!" murmurs Dr. Servet.

Crying softly, Winifred goes to sit down on the edge of the bed, her back turned to them. Carter, looking tired and pained, moves closer to the window, beyond which the great river still flows, dimly lit by the pallid light of the moon.

Suddenly, Dr. Mace's breathing becomes still more laboured. Carter goes to his side and sees the man's eyes staring at the moon framed by the large window. Mace gives a shudder, and Carter draws even closer, as does Dr. Servet.

Cloaked in the glow of the moon, Dr. Mace takes his last breath.

Winifred stops crying and turns to the doctor, who shakes his head, saying, "It is over, he is no longer with us. I'm sorry".

Winifred collapses on the bed in tears. Carter's expression is one of disbelief.

Lowering his voice, Dr. Servet wonders, "Could there be some truth to this curse after all?"

Carter too replies in a hushed tone, "Dr. Servet, as a physician, you cannot possibly believe..."

But Dr. Servet cuts him off, "For the very reason that I am a physician, and yet I am unable to find any explanation for what is taking place, as of this evening, I believe."

All of the area of Deir-el-Bahri, with the cliffs of Deir in the background and the temple of Hatshepsut bathed in the moonlight, has a solemn, mysterious air. Wearing her traditional local garments, Elsa sits at the base of a column. A carriage arrives from off in the distance. The coachman helps Professor Newman get out and points to the young woman, before giving his horses water.

As the Professor walks over Elsa, he also notices Mohammed Hammed crouched on the ground, wrapped up in his cloak, a cross look on his face. Mohammed offers a half-hearted greeting, as Professor Newman, on seeing that Elsa is safe and sound, can barely contain his happiness.

"Elsa thanks goodness! Your mother was too upset, she didn't feel well. I had to call the doctor again."

Elsa admires the landscape for a moment before calmly saying, "I'm sorry. I have caused you trouble as well."

"It has certainly been an incredible experience, Elsa."

She smiles as he continues, "It seems that in a few days, a week at the most, they will be able to open the sarcophagus. They have almost finished taking apart the four shrines. There is very little space, but they are installing the large winches needed to lift the massive slab of quartzite that closes the sarcophagus."

"I don't want to be there when they open it," states Elsa firmly.

"But you have to be there," responds Newman, taken aback. "It could help you remember. Haven't you always wanted to know? You've done so much to understand the reason for that untimely death, and now you could finally get an answer."

"He was only eighteen years old!" says a distraught Elsa.

Mohammed is about to say something, but Professor Newman motions for him to be quiet.

"Ay and Sitamun were glad to see him to rule, but others were opposed, such as General Horemheb, a cruel, ambitious man who dreamed of putting himself on the young king's throne .... and they feared him."

Elsa's account takes Professor Newman way back in time, to a sun-filled day on which Tutankhamun, outside the first courtyard of the Temple of Amun, with the high priest Imhotep and the dignitaries of the temple preceding him, leads a procession into the hypostyle hall found inside the sanctuary.

To his right is the Divine Father Ay, to his left General Horemheb. Right behind him is the Grand Squire Thutmose, followed by Hiknefer and the detachment of bodyguards made up of the king's youthful companions. Then come the scribes, the priests and the representatives of the nobility, while the royal princesses walk alongside the queen, with Sitamun leading the group.

The rhythm of the music, and of the priests' chanting, quickens as the procession nears the portico of the hypostyle hall. Between the two pillars is a large object, from all appearances a statue, though it is wrapped up in a mat tied fast with cords of hemp. The dignitaries pass right by it, not even deigning it a glance, while the queen is unable to hide her sadness. As for Sitamun, she appears to be disinterested.

But suddenly, Tutankhamun stops and sets his eyes on the statue covered by the mat, forcing the procession behind him to come to a halt. Ay motions for them to continue. Imhotep turns and hears Ay say to Tutankhamun: "Divine Lord, today is the day of reconciliation. The High Priest is waiting."

Tutankhamun signals to Imhotep to go ahead, but the high priest, irritated over having to take orders from the young pharaoh, stiffens at the sight of the gesture.

His eyes set in an impenetrable gaze, Tutankhamun begins walking again, and the procession gets back underway behind him. Once they have moved past the corner of the courtyard, Ay and General Horemheb position themselves on either side of the young king, while the Queen and the princesses stand along the opposite side, followed by the state dignitaries.

At that same moment, the Prince of Miam arrives, escorted by two Nubian princes wearing the official garb of the chiefs of Uauat (a feline pelt on the back, two ostrich feathers placed inside a wig that is fastened with a white ribbon). The prince prostrates himself at the feet of the king, who immediately motions for him to get back up.

"Prince Miam, former companion of my studies, I am delighted to see you."

As he looks at the Pharaoh, Prince Miam's eyes fill with sadness. Next comes the tribute from the princes of Kush, whose expressions are serious and downcast, just like those of the other princes. A deafening silence ensues, while everybody waits.

Ay whispers to Tutankhamun: "Whatever your personal feelings, Divine Lord, you must show in public that you accept the will of the old gods, otherwise there will be civil war."

Then General Horemheb lets Tutankhamun know, in a calm, collected voice: "I have organised the Grand Memorial in your name. It is here, in the house of Amun, that you must unveil the sacred stele and start the festivities in honour of Opet."

Imhotep, the dignitaries of the temple and the chief scribe are all waiting anxiously in front of the stele. Tutankhamun, Ay and Horemheb, together with the detachment of body guards, stand facing the temple dignitaries. At a sign from Ay, the priest Imhotep walks up to the stele and cuts the veil covering the offering to the god Amun and his consort, the goddess Mut. Made of quartzite, the stele bears a number of inscriptions.

Imhotep stays alongside the stele, kneeling. Sitamun's gaze is set on Tutankhamun, as the queen waits impatiently.

Turning to the pharaoh, the priest says to him: "Son of Amun Nebkheperure Tutankhamun, this stele shall proclaim your wisdom, your piety, for all time."

Tutankhamun steps forwards, all by himself, stopping in front of the stele. Facing him is Imhotep, who recites the text out loud, so that everyone can hear it.

"When Your Majesty came to the throne, the temples of the gods and goddesses had fallen into a state of neglect."

Tutankhamun listens to the priest's account without any sign of emotion.

"Their sanctuaries had been profaned, and the sacred precincts had become fields filled with weeds. The country lay in a state of cataclysmic disorder and ruin, having been abandoned by the gods."

Tutankhamun turns his eyes towards Imhotep, fixing an expressionless gaze on the priest, who continues with his speech, pointing directly at the pharaoh.

"... He has removed the guilt that weighed Egypt down! The truth has been restored and the heresy has been declared to be the abomination of the country! He has sworn to..."

Tutankhamun cuts him off in brusque, determined fashion, declaring, "This stele will never be erected. I prohibited the speaking of injurious phrases against my father, Amenhotep IV. There can be no damning words spoken against the works of a great pharaoh, as was Akhenaten, who ruled for twenty years. The people will never attend any celebration of this stele!"

The Queen is stunned. Sitamun is beside herself with joy.

Tutankhamun turns to Thutmose and, pointing to the stele, orders: "Destroy it!"

The group of Nubian princes lets out a shout of rejoicing. The Prince of Miam throws himself at Tutankhamun's feet, beaming with happiness. Sitamun raises the sistra she holds in her hands, shaking them in celebration.

The Divine Father Ay, dumbfounded, observes the reaction of General Horemheb warily. The general's eyes remain unmoved, cold, but still profoundly irritated. Thutmose, proud of what his friend the pharaoh has done, advances to the stele with his men and topples it over, causing it to break in two on the ground.

Everyone in attendance is on the side of Tutankhamun. Meanwhile, Imhotep, walking over to the general, murmurs to him, "Now the heresy will break out again, General."

Horemheb offers him a silent, icy gaze, as the priest insists in a whisper, "Egypt will never have peace until every last descendent of that blasphemous heretic is dead."

That same night, a few hours later, Sitamun is leaving the Temple of Karnak, having said her prayers, as she does every evening. But as she walks along a hallway, something catches her attention. From a shadow in which she hides herself, she can see, inside the great hall where the altar is found, a captain of the guard who is waiting for something with an unsavoury, treacherous face. He nervously watches a priest who holds two javelin with their blades pointed in the direction of the Priestess of the Serpents.

The priestess takes a vial and pours a dark liquid onto the two blades. The priest turns and hands the javelins to the captain, who takes them and bows. Then he turns towards General Horemheb and the high priest Imhotep, both of whom were watching him while standing perfectly still and expressionless. Bowing one last time, the captain leaves.

The next day, in a marshy area covered here and there with canebrakes and patches of thick foliage, a gilded tent has been set up. Those inside have finished a lunch consumed during a pause in an informal hunting party. The servants, both male and female, remove the plates and goblets from the table as a group of young woman play music.

Tutankhamun and a number of his youthful friends, including Thutmose and Hiknefer, are sitting on mats, talking and laughing. Queen Ankhesenamun, Tutankhamun's young wife, and also the daughter of Nefertiti, is there too, together with her ladies-in-waiting.

The men, including Tutankhamun, wear white sandals and linen skirts, but nothing on their heads. The female musicians wear transparent veils that reveal their youthful silhouettes. The Pharaoh laughs, looks at the position of the sun and signals to Thutmose that they should get going.

The queen objects, "So soon!" but Tutankhamun is full of energy.

"There are only three hours left until dusk, and we cannot keep the game waiting!"

He checks the arrows in the quiver strapped to his naked chest. The queen tries one more time to change his mind.

"You began hunting at dawn, and you've barely spent an hour with us."

She points to the women in attendance, among whom is a beautiful Nubian princess. The youthful pharaoh smiles. She respectfully lowers her eyes.

"Would you want Thutmose to go around bragging that he came back with more game than I did?"

Thutmose protests in jest, "My Lord!"

A lady-in-waiting helps Queen Ankhesenamun get to her feet, revealing the queen's prominent belly: she is a few months pregnant.

"Which way shall we go?" asks the young pharaoh.

"Northeast," replies Thutmose.

"Tell the beaters," Tutankhamun says to an attendant, who bows and runs off.

Wearing a blue helmet, the pharaoh places a number of ebony boomerangs brought to him by the servants under his belt. The ladies split up, fanning out among the men to pour them goblets of wine.

Even Ankhesenamun pours wine into a golden goblet for Tutankhamun, who contemplates her smiling face as he drinks. The queen raises her arm to take back his goblet, and he kisses the palm of her hand. Then turning around, he leaves for the hunt.

Thutmose, Hiknefer and the others give their goblets back to their women and follow the Pharaoh.

The peninsula holds countless papyrus trees and canals that give its banks a rough-hewn outline. Skirting the edges of the island, the hunters keep their balance while standing in small papyrus canoes that they propel along with long poles. Each canoe holds just one man.

Tutankhamun, standing in his, holds the pole in one hand, moving it slowly, while the other keeps a boomerang at the ready. A few yards further on, along the bank, a crocodile slips silently into the water.

Thutmose and Hiknefer are some distance away, and the others follow behind them, in an irregular formation. From the banks come the distant sounds of the shouts and drumming of the beaters. As they move further into the inlets of the lagoon, the papyrus forest becomes thicker and the waterways follow increasingly twisted and turning paths.

Tutankhamun advances slowly, doing his best to make as little noise as possible. The beaters keep up their shouting, rhythmically pounding their drums. Suddenly, a flock of marsh birds takes wing over Tutankhamun's head. With a smile, the Pharaoh flings his boomerang. At the very same instant, a man who had been following him unseen, his face partially hidden by a turban, gets to his feet.

He is carrying two javelins with him, the ones to which the poison was applied in the temple. He hurls one at Tutankhamun, and the Pharaoh, practically by instinct, turns to avoid it, but the lance hits him anyway, leaving a deep gash on the right side of his face. Losing his balance, Tutankhamun falls into the mud near the bank as the assassin flees through the thick papyrus forest.

Thutmose and Hiknefer are the only ones to have caught sight of the assault, and they run towards their King. Seeing how much blood he is losing from the wound, they gently place him atop a cane thicket. His blood-plastered face fills his two friends with horror and rage.

Thutmose, leaving the young pharaoh in the care of Hiknefer, takes off in pursuit of the assassin, running through the thick forest, until he reaches a clearing where chariots and horses have been stationed.

He jumps into a chariot, and with the same whip later found in the tomb, the one that Callender showed to Elsa in the room at the Winter Palace, he urges the horse on, as the animal immediately gives chase. Thutmose can make out a dim silhouette running through the woods. Changing course, he sets out to encircle the assassin, who, driven by the desperate sensation that he is about to be trapped, turns and raises the second lance.

But before he can throw it, Thutmose has armed his bow and shot an arrow through the chest of the assassin, who sprawls into the mud. Ready to let loose another arrow, Thutmose closes in warily, until he sees the lifeless body stretched out on the ground.

As he flips the corpse over, he notes with surprise and relief that Tutankhamun, supported by Hiknefer, who is pressing a blood-soaked cloth against the Pharaoh's cheek, is coming towards him. The Pharaoh reaches Thutmose and looks at the assassin. Thutmose removes the turban covering the head, along with the veil hiding the face. The assassin is the same devious-looking captain who was in the temple the night before.

Tutankhamun is brought back in a chariot travelling through the open countryside. His dear friend Thutmose holds the reins, guiding the pair of horses with one hand while the other hand supports Tutankhamun, who appears to be in critical condition. Hiknefer follows them, riding in the saddle of a horse upon which the body of the captain of the guard has also been loaded. The others bring up the rear at a gallop.

The group reaches the temple of Karnak. The few priests watching over the temple step aside as Tutankhamun's chariot, driven by Thutmose and escorted by Hiknefer and the Pharaoh's personal guards, rolls in.

Sitamun has been praying, but as soon as she sees the blood on the Pharaoh's face, she understands just how serious the situation is and runs to him. Hiknefer lets the body of the captain of the guard fall to the ground. Sitamun recognises the man, but she forces herself not to cry out in horror. She is the only one who knows the truth: that General Horemheb is behind the crime, but she decides to say nothing.

The young pharaoh asks Thutmose to take him to the statue covered with the mats. Everyone stays where they are, except Sitamun, who joins the two. Bleeding heavily, Tutankhamun struggles to get out of the chariot. He embraces Sitamun, staining her face and clothes with blood. She sobs softly, overcome with sadness.

Gathering together what little strength he has left, Tutankhamun loosens himself from her embrace and turns to the statue. He takes out his sword and, with a single blow, cuts the cords.

The wind blows away the mats, uncovering the gold statue of his father, Akhenaten, whose face was deliberately split in two. The priests and dignitaries of the temple are taken aback at the sight of Tutankhamun kneeling before his father's statue, a gesture in which his personal guards and Sitamun join him.

Tutankhamun slowly lowers his head towards the base of the statue, using his bloodied hand to caress his father's feet one last time. Thutmose walks up to Tutankhamun and kneels beside him, crying. With a sigh, Tutankhamun dies.

Only now can Elsa's voice once again be heard telling the story.

"He had just turned eighteen years old, and he was happy to be expecting a child from his queen, but on that dreadful day, the excruciating pain caused her to lose her second child. All of Egypt mourned. The sovereign's mummy was prepared for the momentous voyage. The Queen placed a wreath of flowers on his chest, and Princess Sitamun laid a blue water-lily in his hands, which were covered in gold."

Professor Newman looks up from his notes to contemplate Elsa as she continues the story.

"More than three thousand, two hundred and sixty years have gone by since that day in April."

Now Elsa falls silent.

Professor Newman is astounded. "So it was a political assassination. Incredible! You have uncovered things that no historian has ever managed to bring to light."

Mohammed, on the other hand, seems less than satisfied with the young woman's words.

"It is definitely a delightful story, but let me point out, with all due respect, that our blue water-lilies only bloom in October and December."

After a moment's hesitation, Elsa replies, "The blue water-lily was grown in Princess Sitamun's covered gardens, where it had blossomed ahead of time."

Sailing on the Nile in the first hours after dawn offers travellers an extraordinary spectacle: the chirping and warbling of the birds that seem to race each other as they skim along the water, leaving marvellous patterns on the surface. Elsa is on the ferry, travelling back towards the banks of Qurna, in the company of Newman and Mohammed.

CHAPTER XII
The Wedding

Newman, together with Elsa and Mohammed, who are dressed in traditional native garb, step out of a carriage that leaves them in front of the Winter Palace Hotel in Luxor. An Egyptian member of the hotel staff, dressed in an impeccably clean white tunic, with a bright red fez on his head, sees Professor Newman in the company of those two figures covered in dust and dressed like locals and stops him a second, asking in a worried tone, "Is everything alright, Professor Newman?"

Then he adds, in a hushed, confidential tone, "They're not bothering you, are they?"

At first Newman fails to understand, but the hotel employee continues, whispering under his breath, "... They're not to be trusted, these people. They'd kill their own mothers for a drachma or two."

Only then does Professor Newman realise that Elsa's veiled face and Mohammed's style of dress could be cause for alarm and suspicion. Elsa, having understood the situation, removes the veil, showing her face, at which point the hotel employee bows obsequiously, repeatedly asking her to forgive him.

"My Lady! Effendi, I apologise! Welcome back, My Lady. I beg our forgiveness, but seeing you dressed like that... I am mortified!"

Professor Newman answers with a smile, "It simply means that you're paying attention to your work. No problem whatsoever!"

Newman and Elsa enter the hotel. An extremely irritated Mohammed follows them, giving the hotel employee's shin a kick when Elsa is not looking.

"Tanzif almutasawil aldhy yunkir earaqak!" hisses Mohammed at the man, who hears the phrase, which translate as, "Craven traitor to your own race!" while doubled over in pain.

The three of them reach Olga's room. Professor Newman knocks on the door, which is opened by Muna, who hugs Elsa the moment she sees the girl.

"At last! What a relief! We were so worried!"

Olga, who can hear them talking, wants to get up from her bed, but Dr. Servet urges her to stay where she is,

"Please stay put. Here she comes..."

A worried Newman studies the doctor's face, looking for signs of what condition Olga is in. Elsa sits down on the bed, alongside her mother, and hugs her.

"Elsa, you simply vanished. I was terribly afraid. Thank goodness you're back, my dear!"

"I'm sorry. I didn't mean to cause you such pain, but you know the trouble I've had sorting out what's in my head. I've been searching for so long..." Olga holds her close.

Mohammed asks Muna where he can go to wash his face, and she leads him to the bathroom, handing him a clean towel. Professor Newman nods to the doctor, who understands that he wishes to speak with him and follows him out onto the terrace.

"Thank you. I don't want Elsa to worry. She already has so much on her mind. But how is Olga?"

After a brief moment of indecision, the doctor smiles at him and says, with a knowing air, "... She is fine, in excellent health. And you too, I imagine?"

Professor Newman is both puzzled and concerned.

"But are you sure she is alright? The frequent dizzy spells? The vomiting?"

Dr. Servet is still smiling, "I suggest you have her rest. She has been under a lot of emotional stress for a pregnant woman... but there's been nothing more than a little bleeding."

Professor Newman's legs almost fail him.

"Pregnant?! Are you sure, Doctor?"

The doctor reassures him, again with a smile.

"Yes, and let me be the first to offer my congratulations! But rest easy, no one else knows. And as I said, there's no need to worry, though she should rest."

Professor Newman, visibly shaken, goes to the balcony railing, looks out at the river and then turns around, smiling happily.

"A child... my child!" he states emphatically. "What wonderful news, Doctor!"

It is a delightful evening. Professor Newman has asked the concierge to have a table set out on the terrace of their apartment. Muna is happy to have Elsa back. She softly sings a Sudanese song while overseeing the two waiters who are putting the finishing touches on the table. Muna positions the candelabra.

Professor Newman, looking exceptionally well groomed, is wearing elegantly scented evening clothes. Smiling broadly, he opens a bottle of Bollinger champagne, which the prestigious hotel is able to offer thanks to the labours of Jacques Bollinger, who in 1920, at the age of only 24, assumed control of the family business, founded in 1829, initiating the third generation of Bollinger vintners.

Professor Newman opens the prized bottle and asks Muna, "Would you please let Mrs. Olga know that I would be delighted to have the pleasure of her company, as soon as she can come out here on the terrace?"

Muna hurries off inside the apartment. When Olga comes out on the terrace, the Professor has just finished pouring two cups of champagne. She looks beautiful in a French dress, her cheeks powdered red and her lips coloured a deep, sensual shade.

"Muna said you wanted to see me."

He smiles, pours her a cup of champagne and says, "Dearest Olga, I can't imagine a better place, or more suitable company, to ask if you will marry me!"

Olga feels faint, she struggles to keep her footing, smiling in surprise, though deep down this is exactly what she dreamed of hearing.

"I'm... I'm flattered, Carl... Marriage?"

He replies enthusiastically, "Yes, marriage! Let's toast to it while looking out on the river that has made this land so happy! Just as I now ask you to make me happy."

She is both delighted and pleasantly confused.

"Carl you are always so full of surprises, and this is wonderful, but why the hurry? Elsa has only just returned, so many things are happening, so many emotions..."

He draws closer to her, kisses her softly and whispers in her ear, "Yes, intense emotions, such as the doctor telling me that you are pregnant and we'll be having a handsome son or a lovely daughter, whichever the Good Lord decides to send us!"

Moved nearly to tears, Elsa hugs him tight. They kiss. He raises his glass and proclaims, "To the glorious days of our future!"

Muna is about to step out on the terrace, but sensing the intimacy of the moment, she turns right around, bumping into Elsa, who was headed that way too. Elsa is also a study in elegance, wearing a lovely western-style dress and fine perfume.

"It's delightful out here this evening, the perfect temperature for dining in the open air. Was the idea yours, Professor Newman?"

Just then Mohammed makes his appearance, dressed in fine evening wear that Professor Newman has graciously lent him, though the buttons of the shirt are struggling to keep his sizeable stomach from bursting forth.

"I am most worried about what will become of these buttons by the end of the meal!" he says in a playful tone, at his own expense.

Everyone breaks out laughing, as Olga shows them where they should sit. Professor Newman pours four large glasses of Bollinger and passes them around.

"I wish to share my great happiness, or rather our great happiness, with you."

Everyone is paying close attention.

"I have asked Olga, that is, I have asked your mother, dear Elsa, to marry me, and she, thank goodness, has accepted, making me, after Carter, the happiest man in all of Egypt!"

Elsa, her mouth hanging open in wonder, is disoriented at first, while Mohammed nearly chokes on his champagne. Olga smiles as Muna, her eyes almost popping out of her head, covers her mouth with her hands. Professor Newman is anxiously waiting for Elsa to give her opinion. With a lengthy sigh, she slowly gets to her feet, lifts her champagne glass and says, "A toast to the best news I could ever wish to hear. Your happiness leaves me overjoyed, and I wish all the best to you, Professor Newman, a big-hearted man if there ever was one, and to you, Olga, an incredible woman and mother who certainly deserves every possible love and happiness!"

Olga is touched, Muna is in tears. Even hard-bitten Mohammed is visibly moved. Clearing his throat, he declares, "I too toast this splendid evening, in which I have been so graciously asked to take part! Here's to you bizarre people of the West, and to the love that brings life into the world!"

Everyone applauds and drinks their champagne with gusto.

Inside the Office of Antiquities in Cairo, Carter, assisted by two English lawyers, is discussing the renewal of the license. Also in the room are two lawyers representing the Egyptian authorities, as well as a notary public and Pierre

Lacau, who reads with satisfaction from a document: "The concession is renewed, but under two conditions: 'a. There shall be no exclusive arrangements with any news publications; and b. Any and all objects found in the tomb shall remain in Egypt'. If you would be so kind as to sign, Professor."

Carter hesitates, wondering if his patron would have approved, and then, despite his annoyance, he signs the document.

Inside the tomb, in the Valley of the Kings, the skilled workers are busy taking apart the four gilded shrines, under the attentive supervision of the archaeologists. Professor George Bénédite, head of the Department of Egyptian Antiquities at the Louvre Museum, is helping the technical experts with the difficult task of dismantling the shrines. Down on all fours, he awkwardly moves backwards, causing the seat of his pants to bump into the head of a sweaty Carter, who breaks out in laughter.

"Working like this," says Carter, who has stripped down to his undershirt, "packed in here like sardines, I must say, it can lead to no little embarrassment!"

Taking the shrines apart, in order to bring to light the stone ark, which is thought to hold the king's coffin, has been an extremely difficult task calling for great skill and knowledge. The shrines have been divided up into no fewer than fifty-one different sections, each wrapped in soft cotton padding and taken to the museum in Cairo.

After eighty-four long, gruelling days of work, there is finally enough space in the funeral room to admire the wall paintings. Strangely enough, this is the only room whose walls are decorated, as it would almost appear that the Pharaoh was buried in great haste, so that there was no time to embellish the rest of the tomb. Perhaps his death at such a young age had surprised everyone responsible for preparing what was to be his dwelling place upon his death.

Painted on the east wall is a scene were the Pharaoh's mummy, laid out inside the ark, is being transported in a funeral vessel hauled by twelve slaves. Depicted on the north wall of the room is the vizier, the Divine Father Ay, wearing a leopard pelt as he prepares for the ceremonial opening of Tutankhamun's mouth. The Pharaoh himself, represented as Osiris, is shown alongside the goddess Nut, the great deity of the sky, who welcomes him. Finally, Tutankhamun enters the realm of the afterlife, followed by his spirit, his "Ka", or vital force. There he encounters Osiris wearing his crown, known as the "Atef". Osiris is the supreme god and judge of the dead, responsible of maintaining order in the world while also serving as the ruler of the afterlife and resurrection.

Painted on the west wall are the divinities who await the Pharaoh in his first moments in the underworld. On the south wall is Hathor, the goddess of maternity, who rules over births and regeneration in the afterlife, as well as the sun and joy. She is shown wearing the disk of the sun atop her head, in between a pair of horns. In her left hand is the "Ankh", an ancient symbol of life, in the form of a cross topped by a loop.

Hathor is bringing another Ankh close to Tutankhamun's nostrils, to start the rite of mummification. Behind him is Anubis, the god of mummification and the afterlife, depicted with the head of a jackal. In his right hand he holds a key, the symbol of life.

Left all by itself, in the middle of the room, is the massive ark, the great sarcophagus of stone thought to contain the coffin and the body of the Pharaoh.

Professor Newman is sitting on a bench. Lost in his thoughts, he fails to notice that the others have all gone. As Carter is leaving the "treasure" room, he sees him and comes over. Callender joins them as well.

"It was a thrilling moment, unforgettable," says Carter with satisfaction.

Professor Newman points at the sarcophagus and says, though somewhat hesitantly, "There ought to be a wreath of flowers in there too, on his chest."

But Carter, barely letting him finish the phrase, clarifies, "Bouquets and wreaths of flowers were always placed on mummies."

Professor Newman insists, "Apart from the wreath, you should find a blue water-lily in his hands, one that blossomed prematurely in the covered gardens of the royal princess Sitamun!"

At Carter's home, everyone is busy studying the mechanism, designed with the utmost sophistication, to be used in removing the heavy, yellow quartzite cover of the ark, which all by itself weighs three hundred and fifty kilograms, out of the ark's total weight of one thousand, five hundred kilos. Callender, who is an engineer, has the best grasp of how all the levers, cables and pulleys work. He explains a technical drawing to some carpenters, showing them exactly how to attach the pulleys to the winches, to keep them from collapsing. Carter also takes a close look at the drawing, which strikes him as being well done.

Callender presents copies of the drawings to the head carpenter, noting, "You have to build it outside the tomb and then assemble it in the funeral room. Work quickly, but without overlooking anything: we can't afford any mistakes. Thank you everyone."

As the team of carpenters leaves, Alì come up to Carter, "Excuse me, Effendi, but they have delivered this envelope, saying it is very important."

Curious to see what it is, Carter opens it, exclaiming with a broad smile, "Finally some good news! Professor Carl Newman is marrying Mrs. Olga Mittieri. It says here that the wedding ceremony will be celebrated in honour of the ancient goddess Hathor!"

Callender points out, in amused appreciation, "If I'm not mistaken, she is the goddess associated with worship of the celestial god Horus. In fact, her name Hathor means 'home of Horus', and she is shown with the disk of the sun on her head, framed by two horns."

Carter adds to that, "You're right, but she was also the divinity of love and maternity, ruler of births and regeneration, as well as the goddess of music. But what stands out here is that the invitation comes from the bride's daughter, Miss Elsa. And it would appear that the reception is to be organised by that rascal Mohammed Hammad, in the hills of Qurna."

Callender notes whimsically, "Finally something to take our minds off work!"

The night of the wedding, Carter and Callender reach the slopes of the hills of Qurna in a carriage. Strangely enough, the lights of the hundreds of fires that normally set the local caves and homes aglow are not to be seen. Only one house, halfway up the hillside, is resplendent with the light of hundreds of lamps.

A group of people riding donkeys that are being led by the reins by local youngsters draws near. They turn out to be other western guests, including Dr. Servet, who waves to them with his hat as his wife, on the donkey behind his, barely manages to stay in the saddle. Among the other riders, who number roughly thirty altogether, are La Fleur and Winifred, wife of the late Arthur Mace, along with other distinguished guests.

A boy approaches Carter and Callender with a pair of donkeys, shouting, "Effendi, go ahead, get on. With donkeys it takes less time, and you don't tire yourself out. Tonight, Zeffa! Raks Shamadan, simply wonderful!"

The two quickly take leave of the other guests and get on the donkeys. Thirty-two people wearing lace, jewels, top hats and other finery are riding on donkeys towards the infamous hills, their destination the brightly lit home. Callender looks over his shoulder at the line of guests bouncing up and down on their less than steady mounts, as the barefoot, dark-skinned young boys flash their bright–white smiles in amusement at the sight.

"If you were to try and describe this scene, who would ever believe you!" says Callender to Carter.

"Like something out of an Agatha Christie novel!" the two of them laugh, delighted by the spectacle.

When they are close to the home, one of the youngsters runs up and knocks on the door, which opens. Out come six boys dressed in pristine white tunics, with handsome red fezzes on their heads, carrying large trays of crystal glasses filled with a beverage meant to refresh the guests who are struggling to dismount from their donkeys.

"For you, Effendi, something cool to drink, flavoured with lemon and mint. Enjoy!"

The guests consume the beverage with pleasure. Then the rhythmic sound of drums inside the home catches their attention, Out of the door comes a group of musicians playing a lively Arab-Egyptian folk tune, followed by six girls dressed as odalisques, their bodies covered in pink veils, gold belts on their bellies, their sensual movements keeping time with the beating drums. Each of them balances atop her head a shamadan, a large, gilded candelabra with nine lighted candles, metaphorically taking on the challenge of light or darkness with her gifts of balance, control and elegance. The guests applaud in amazement.

Following the odalisques, a radiant Olga Mittieri makes her appearance. Dressed in white chiffon, she wears a crown of pearls on her head, with Muna, smiling as if she never meant stop, helping her keep the long lace veil attached to the crown in place. The bride's belly makes no secret of its rounded state.

She smiles at the guests, who shower her with their admiring applause. Behind her come six more dancers dressed in pink, also balancing the heavy, lit candelabras on their heads. The music is lively, invigoratingly festive. As the magical procession moves up the narrow street, the 'Raks Shamadan' candelabra dance, a classic of local folklore, takes shape.

The luxuriant, noisy nuptial parade proceeds, with youthful bridesmaids positioning decorated candles along the sides of the route to symbolically light the bride's new path, as was done in the "Zeffa", or traditional Egyptian wedding ceremony. The procession reaches a slightly wider portion of the street, where a sumptuous banquet has been laid out beneath a large tent. Carpets and comfortable cushions cover the ground. The white-gloved waiters, who are ready to begin serving the banquet, also smile at the bride.

From another home, symbolically that of the groom, appear four men who do a spinning, whirling dance that turns the large skirts they are wearing into four colourful wheels. Then, finally, Professor Newman comes forth, wearing the traditional "Kandura", a tunic that comes down to his ankles, on top of which he has on a "Bisht", a cloak of dark linen adorned with a broad strip of embroidered gold along the collar, while his head is covered by a "Ghutrah", a white, linen rectangular scarf folded into a triangle and held in place by an "Agal", a double headband divided into eight parts and coloured, for this occasion, gold.

All at once, the music stops playing and the odalisque dancers step aside, clearing the way for Olga to walk up to Professor Newman and hold out her hand. He takes it, smiling at her in tender expectation. Immediately after, Mohammad Hammad and Elsa, both dressed in richly adorned garments traditionally worn in Qurna, come out of the house.

Mohammed solemnly states, "I am getting old, and so I feel the need to hand down the wisdom and virtues of my ancestors, such as truth, gentility and knowledge."

The local women make the shrill, vibrant sounds with which women throughout the Arab world accompany celebrations.

Elsa speaks, "Thank you, Hathor, for the gift of music. And thank you for the love you have given us," she adds, pointing to her mother's belly. "You, the goddess of maternity, who rule over birth, thank you for having given my mother the gift of new life, restoring the strength and joy that had left her."

Olga is deeply touched. Elsa continues her recitation, stating, "Ptahhotep, who was vizier to Djedkare Isesi, the next to the last pharaoh of the 5th dynasty in ancient times, wrote a number of teachings of universal value, received by us in the Prisse Parchment: 'May your heart never be vain because of what you know. Take counsel from the ignorant as well as the wise. Follow your heart all your life. Do not use time set aside for pleasure for anything else, as there is nothing more hurtful to the soul than to be deprived of its time."

The women once again make the shrill, pulsating sound, in approval of these sentiments. Mohammed adds, "Love your wife as you should, feed her and dress her. Build a house and establish a home. Now you may kiss.

Professor Newman kisses Olga. The shrill sounds start all over, mixed with the applause of the guests.   The banquet begins, as the musicians return to playing their rhythmic tunes while the waiters pour champagne and serve small portions of surprisingly delicate local dishes.

At the Luxor train station, Carter, Professor Maspero and Pierre Lacau are waiting for Countess Almina and Lady Evelyn to appear from inside their train. When the ladies do get off, they are dressed in mourning, though Lady Evelyn wears a small pink rose on her chest. Their private secretary is with them, and a group of photographers gets off the train at the same time as they do, leading to a flurry of magnesium flash bursts.

"I am delighted to see you again, Lady Carnarvon", Carter greets Countess Almina.

"My husband would have wanted me to come."

"Welcome," says Maspero enthusiastically. "Allow me to introduce you to the new director of antiquities, Pierre Lacau."

The Director bows. "It is wonderful to have you back in Luxor, Countess."

"I have heard tell of you even back in England, Sir," answers Lady Carnarvon with a subtle hint of irony.

Failing to catch the wry undertone, a grateful Pierre Lacau responds, "The glory of this discovery will keep Lord Carnarvon's name alive forever!"

"I am extremely glad to see you," says Carter to Evelyn. "It was my hope that you would come back."

She replies with a smile, "Did you ever doubt I would, Howard?"

Outside the dig area, in the Valley of the Kings, the crowd of journalists waits in keen expectation. There are also a good number of tourists, newsreel photographers with their bulky cameras, and photographers. Mohammed is wandering through the crowd. The bookmaker points to his chart with the list of names for the wager on the curse.

The inside of the tomb is lit by the artificial glow of electric lamps. The shrines have been removed from the room. The ark, 275 centimetres long and 147 wide, with the goddesses who serve as its guardians at the four corners, and the further adornment of the Eye of Horus, or Udjat, is positioned at the centre of the room. The winches begin to lift the heavy cover of pink granite, which was painted a shade of ochre in ancient times, to match the body of the ark.

Numerous illustrious figures of the Egyptian government are on hand at the tomb, along with archaeologists and scientists, plus the ladies who have accompanied them to the event. Occupying central positions are Lady Almina and Evelyn, along with Lee Stack, the former British officer appointed supreme commander of the Egyptian armed forces, together with his adjutant, plus Field Marshall Lord Allenby, whose adjutant is also with him.

The silence is absolute. Carter, Callender and the other specialists are standing near the sarcophagus. Miss Elsa, Professor Newman and Olga are seated with the rest of the guests. Turning to those in attendance, Carter says, "Ladies and gentlemen, the work whose results we are about to witness is dedicated to the memory of Lord Carnarvon".

He bows, everyone applauds, and then he returns to the painstaking, difficult task of raising the sarcophagus.

Elsa watches with a gaze of intense concentration. Painted on the front wall of the tomb is the sled on which the royal funeral bier was laid, to be hauled along by a group of slaves. Elsa, lost in her thoughts, remembers how, in ancient times, outside the Valley of the Kings, the bier was at the centre of the procession, with the mummy laid atop it, pushed along on a sled.

The princes followed the bier, while Thutmose walked out in front of the sled, which was pulled by four oxen with red fur. The nine Friends of the King were wearing the ritual cloak and holding the pommel of a walking stick. Leading the group was the prince "Mouth of God", the exalted dignitary responsible for supplying all the oxen to be sacrificed for the pharaoh. The priests uttered their laments.

The men carried long steles made of papyrus, symbolising the reign of the goddess Hathor. The sizeable group of women included the Queen, dressed in white, the colour of mourning, her hair gathered up in white bandages, as was the case with everyone in the procession.

The young widow recited the formulas of rebirth in front of the bier, carrying out the duties of the goddess Isis, the mediator between the terrestrial world and that of the afterlife. Princess Sitamun was praying intently. Preceding the courtiers came the servants, carrying the key furnishings to be placed in the "house of eternity": thrones, beds, cases filled with jewels and ritual headpieces, vases and flasks filled with ointments, jugs of wine, gilded carriages, weapons, games, ritual statuettes and funerary figures, lamps and ships.

A servant carrying a luxuriant armchair, the same one in which Tutankhamun had sat, walked ahead of Sitamun. The priests scrupulously sprinkled milk in front of the two conveyances, reciting, "For rebirth and entry into the world of the gods."

Off in the distance, the chants and laments of the courtesans could be heard. A priest read from a roll of papyrus in his hands, "He who knows this books goes out by day and walks the earth in the midst of the living. He shall be saved for all eternity."

Once they reached the necropolis, everyone fell silent. They all waited in anxious expectation, as if something was about happen. Suddenly, a deep, brooding drum roll filled the air, while the dancers known as the "MUU" came out from a sort of cabin, wearing loincloths and tall headpieces of bamboo. They moved towards the procession, performing a ritual dance to the rhythm of the drums.

Alongside the tomb, a priest dressed as the god Anubis carried out the rites for the acceptance of the deceased in the afterlife, holding the sceptre associated with kings and gods. The dancing stopped, while the sombre drum roll continued. The procession came to a halt. The mummy was taken out of the sarcophagus and placed in a standing position on a platform of sand in front of the tomb.

The Divine Father Ay, wearing a panther pelt on his body and a blue crown on his head, walked up to the mummy and touched its mouth with a small iron instrument, pronouncing the sacred formula, "Now you have power over your heart. You have power over your arms. You have power over your feet. You have power over your mouth. You have power over your limbs."

As he said the words, Ay touched the various parts of the mummy with the instrument. The priests burned incense while pouring scented oil onto the mummified body from small flask. Slaves held large sheets of metal in front of the tomb, in order to reflect light inside. The priests oversaw the arrangement of the funeral decorations, based on the position carefully chosen for each element. Artists, working by the light that reflected off the massive sheets of metal, completed their paintings on the wall of the room where the body of the king was to be laid to rest.

Sitamun, together with the queen and the other princesses, prepared to enter the sepulchre, reciting in chorus, "Oh Sovereign, great Sovereign! Return to us in whatever garden you choose. Return to us, great Sovereign, once you have seen the shadows of the afterlife."

The king's mummy had been placed standing up straight, at the entrance to the funeral chamber. The Queen began reciting her prayer, "I am your bride, oh great one, do not leave me! Is it your wish that I go away from you? Why must I go off on my own? I say that I will come with you, oh you who were so fond of speaking with me, but you say not a word."

Princess Sitamun also began praying, "Handsome voyager who has left for the land of eternity."

The princesses took up the prayer, replying to her as a chorus, "You who were surrounded by so many, now you find yourself alone in the land that loves solitude. You who so enjoyed moving your legs, now you are bound tight. You who had so many clothes, here you lie, wearing those from the day before."

Sitamun repeated her prayer with ever greater feeling, "Oh handsome voyager who has left for the land of eternity."

While the last of the four shrines was being closed, and the seal was placed on the necropolis, a servant positioned the armchair in the space indicated by the official in charge of the ceremony. Princess Sitamun moved it ever so slightly, to make sure the position was just right. Meanwhile the Queen, followed by the guests, left the room. The wall had been constructed, with the smoothing of the plaster the last step. Once everyone had left, Sitamun placed a bouquet of flowers on the ground and, after standing up straight again, pressed her hand against the still wet plaster, leaving a print...

Back in the present, in the tomb, Elsa smiles in a sweet but melancholy way at the thought of that memory. It is then that she finally understands that she belongs to a different time and world. She looks at her hand, and then at the handprint on the wall. Her sad smile makes it clear that she no longer has any reason to live in the present, and now she is sure of it.

Meanwhile, the heavy slab is about to be lifted. Everything seems to be going smoothly, when suddenly, in the middle of the operation, a creaking sound is followed by some small pieces of the external decoration coming loose and falling to the ground. Everyone is on edge. The winches finally stop. The slab has been lifted, moved to one side and laid on the ground.

Carter, Callender and the two other scholars look inside the sarcophagus, their faces showing disappointment, as inside they see nothing but linen cloths. Carter reaches in and removes them, one by one. Underneath, instead of a body, there is a magnificent sarcophagus of gilded wood, decorated with a likeness of the young king, who holds in his hands, which are clasped across his chest, the 'Heqa' sceptre and the flail.

Carter sees that a small garland of flowers had been placed on the 'Nemes', or headpiece, presumably during the funeral ceremony, so that it surrounds the royal insignia of the vulture 'Nekhbet' and the cobra 'Uto'. He turns to glance at Elsa, who is following the scene calmly and attentively. Evelyn also turns towards Elsa and hears her murmur, "The resting place of his spirit".

Everyone present observes the scene in absolute silence. Lady Evelyn leans forward, hoping to catch sight of the coffin, as Countess Almina leans closer too. Professor Newman also glances in that direction, before looking back at Olga, who, her massive belly sticky with sweat, is waving her fan in search of relief from the heat.

The coffin, 224 cm in length, is shaped like a mummy. The technicians remove its cover with the winch, revealing a second coffin that is 204 cm long. It also bears a likeness of the sovereign, though this time the expression on his face is sad and dejected. The second coffin is likewise made of gilded wood, together with the further adornment of small fragments of glass and precious stones. The sovereign's head is covered by the traditional 'Nemes', while his braided beard is decorated with lapis lazuli. All over the coffin are inlays in the form of gold feathers, complete with coloured stones applied by means of an especially sophisticated procedure.

Those present in the tomb murmur their appreciation. Burton of the Metropolitan Museum of New York painstakingly photographs each phase of the work, as Carter oversees and directs the delicate operation of opening the second coffin and removing its cover.

Incredibly enough, a third, resplendent coffin is found inside. It measures 188 cm in length and shows the pharaoh with a sad expression, his face looking younger than the one depicted on the coffin that came before. Carter asks the carpenters to remove the cover of this last coffin as well, only the winches, placed under too much stress, began creaking, apparently on the verge of giving out.

Edward speaks up, observing, "Wait! The winches aren't up to the job. It doesn't make sense.... my goodness, this is gold! The coffin is made of solid gold!"

All those present move closer to the coffin, to admire the master craftsmanship of the sculpted gold, which features the great vulture "Nekhbet", its wings unfurled to cover the coffin, as though to protect the pharaoh.

The expression on this last mask of the pharaoh is solemn. Pointing to the other Masks, Carter notes, "Each of the three expressions obviously has a meaning of its own, corresponding to the different stages through which the pharaoh passed. The first shows a sense of absolute peace and serenity, symbolising the eternal youthfulness that the sovereign must leave behind him. The second appears tragic and fatigued, as if the king had been fighting hand-to-hand with death. And here, in the third likeness, he is preparing to be reborn as Osiris, the god of death, the ruler of the great beyond. By this stage, he has already been through the death and suffering in the afterlife that he needed to sustain in order to triumphantly return to life, having transformed himself into a divine substance."

Elsa smiles in approval, as if Carter had done an excellent job with his schoolwork, while Carter continues with his explanation, "The cover of the third coffin is made of solid gold, displaying the pharaoh's features, together with the motif of the winged divinities protecting the sarcophagus adorned with precious stones."

The astonished onlookers are left speechless. Also engraved on the sarcophagus, winding upwards from its lower portion, are a pair of ribbons that contain writing. Callender and two other experts in hieroglyphic characters lean over to decipher the meaning.

Elsa, her face a study in concentration, murmurs as she reads the lettering: "Oh Nut! Great goddess of the sky, spread your wings over me until the stars that never set begin to shine."

Lady Evelyn hears Elsa's murmuring, as do Professor Newman and Olga, who are right next to her. Olga rubs a hand on her face, where her emotions are on clear display.

Pierre Lacau moves closer to the sarcophagus, delicately tapping it with his signet ring, in order to judge the state of the gold.

"Solid gold!" he calls out ecstatically.

Elsa looks at Evelyn and says, "Gold is the flesh of the gods."

The cables that were originally used to close the coffin are attached to the four gold handles on the cover. The pulley screeches as the lifting operation required to remove the sarcophagus gets underway.

Visibly worried, Carter notes, "It's so heavy. Let's hope the winch can take it."

Then, turning to the technician, he asks, "What is the weight?"

The technician looks at the needle on the gauge and answers, "The winch is carrying 110 kilos and 400 grams".

Once the cover has finally been lifted, Carter states in a tone of restless expectation, "Now he should finally appear!"

Elsa does her best to hide the worry that fills her face all the same. Lady Evelyn is waiting anxiously. The opening of the coffin promises new and added emotions for all those present. Elsa's eyes can barely contain their burning misgivings, while the other onlookers murmur their astonishment.

Burton continues to take photographs, working silently while wiping the sweat from his brow. The mummy is covered with a spacious linen shroud held fast by four horizontal strips and three more set lengthwise. Lying atop the shroud is a wreath of withered flowers, almost intact, the colours still vivid. The sight draws expressions of admiration and wonder from those present.

Carter delicately lifts the wreath, using a linen cloth suited to the purpose, and hands it to an archaeologist, an expert in fabrics, who immerses the wreath in a container of lukewarm water. Carter slowly lifts the shroud, revealing the mummy. Everyone is standing. The mummy's head and face are hidden by a large mask of solid gold decorated with glass and precious stones, including fragments of lapis lazuli, quartz, obsidian and feldspar, inlaid in twelve precisely arrayed rows surrounding the ample collar. Atop the head is the traditional 'nemes', with 'Nekhbet' the vulture goddess and 'Wadjet' the cobra goddess, who respectively protect upper and lower Egypt, depicted on the front.

The English commander of the Egyptian army, Lee Stack, stands at attention, together with his aides, and salutes. Lord Allenby and his adjutant also get to their feet, clicking their heels as they too salute the sovereign.

Draped around the pharaoh's neck are three necklaces made from disks of yellow and red gold. On his chest is the "Khepri", the large beetle of black amber that symbolises rebirth. In his two hands of gold, clasped together atop his chest, he holds the flail and crook of Osiris. Just below the hands, practically intact, is a blue water-lily!

Carter and Callender look at each other in astonishment, and then turn to seek out Elsa's gaze, but her lowered head remains motionless. Professor Newman moves closer to the sovereign, peering at the water-lily in bewilderment and wonder. Carter, looking shocked, moved and confused, finds the wherewithal, with the assistance of Callender and two other experts, to remove the mask, a work of gold that weighs roughly eleven kilograms, from the pharaoh's head.

The face is covered by a light cloth. Carter reaches into the coffin and pulls away the red fabric embroidered with gold and pearls, revealing the king's young, innocent, peaceful face, left taut out and burned by the holy oils, possibly because the quantities used were excessive. The eyes are hallowed out and covered, at the spots where the pupils should be, and a crown sits on the head.

The breath-taking, almost unimaginable sight sends a shiver running through the entire room. One of the ladies, the wife of Ali Kamel Fahmy Bay, lets out a muffled cry and faints away. Another has to cover her eyes. Out of respect, Lady Evelyn bows her head.

Carter moves closer to the face, looking like he has trouble believing his eyes. He turns to glance at Elsa, but realises that her chair is empty. The young woman has left.

Professor Newman, also surprised to find that Elsa is no longer there, goes up to Lady Evelyn and asks, "Would you be so kind as to look after my wife for a moment? Elsa has left, I must go...."

"Yes, certainly. Go to Elsa..."

The newsreel cameramen continue to film the scene, the electricians bring other portable lights, and Burton continues to immortalise the historic moment with his photographs.

Professor Newman leaves the tomb and, not seeing Elsa anywhere, gets on a donkey and heads out of the valley, towards the river. A number of hours later, as the first rays of dawn start to light the darkness of night, a skiff is sailing south from Luxor, its large, trapezoid-shaped sail filled with wind.

Aboard the boat, Elsa and Mohammed are contemplating the sacred river, when suddenly they catch sight of Professor Newman motioning to them from the shore. Elsa asks that the boat be stopped. The sail is turned into the wind and the vessel comes to a halt.

Newman standing in mud up to his ankles, reaches the skiff and, with the help of the helmsman, comes aboard.

"Thank you for waiting, Elsa. I'm sorry, but I absolutely had to talk to you. The water-lily is exactly as you remembered it. Unbelievable!"

Elsa says with a smile, "Professor Newman, you've got mud all over you! You should worry about my mother, rather than running after me. Before long, you'll have a little boy or girl to take care of, definitely a source of joy for my mother and yourself, whereas I have brought you nothing but suffering."

Newman cleans himself off as best he can. "What suffering, Elsa? Why you mean everything to your mother! I must say, this mud is terribly sticky, it simply won't come off."

Mohammed takes a deep breath, as if he were savouring a fragrance. Then he declares with a smile, "I love this river! I hope the spring flooding will be heavy this year, that way the harvest will be especially rich!"

Elsa observes in a calm, tranquil tone, "Along the Nubia with its desert-like banks, here was where the Hyksos were defeated and driven out of Egypt. Thutmose III managed to advance as far as the fourth cataract, but rebellions continued to create havoc in these lands which, though arid, contained rich deposits of gold. Not until the reign of Amenhotep III, the father of Sitamun and Akhenaton, did the region find peace."

Mohammed joins the conversation in typically jocular fashion, "If only I knew where that gold was found! That would be quite a stroke of fortune! If you happen to remember, could you let me know?!"

Elsa smiles, having become quite good friends with the portly fellow. "It would be an excellent way to keep you from plundering tombs."

Mohammed laughs in amusement. Elsa points to a cluster of ruins on the west bank of the river.

"Do you see those? In this land, along the Nubia, Amenhotep III had the largest funerary temple of them all built. He called it 'Maat', which means order, respectability, ethical values and justice, culture and creation. The direct opposite of you, Mohammed, who are wild and disorganised, destructive and blasphemous. In a word, chaos. But you have a good heart, and this saves you.

"You are respected in Qurna, but remember, a good ruler must ensure that his people have 'Maat', he must think of their future."

The sun begins to timidly present itself on the horizon.

"Where are we headed?" asks Mohammed.

But Elsa continues with her tale.

"He had dedicated the temple to Amun Ra and to himself, as the divine masters of the Nubia. Tell them to dock here, this is where we want to get off."

The skiff stops, letting off its passengers. Professor Newman looks back through what he has been writing in his notebook before timidly asking, "You said that, in your memories of the events, the Royal Princess Sitamun knew who had killed Tutankhamun. But why did she do nothing about it? Why didn't she reveal who the guilty party was?"

Elsa sits down and, after running her fingers through her hair, answers, "She did a lot more than that. She loved Tutankhamun dearly. She had raised him during his childhood, and was his first lover. She had the privilege of introducing him to the joys of passion, turning herself into his first recollection of love.

"It is true, she did not reveal who the traitor was, but only because she knew that the man in question could count on the support of a powerful faction of the clergy. Ultimately, however, she did much more.

"After the death of Tutankhamun, his wife, Ankhesenamen, lost her second child, meaning that she had no heirs and could not trust anyone. Out of desperation, as well as a wish to get even, she made a dramatic error, writing a letter to the Hittite ruler, King Suppiluliuma, to inform him that she was a widow with no male children who could on the throne. She did not trust anyone in the royal court, and choosing a subject as her husband was out of the question, so she wanted to ask the king if he would marry one of his many sons to her.

"Suppiluliuma was wary, but he was curious to know more, and so he decided to send the royal chamberlain, Hattusa-Ziti, to personally control that the contents of the letter were sincere. The chamberlain came back to the king with another letter from the Queen of Egypt, in which she objected to him thinking she might be a liar, but she renewed her offer to marry his son all the same.

"The Hittite king, realising just how attractive an opportunity this was, given the sizeable political advantages he would obtain once he had placed his son on the throne of Egypt, agreed to the idea, choosing from among all his sons Zannanza, the fourth-born, whom he sent to Thebes, together with an escort of soldiers. But the young man never reached his destination, for when the queen's political enemies caught wind of her scheme, they sent a squad of assassins out to kill the young prince in an ambush in Egyptian territory. Once the Hittite king learned of the dramatic turn of events, he went into a rage, ordering a violent reprisal against Egypt.

Horemheb, the strong man and chief commander of the Egyptian armies, was forced, along with the other generals, to fight to defend their borders. It seemed likely that the war would be a violent, drawn-out conflict. Queen Ankhesenamen feared for her life..."

Elsa's memories come to life in her mind, taking her back to a moonless night when Sitamun is making her way to the home of the elderly Ay. On her arrival, a servant accompanies her to the main hall of the palace, where Ay is eating dinner with his wife Tey.

Upon seeing Sitamun, Ay immediately gets up from the table and, despite his advanced age, kneels down before the royal princess. Sitamun walks to his side and helps him get back to his feet.

"Great Father Ay, forgive me for the disturbance, but I need to talk to you, and right away."

Ay answers her respectfully, "Princess Sitamun, you are always welcome. Come, let us step out on the terrace."

Once they have gone outside, Sitamun, her eyes brimming with emotion, hesitates for a second before finding the right words.

"I know who killed my nephew, Tutankhamun. I saw him scheming with my own eyes. It was Horemheb. He wanted to become king, but we cannot let him. Do you not agree?"

Ay is shaken by the dramatic news, even though, deep down, he has always harboured certain suspicions.

"My Princess, what can we do? He has become a great general. The pharaoh publicly appointed him "Idnw", and he was officially proclaimed the king's representative for the entire country. He has even had that status written on the walls of his funerary temple in Saqqara, in Memphis. He fully expects to take the place of the pharaoh."

Sitamun replies in a sly tone, "Nobile Ay, right now his mind is on the war. He has lost a battle in Kadesh. He is not of royal blood. His parents were simply government officials. You are the stepbrother of the Great Royal Wife Tiye, who was married to my father, Amenhotep III. You are my uncle, as you were to Akhenaten... You have royal blood, and so you should marry Ankhesenamen, the widow of my nephew Tutankhamun. You would be entitled to the throne."

An anguished Ay objects, "But I am too old... and he is too powerful."

But Sitamun insists, "Yes, you are along in years, but don't forget, you have a son, Nakhtmin, who would rightfully succeed you on the throne after your death!"

Ay still has his doubts, but Sitamun keeps after him, "Divine Ay, you cannot let Horemheb, that traitor, that assassin, take the throne!"

Elsa contemplates the banks of the river in silence. Mohammed is watching her closely. After a moment's hesitation, Professor Newman gathers up his resolve and asks her, "What happened? What did the Divine Ay do?"

Elsa lifts her eyes sadly. A tear slips down her face.

"He did what Sitamun had said he should and married the young widow of Tutankhamun, and so he became pharaoh..."

Mohammed observes with satisfaction, "Serves Horemheb right! The traitor got what he had coming!"

Elsa goes on with the story, an increasingly sad tone to her voice.

"Horemheb had come up from nothing, driven by his thirst for power, and Sitamun had underestimated him. The young Royal Wife Ankhesenamen was sad, broken-hearted, on the day she was married to the Divine Ay. Though afflicted, she neglected her health, and only a few months later suffered a grave infection that led to her death.

"Meanwhile, Horemheb continued to win victories in his war against the Hittites. A sly individual, he had everyone believing that he had willing accepted Ay as his pharaoh. Yet upon returning to Thebes, after one of his victories, he did not hesitate to ask Ay for the hand of the older man's daughter, Mutnedjmet. The Divine Ay, wishing to stay on the good side of the victorious general, and hoping that they might soon reach an understanding, agreed to the request.

"Unfortunately Ay's advanced age had dulled his once astute powers of reason, and led him to commit a regrettable error..."

Professor Newman, who has been taking notes, cannot stop asking the young woman questions.

"What exactly do you mean? What was this fateful error?"

Mohammed speaks up, "She means that you can forgive, but you should never forget the face of your enemy."

Allowing herself a bitter smile, Elsa answers, "You are right, Mohammed: never forget their faces. Horemheb called a meeting of the Council and put it to them that, apart from the problem of the Hittites, with whom they were still at war, there had also been disturbances among the Syrian-Palestinian tribes, who were dangerously inclined to strike up alliances with the Hittites. He said that he would go control the situation himself, taking with him a group of valiant soldiers, to see if there was any truth to the rumours.

"He was crafty enough to take Ay's son with him, claiming that the military operation would add lustre to the young pharaoh's reputation. What he did instead was to set up a false ambush by Shasu Bedouins, during which Nakhtmin, the young heir to the throne, was killed, along with other soldiers. Horemheb held the Bedouins and the Syrian-Palestinians responsible, and with the pretext of avenging Ay's son, declared war on them, invading their lands and winning an impressive victory.

"And while he covered himself in glory on the field of battle, Horemheb plotted, conspiring with the Oracle of Amun in Thebes, to poison the Divine Ay and his Wife Tey. The Oracle described in public a vision in which the two elderly parents had been separated from their "Ka", the vital, creative force that animates any individual, symbolising the inexhaustible power of the sprit, which springs forth from the individual, surviving even in the afterlife. In their case, this would supposedly help them be reunited with their young son Nakhtmin, allowing them to live in eternity."

An indignant Professor Newman stops taking notes and says between clenched teeth, "What a scoundrel! He had everything figured out. He had married the daughter of the Divine Ay, establishing ties to the royal family, so that he could finally sit on the throne!"

Elsa sadly responds, "In fact, he did indeed become the last pharaoh of the 18th dynasty, only the Royal Princes Sitamun never stopped hating him. His vile, underhanded ways had caused her too much pain. During his reign, Horemheb destroyed all the public records and memorials of the Amarna period, meaning those of Ay, Nefertiti and Akhenaten, further reinforcing the power of the clergy who had lent him their support.

"He had all the statues of the period destroyed, taking credit for a series of projects commissioned by Tutankhamun and Ay, replacing their names on the finished works with his own. But the gods did not forgive him, leaving him without any male children. Worse yet, he himself killed his only potential male heir, when he stabbed his wife in a fit of anger, little knowing that she was carrying a future son in her womb."

Professor Newman listens with rapt attention to the rest of the account.

"During one of the national holidays, the 'Tekhi', celebrated shortly after the start of the year...."

Mohammed interrupts, noting with a smile, "'Tekhi' means drunkenness! It's an ancient feast that we in Qurna still celebrate, a good excuse for imbibing wine until you're drunk! It came after the feast of "Thoth", when honey and figs, usually eaten only by the priests, were feasted on by everyone. Both celebrations were tied to the annual return of plant shoots and blossoms, following the flooding of our generous river!"

Elsa clarifies, "These were feasts tied to the cyclical processes of death and rebirth, and they concluded on the last day of the fourth month of the harvest. On that evening, the meal known as 'mesit' was eaten, and during the celebration of lights, the glow of the lamps and candles was offered up as a sign of gratitude to the gods, to ward off misfortune..."

Elsa's memories of the ancient nocturnal celebration come to life, with scenes of lighted lamps, people in joyful celebration, candles, freely flowing wine ... Sitamun walks up to a group of guards watching over a cream-coloured tent. They too seem numbed by the fumes of drink. Bowing to the royal princess, they let her enter...Inside is Horemheb, who has been pharaoh for a number of years. With him are two young Nubian women no longer wearing clothes. As they pour wine into a cup, they offer their intimate parts for Horemheb to touch.

As soon as he sees Sitamun, Horemheb turns serious. Then his drunken smile returns to his face and he raises his glass with a satisfied expression. For far too long he has desired that princess, and there she is, standing before him as she slowly takes off the gold diadem adorned with interwoven lotus flowers and attached to the veils covering her body... the pharaoh motions to the two Nubian women to leave the tent, and they immediately obey... The princess is completely nude, and strikingly beautiful, her skin milky white, her legs long, her breasts large and firm. She wears a gold bracelet on one ankle and two on her wrists.

Taking a cup of wine, she moves closer to Horemheb, letting her hair fall loose while placing a foot on his pelvis, as if to dominate him. He smiles in suggestive fashion, takes the glass and slowly pours the wine on her knee, so that it trickles down to her foot, which he takes in his hand and kisses...

Sitamun flashes him an alluring smile, as he motions for her to hand him another glass of wine that she now has in her hands. At first, she refuses, but then she smiles and obeys. Horemheb drains the glass quickly and throws it away. She presses her foot against his chest. Suddenly, he can no longer breathe, as if he were suffering from a massive allergic reaction that has caused his throat to swell, cutting off the airway. He twists, he gasps, unable to cry out. She presses with her foot, as if she meant to crush him. He trembles, groans and then nothing...

Shaken by the impact of the memory, Elsa's eyes swell up with tears, her breathing is laboured. Then she slowly returns to normal.

Mohammed and Newman, taken aback, are left without words as they gaze at her. Finally, the young woman resumes her account, "She had no other choice. He did not deserve to be king."

Elsa gets up and walks to the riverbank. Sighing, she looks out at the water and says, "We called the Nile 'Iteru', which means "The Great River", the house of Hapi, the god of fertility and life."

She seems at peace. She takes off her shoes and puts her feet first in the mud and then in the water.

Mohammed offers, "Neither of you knows this, but everyone in my family is a farmer. I am the only exception. I just never wanted to be one."

Elsa responds with a smile, "The Nile is so splendid... Every year, at the start of the flooding, toward the middle of June, the Pharaoh would go to the island of Elephantine and, after completing the sacrificial ceremony, he would throw flowers, bread and meat into the river, and finally a rolled-up sheet of papyrus that was a treaty establishing an alliance between the sovereign and Hapi, the spirit of the Nile."

Elsa's feet begin to sink into the mud. Mohammed looks around, in search of a sandal he has lost in the muck. Absorbed by his notes, Professor Newman starts to write again. Elsa goes back to her account.

"The Nile is so generous that it gives eternal life and divine essence to all those who lose themselves in its waters. Iteru was the passageway for those going from life to death, and then to the afterlife, so that they could be reborn in the east, like the sun."

The young woman keeps moving towards deeper water. Mohammed watches her with a worried look.

"What are you doing, Miss? There could be crocodiles, other kinds of beasts!"

Peaceful, serene, she recites in a whisper, "Welcome, God Hopi. You who every year arise from the earth and flood everything that thirsts, giving life to the living..."

The sound of the backwash of the river mixes in with the words that Elsa continues to murmur in her unknown language... Only then does Professor Newman, realising that the girl is in water up to her waist, call out with worry, "Elsa, stop! You'll sink into the mud. It's dangerous!"

Mohammed tries to follow her, so that he can hold her back, but he too sinks into the mud, struggling to get back up again. Weighed down by the muck in his clothes, he can barely move. Newman also tries to make his way, but a foot gets stuck in the mud and he falls face-first into the water, just as Elsa disappears beneath the surface.

Mohammed makes one last desperate effort, diving beneath the water, but he can barely see a thing. He thrashes around, but cannot find her. Returning to the surface, he chokes and sputters. On the verge of drowning, he cries out, "Miss, Miss Elsa!"

Newman is petrified. Mohammed holds his face in his hands, closing his eyes in prayer, as the sound of the lapping water echoes the flowing river.

Mohammed reopens his tremulous eyes. The first rays of the sun are painting the sky red. The water sparkles. Elsa has disappeared.

It is night, and in Carter's house in Thebes, Carter, Callender and Lady Evelyn have just finished dining and are about to move to the sofa. As always, Alì is preparing to serve them coffee.

Beyond the window stretches the desert, with its countless voices. Lady Evelyn notes in a sorrowful tone, "I've looked for her, and I've had others do so. I went to Qurna, but no one could tell me anything. Mohammed and Newman are nowhere to be found either. They seem to have disappeared.

With considerable worry, Carter replies, "I do believe that Mohammed is the only one who knows anything of her whereabouts. Lately he's served her quite faithfully, that godless thief."

"I just can't get over it," observes Callender, pondering the mystery of the girl's behaviour. "She has a tremendous depth of feeling, she is truly, incredibly authentic. And what she has told us matches what actually took place, so we have to wonder exactly who she was in the past.

Lady Evelyn interjects, "Newman told me that, in the museum in Cairo, she lay down on the floor, prostrating herself in front of the mummy of Amenhotep III. That detail has stayed with me. He said that she murmured, 'Amenhotep the Third, father and husband', as if she were wrestling with some strongly felt emotion."

Carter says nothing. Then he picks up an ancient object sitting on a table, the Anhk, or symbol of life, and muses with a pensive air, "If she said, 'father and husband', that would be because Amenhotep III, who had a number of daughters, married not just Queen Tiye, but also Sitamun, his first-born daughter, in order to give her the rank of Great Royal Spouse."

Callender attempts to clarify the situation, "So Sitamun was Akhenaten's sister, as well as Tutankhamun's aunt."

Lady Evelyn listens in near disbelief as Carter adds, "A cosmetics box of blue faience pottery was found, bearing scrollwork engravings with the names of Amenhotep III and his daughter, which would make it seem as if the two of them had been joined in marriage. An alabaster chalice was also found, from the Malkata Palace in Amarna, with the same inscriptions. All this would explain why Sitamun went on living in the same rooms in the royal palace."

"In the Egyptian Museum in Cairo," points out Callender, "there is a statue of the scribe Amenhotep, son of Hapu, who performed certain administrative duties involving the properties of a 'Queen Sitamun'. And the same statue was originally found in Karnak, where Sitamun is referred to as the Great Royal Wife."

Carter and Lady Evelyn meet the following afternoon in the well-appointed bar of the hotel in Luxor. They chat in friendly relaxed fashion as he sips a brandy while she enjoys a cup of Rooibos, a tisane mix originally from South Africa, with excellent anti-oxidant properties and no theine whatsoever.

A houseboy begins to discretely refill her cup, when Evelyn interrupts him to ask, "Has none of you here seen Professor Newman? It's incredible, he's simply vanished. He thought that Elsa really had been part of a reincarnation. What do you make of it?"

For the first time, Carter seems to harbour some doubt.

"What can I say? The things she told us turned out to be true, even though they were contrary to all logic, to every scientific assumption and reasonable conjecture. It all seemed impossible, but then the water-lily..."

Carter, wrapped up in his thoughts, continues to ponder what took place. Meanwhile, the houseboy is still standing there, holding the teapot with his white gloves, and looking quite embarrassed, until Lady Evelyn finally notices him.

"I'm sorry! That's fine. Thank you."

The boy bows and walks away.

Evelyn offers, "I saw her kneel down and place her hand on that handprint on the wall. It fit perfectly, as if it could very well have been her hand."

Carter wonders in a sombre tone, "But why would she disappear like that? It was all over."

"She was in such torment. Who can say what she was really looking for, poor girl. I would have liked to have had the chance to say goodbye to her before going back to London," notes Evelyn with regret.

Taking a sip from her cup of tisane, she adds, "Howard, you know how much respect and admiration I have for both you and your work."

An appreciative Carter answers, "Thank you. Of course we both know that your family deserves all the credit. I do hope that you and Lady Almina will be at the Cairo Museum for the inauguration of the special section devoted to this extraordinary discovery of ours."

With a hint of disappointment, Evelyn answers, "I'm not sure my mother will feel like coming. She is still quite upset over my father's passing."

"But you'll be there, Evelyn, won't you?" asks Carter anxiously. "All the work of cataloguing, publishing reports of the finds and arranging the pieces themselves will still take a good deal of time."

Evelyn answers with a winsome smile, "Of course I'll be back, Howard. Despite the fact that this discovery is tied to a very painful loss, it has added a great deal to my life."

Changing to a more serious tone, "But I must ask you an enormous favour, Howard. Would you please do everything in your power to ensure that the body of the young pharaoh remains in his tomb in the Valley of the Kings? If you need our help, just send a telegram. We still have a number of close friends in the English government, and in the Egyptian administration too. But Elsa made a point of asking me that favour, and I promised her I would see to it."

"I assure you, I will do everything in my power, Lady Evelyn, to make sure that the sovereign never leaves his tomb. I give you my word," states Carter resolutely.

In return, she shows him an alluring smile, saying, "Even from afar, I will be close at hand, whenever you need me."

"Lady Evelyn, throughout this effort, you have always played a key role."

"And does that mean that I will always have place on your heart," she asks in a slightly mischievous tone.

Taken by surprise, Carter blushes before answering, "Why of course...... we have worked together on the greatest discovery of the century. Unfortunately, the enjoyable part of the effort is over. Scholars are waiting impatiently to receive a full report....officials in Cairo are applying pressure to have the objects on display at their museum, and the Egyptian government wants to open the tomb to tourists as soon as possible."

In a light, teasing tone Lady Evelyn notes, "So you've become nothing more than an administrator, Howard?!"

"Yes," answers Carter with a smile. "A mere bureaucrat carrying out routine, everyday tasks."

"But an exceptionally romantic bureaucrat all the same, wouldn't you say, Howard?" she says with a smile.

He nods. She looks around, making sure that there are no indiscrete eyes in the vicinity, and adds, "But if the bureaucrat, in a sudden fit of passion, were to say goodbye to me with a kiss?"

Carter looks her in the eyes, draws closer and gently kisses her.

Inside the tomb in the Valley of the Kings, on the day after that unforgettable, truly excellent brandy, Dr. Derry, professor of forensic medicine, expounds on his findings to Carter, Callender and the other archaeologists and scientific experts gathered around the dissected body of Tutankhamun.

"If we look at the knee socket, the space inside the joint, measured from the end of the femur, leaves no room for doubt: the cartilage tissue of the joint develops at age twenty, and yet here it is missing."

The physician's presentation has Carter's full attention.

"At the upper ends of the femur bones, on the other end, the cartilage of the coxofemoral joints is clearly visible, and its definitive growth begins at the age of eighteen. Similar anatomical observations were recorded for the tibia and the humerus as well. It follows that this youthful sovereign may have died at the age of seventeen or eighteen, though the most likely age, based on all the available data, would be..."

Carter finishes the phrase for him, "Eighteen."

Dr. Derry agrees, "Yes in all likelihood".

Carter rubs at his tired face with a hand. Callender is paying close attention to what is being said. Professor P. C. Newbarry presents his report in a folder, commenting, "Based in the flowers, it can be established that the sovereign was buried in March or April. What we have, for the most part, are fleurs-de-lis and mandrakes, which blossom in Egypt in those months. And then there is the blue water-lily, which is strange, because it only blooms between October and November."

Carter exchanges a knowing glance with Callender, when suddenly, to everyone's surprise, Professor Newman rushes in. Looking extremely worried, he whispers something in Carter's ear.

CHAPTER XIII
The Water-Lily

Elsa's body has been found along the riverbank by ancient Thebes, amidst the papyrus plants and lotus flowers of the Nile. Her garments are pasted to her body, on account of the mud that stuck to her as it dried. Carter, Callender and Professor Newman look on in pity and sorrow as the body is recovered. Olga Mittieri, her pregnant belly enormous, is kneeling in the mud, cleaning the encrusted muck off Elsa's face while softly sobbing.

"...My baby... you look so calm... and my heart is bleeding..."

A sorrowful Professor Newman tries to ease her pain, "Darling, come on, let's get you in the shade."

Professor Newman helps her up, while the military personnel attend to the body. Callender gazes at the corpse with a distraught air. Its appearance, encased in the mud, resembles that of... a mummy.

And then it hits him. He murmurs to Carter, "...Now I remember where I've seen her."

Carter gets to his feet and, together with Callender, moves a short distance away, as Callender adds, "It was in the valley, in tomb KV55, the one discovered by Theodore Davis, the American. Do you remember?

In the Valley of the Kings, at a remove from the most frequently visited tombs, a roughly made sign lodged in a cleft in the rock reads: "FUNERARY CACHE KV55". Scattered everywhere on the uneven ground are pieces of jars, hemp and other fragments. On a platform are the remains of the coffins of three "Unknown Princesses". Only one has survived in anything like its original form, though the wood is cracked and just bits and pieces of the writing remain. But the mummy is intact, still wrapped in its bandages, beneath a heavy shroud folded in a triangular pattern.

Around the neck is a gold diadem decorated with intertwined lotus flowers, identical to the one Sitamun wore when she bared her body to avenge Tutankhamun. The mummy's clasped hands hold a blue water-lily. Carter and Callender move closer, while Professor Newman stays back with Olga, comforting her as she holds onto her pregnant belly.

Callender points out, in discrete but satisfied tone, "I was right when I said that I knew her, that I'd seen her somewhere..."

Carter agrees, "They do look very much alike..."

Professor Newman draws closer, together with Olga, who barely stifles a scream.

"Oh my god! They're identical ... she looks just like my Elsa..."

Carter moves even closer, to get a better look. "... She's holding a blue water-lily too."

Carter face is a study in anguish, while Callender also looks grief-stricken.

Olga, not even trying to hide her feelings, goes up to the mummy and, giving it a gentle caress, asks, "Who was she?"

Carter, "... All the registry entry says is: 'UNKNOWN PRINCESS'. Their coffins were robbed and their names were cancelled. I'm afraid that is all we know."

Olga whispers sweetly, "May you find peace, unknown Princess...."

Callender offers, "Actually, I think I know the name of this princess: she is Sitamun, the daughter and wife of Amenhotep III, the aunt of the Pharaoh Tutankhamun. It was she who put the blue water-lily in the hands of the pharaoh upon his death... she grew them in an enclosure, a sort of greenhouse, which explains why the things of value that she took with her include this blue water-lily.

Professor Newman rips a page out of the diary he keeps in his pocket and folds it. Then, with great care, he takes a petal from the water-lily and places on the paper. He closes the diary and hands it to Olga, who smiles as she takes it, placing it in her purse before slowly heading towards the exit.

Suddenly she feels a sharp pain in her pelvis, then another. She leans against the wall, breathing heavily. Professor Newman runs to her side.

"Olga, what is it?"

Starting to gasp, Olga barely gets out, "I think the time has come... this is it, Carl..."

The two of them leave. Callender follows, in case he can be of assistance. Carter, the last one to walk out, turns and takes a long look at the mummy before finally heading off, his shadow growing smaller with each step, until it disappears, leaving behind the face of a young woman who truly seems at peace.

"My second-born, Giorgia, came into the world that same evening, after a lengthy labour, thanks in part to Professor Ernesto Schiapparelli, an archaeologist and benefactor who, while working on his digs, also found the time to establish the hospital of the National Association for the Assistance of Italian Missionaries in Luxor. The baby gave me the strength to carry on and once again smile at the future. Losing Elsa was the greatest sorrow of my life, as a child should never pass away before its mother. Even though, in some incomprehensible fashion, she had somehow lived another existence, in a whole other era, she was, and always shall be, Elsa, my beloved daughter."

In room number 123 of the Royal Children's Hospital, Olga's great granddaughter, the new Elsa, the young girl wounded in the Manchester terrorist attack, seems to have forgotten her wounds and her pain. The story her grandmother has just finished telling her has left her deeply moved.

"Here is something else for you..." says her grandmother, delicately removing a blue water-lily petal from the pages of her diary and holding it out to the girl.

"... Take it, it was meant for you. You'll see .... It will bring you luck-

Elsa smiles, taking the petal as if it were the most precious object in the world. She instinctively holds it up to her nose to smell the fragrance, only to say, "... It has no smell, Grandma, like the desert."

The elderly lady smiles while softly caressing her granddaughter. "So you see, darling, I was born thanks to my sister. Meaning that it was the extraordinary events of her life brought together my father and my mother, so that now I have the great good fortune of being able to tell you the story. At last, you know why your name is Elsa.

The noise of the door opening behind her causes Giorgia to turn around. A young nurse comes into the room and murmurs something to her before controlling the medical equipment hooked up to Elsa.

Getting to her feet, Giorgia says, "Try to get some rest now. I'll be right back." She kisss her granddaughter's forehead and leaves the room.

David is sitting in the drab waiting room. Distraught, his eyes red from crying, he cannot work up the nerve to go into his daughter's room, for fear of disturbing Elsa in her delicate condition.

Seeing him like that, Giorgia fears the worst. She sits down beside him.

"David, tell me..."

Drying his tears, David speaks, his head still hanging low.

" ... nothing yet. They're afraid she's still too weak to do anything. From the X-rays, it seems like, even if she does wake up again, she'll never walk again.

"After the first explosion, the one furthest away, she tried to protect Elsa, shielding her with her body, but the force of the second blast hit her full on. How do I tell Elsa that her mother sacrificed herself for her? Help me Mother!"

He breaks down sobbing, like an exhausted, fragile, defenceless child. Giorgia does what any mother would in such a situation, holding him close.

"We'll find a way," murmurs his mother. "We will... But right now, you have to be strong, the way she would be."

Giorgia hugs him even tighter, as the son says, in little more than a whisper, "... she shielded Elsa with her body... she risked her life to save our daughter..."

Giorgia, her voice filled with emotion, "The greatest sacrifice of all..."

Suddenly an alarm goes off, a shrill, unsettling, disheartening sound. It distracts them from their pain, focussing all their attention on the doctors and nurses who come rushing down the hallway and into Elsa's room.

Giorgia and David, sick with worry, also rush over to the door. The shrill alarm is coming from the electronic machinery. The monitor shows the tragic sign of a long, flat, uninterrupted line. Elsa's heart has stopped!

The doctors shout to each other, preparing the defibrillator, while the most experienced of the group begins a cardiac message ... The defibrillator is primed. The doctor rubs the two metal paddles together. Everyone steps back. A nurse bares the girl's chest and spreads a gel on it. The paddles are pressed onto her. The first charge makes her jump, but the monitor stays flat.

The shrieking alarm pierces Giorgia's heart. She leans against her son to keep from fainting. The defibrillator is recharged, but in that very instant, everything goes off: the monitor, the neon lights, the entire hospital. Everybody looks shocked, dumbfounded, unable to understand.

"What's going on?!" yells the doctor.

Then complete silence. Until one by one, with a soft, buzzing sound, the neon lights in the hallway come back on, then those in the room.

The monitor that showed the flat line of the failed heart comes back on too, but miraculously, to everyone's astonishment, the glowing line has returned to the rhythm of a normal heartbeat.

They all exchange glances of disbelief. The doctor presses two fingers against the artery on Elsa's neck, smiling in satisfaction as the girl slowly opens her eyes.

David hugs his mother, "Thank god!"

Then he goes up to his daughter, holding her gently in his arms. The girl murmurs, "TS08 PBS..."

Slowly shifting himself so that he can see her, David asks, "What did you say, sweetheart?"

She repeats, "TS08 PBS...the license plate ... the van that drove away, just before the explosion, I saw it from the lobby... the license plate of the van, Papa..."

Her grandmother gazes at her, her eyes full of tears, before exclaiming in a stunned whisper "... Dear lord..."

The next day, the British government raises the terror alert to "critical", the highest level, based on the latest information received. "Critical" means that the authorities hold a new attack may be likely in the near future. In Manchester, the investigative work continues, in order to uncover all the members of the terrorist network that included Salman Abedi, the young man identified by police as the bomber.

So far, a total of eight people have been arrested. Two of them were detained in Tripoli, in Libya, the home country of the parents of Salam Abedi. They are his father, Ramadan, and his younger brother, Hashem. It would appear that both arrests were made by men of the RADA, a special anti-terrorism unit under the command of Libya's Ministry of Interior Affairs, but reports of the news are still incomplete.

A few days later, in Manchester, the English police arrest a 23 year-old man suspected of having ties to Abedi. Some papers report that the man may be Abedi's older brother, Ismail, but the investigators have yet to confirm the news.

Elsa's mother goes on to regain consciousness after a total of twenty-three days in a coma, and she appears to be reacting well to her physical therapy. Amazingly enough, she is able to move her legs again. Elsa is well. She says that, "When mamma is better, I want to go to the new Grand Egyptian Museum in Cairo."

Printed in Poland
by Amazon Fulfillment
Poland Sp. z o.o., Wrocław

80806399R00218